PRAISE FOR THE PEPPER MARTIN MYSTERIES

Tombs of Endearment

"A fun romp through the streets and landmarks of Cleveland...A tongue-in-cheek...look at life beyond the grave...Well worth picking up."   —Suite101.com

"[A] PI who is Stephanie Plum-meets-*Sex and the City*'s Carrie Bradshaw...It's fun, it's 'chick', and appealing...A quick, effortless read with a dash of Bridget Jones–style romance. [Martin is] a hot redhead who always manages to look good...and suffers the emotional catastrophes that every woman can relate to."   —*PopSyndicate*

"With witty dialogue and an entertaining mystery, Ms. Daniels pens an irresistible tale of murder, greed, and a lesson in love. A well-paced story line that's sure to have readers anticipating Pepper's next ghostly client."   —*Darque Reviews*

The Chick and the Dead

"Amusing with her breezy chick-lit style and sharp dialogue."   —*Publishers Weekly*

"Ms. Daniels has a hit series on her hands."

—*The Best Reviews*

"Ms. Daniels is definitely a hot new voice in paranormal mystery...Intriguing...Well-written...with a captivating story line and tantalizing characters."   —*Darque Reviews*

"[F]un, flirtatious, and feisty...[A] fast-paced read filled with likeable characters."   —Suite101.com

continued...

Don of the Dead

"Fabulous! One of the funniest books I've read this year...Pepper is a delight."

—MaryJanice Davidson, *USA Today* bestselling author

" 'Spirited' Pepper Martin brings a delightful new dimension to sleuthing. There's not a ghost of a chance you'll be able to put this book down. Write faster, Casey Daniels."

—Emilie Richards, *USA Today* bestselling author

"One part Godfather, one part Bridget Jones, one part ghost story, driven by a spunky new sleuth...A delightful read!"

—Roberta Isleib

"[A] humorous and highly entertaining expedition into mystery and the supernatural."

—Linda O. Johnston

"A spooky mystery, a spunky heroine, and sparkling wit! Give us more!"

—Kerrelyn Sparks

"[F]unny and fast paced; her sassy dialogue...her bravado, and her slightly off-kilter view of life make Pepper an unforgettable character...The only drawback is waiting for book two!"

—*Library Journal* (starred review)

"[A] tightly plotted story with a likable amateur sleuth."

—*Romantic Times*

"[A] fun cozy with a likable heroine and a satisfying plot."

—Suite101.com

"Fans of Buffy ought to enjoy this one...original, funny, and shows plenty of scope for future books (all of which I aim to read)...[A] highly enjoyable debut."

—MyShelf.com

Night of the Loving Dead

CASEY DANIELS

BERKLEY PRIME CRIME, NEW YORK

THE BERKLEY PUBLISHING GROUP
Published by the Penguin Group
Penguin Group (USA) Inc.
375 Hudson Street, New York, New York 10014, USA

Penguin Group (Canada), 90 Eglinton Avenue East, Suite 700, Toronto, Ontario M4P 2Y3, Canada
(a division of Pearson Penguin Canada Inc.)
Penguin Books Ltd., 80 Strand, London WC2R 0RL, England
Penguin Group Ireland, 25 St. Stephen's Green, Dublin 2, Ireland (a division of Penguin Books Ltd.)
Penguin Group (Australia), 250 Camberwell Road, Camberwell, Victoria 3124, Australia
(a division of Pearson Australia Group Pty. Ltd.)
Penguin Books India Pvt. Ltd., 11 Community Centre, Panchsheel Park, New Delhi—110 017, India
Penguin Group (NZ), 67 Apollo Drive, Rosedale, North Shore 0632, New Zealand
(a division of Pearson New Zealand Ltd.)
Penguin Books (South Africa) (Pty.) Ltd., 24 Sturdee Avenue, Rosebank, Johannesburg 2196,
South Africa

Penguin Books Ltd., Registered Offices: 80 Strand, London WC2R 0RL, England

This is a work of fiction. Names, characters, places, and incidents either are the product of the author's imagination or are used fictitiously, and any resemblance to actual persons, living or dead, business establishments, events, or locales is entirely coincidental. The publisher does not have any control over and does not assume any responsibility for author or third-party websites or their content.

NIGHT OF THE LOVING DEAD

A Berkley Prime Crime Book / published by arrangement with the author

PRINTING HISTORY
Berkley Prime Crime mass-market edition / January 2009

Copyright © 2009 by Connie Laux.
Cover illustration by Don Sipley.
Cover design by Judith Lagerman.
Interior text design by Laura K. Corless.

ISBN: 978-0-425-22555-4

BERKLEY® PRIME CRIME
Berkley Prime Crime Books are published by The Berkley Publishing Group,
a division of Penguin Group (USA) Inc.,
375 Hudson Street, New York, New York 10014.
BERKLEY® PRIME CRIME and the PRIME CRIME logo are trademarks of Penguin Group
(USA) Inc.

PRINTED IN THE UNITED STATES OF AMERICA

10   9   8   7   6   5   4   3   2   1

In loving memory of
Mary Cihy Morrish,
who liked nothing better than
a good ghost story.

1

At the risk of sounding way too full of myself, I'll admit it right now—I'm used to guys checking me out. It comes with the territory when you're five-foot-eleven, boast a cascade of carroty-colored hair, and have a sense of fashion that's cutting-edge but never crosses the line.

A 38C bust doesn't hurt, either.

That's why when Doctor Hilton Gerard's gaze slipped from my face to the peachy cashmere sweater I was wearing with black pants and Miu Miu booties with four-inch heels, I never even flinched. Big points for me, because used to it or not, that took a lot of guts.

Why?

Well for one thing, from the moment I walked into his office and saw the way Doctor Gerard ogled me, I knew he was a dirty old man. And for another . . . well, there's no getting around the truth, even when it isn't so easy to admit, and the truth is simply this: the reason I was sitting across from the doctor's desk at the Gerard Clinic was because a dead woman who used to work there had flimflammed me into getting embroiled in another investigation. Her name was Madeline Tremayne and yes, I did say she was dead. In fact, I'd met her at her grave.

But that, as they say, is another story. Or at least it's another part of this story, and not something I had time to worry about. Right then and there, the only thing I had the luxury of thinking about was what Madeline had told me about Doctor Gerard. He was a successful psychiatrist from a wealthy and socially prominent family who had devoted his life to making sure Chicago's homeless and indigent had dignified, state-of-the-art, and (most importantly) free mental health services. He'd built this clinic with his own money, and for more than twenty years, he'd kept it open because he was smart and economical and he worked like a dynamo at fundraising and grant writing. Some days, he was down in the trenches with his employees getting his hands dirty. Others, he was schmoozing on the Gold Coast, convincing the city's movers and shakers to open their hearts—and their checkbooks—for the sake of the poor and mentally ill.

Oh yeah, Doctor Gerard, he was Mother Teresa in a tweed suit, all right.

But remember what I said about Madeline? Talking to the dead can be a big ol' pain in the ass. Believe me when I say this. But thanks to Madeline, I had the inside track, and I knew what the society pages and the news stories didn't report, and what they didn't report was what brought me to the Gerard Clinic in the first place. Not the bit about how Doctor Gerard had a secret set of books and siphoned money from the clinic to build a sweet little bungalow for himself in the Bahamas. Hey, I might not condone it, but I had a felonious gene or two in my own family; I understood.

No, what brought me to the clinic on that frosty winter afternoon was something else Madeline had told me. She was Doctor Gerard's assistant. At least while she was alive, anyway. She knew a whole lot about what was up around there. Like that the doc was conducting a special study with some of his homeless patients, and that this special study of his was looking more and more like it wasn't on the up-and-up.

Why would I care?

Honestly, I wouldn't. Not usually, anyway.

Except for three things. Or I should say three people: Dan and Ernie. And Stella, of course.

Really, there's no time to explain about them. For the record, let me say that I barely knew Ernie or Stella, and we had just about nothing in common, what with them being homeless and all, but I felt a weird connection to them, anyway, and an obligation, too, seeing that I was the one who was responsible for Ernie's disappearance, and Stella's murder.

I guess I owed Dan, too, on account of how he'd once saved my life and how another time, he'd provided me with a key piece of evidence that helped me solve not one, but two murder investigations. I first met Dan in a hospital ER where he said he worked only I found out later he didn't. He claims to be a brain researcher, and I knew for a fact that he was mixed up in the whole Doctor Gerard/clinic thing. Dan is the only guy I know who shows up out of nowhere to issue dire warnings about how dangerous it is to talk to ghosts and disappears just as quickly. (Oh yeah, and by the way and not incidentally, he is also one of the best kissers I've ever had the pleasure of meeting lip to lip.)

"So, Miss Martin…" The good doctor's voice snapped me back to the matter at hand. He was a thin man with high cheekbones, a long nose and dark, wavy hair shot through with silver. In spite of—or maybe in defiance of—the fact that his office was nothing more than a fifteen-by-fifteen square with utilitarian metal furniture, a pitted linoleum floor, and cinder-block walls, he was wearing a tailor-made suit, a crisp white shirt, and a tie I recognized as Italian silk and expensive. Joel—my ex-fiancé—had one just like it.

The doctor thumbed through the forms I'd filled out as I sat in the waiting room, side by side and way too close for comfort with what seemed like the entire homeless population of Chicago.

"You'll have to forgive me for being so forward," he said, "but you don't look like one of our usual clients. You say you were referred here?"

"That's right."

I knew what was coming and reminded myself that this was no time to lose my nerve. Or spill my guts. Not if I intended to find out what was really up at the Gerard Clinic and in the bargain, keep Dan from joining my dad in the federal pen.

"May I ask who recommended you talk to me?"

Yes, I had every intention of stringing the good doctor along so no, this wasn't the time to tell him about Madeline. For now, I needed to sound helpless and just a little needy. That wasn't too much of a leap. If I was going to help Ernie, Stella, and Dan, I needed to get accepted into Doctor Gerard's study.

Yeah, yeah, I know, this wasn't the smartest plan. It

was harebrained, and if what happened to Ernie and Stella was any indication, it might be dangerous, too. But that wasn't going to stop me. I guess the stubbornness goes along with the red hair. It also serves me well as the world's one and only private investigator to the dead.

Like I was embarrassed, I giggled when I answered. "It's that whole doctor-patient confidentiality thing. You know, all those complicated new laws that say no one can know what goes on between a doctor who's conducting a brain study and his test subjects. Oh!" If years of dating had taught me nothing else, it was how to blush on command. I put one hand to my flaming cheek. "I guess I've already told you more than I intended. Now you know I've been part of a study."

Doctor Gerard nodded. "That's very interesting. A study. But your forms say you're not in therapy at the moment. That you never have been. You're a little old for a schizophrenia diagnosis." He looked me up and down, and good thing I was trying to get on the doctor's good side, or I might have pointed out that I'd just had my twenty-sixth birthday and that hardly qualified as *a little old*. "How did this researcher find you?"

"Head injury." I pointed to my skull and instantly felt like an idiot. As if a guy with that many diplomas on his wall needed help finding my head. "I guess my brain scans were a little weird."

He looked at me over the frames of his tortoiseshell glasses. "A little weird? Or a lot weird?"

I wrinkled my nose. "There was some talk about occipital lobes. And aberrant behavior."

"Which manifests itself as . . ."

"Voices." I shrugged. "People who talk to me. And

sometimes..." I looked away like I was embarrassed and this wasn't a complete put-on. I'd never actually come right out and explained the whole thing to anyone. Not anyone who was alive, anyway. "I see the people, too. You know, the ones who talk to me."

Doctor Gerard's eyes lit with interest. "You didn't mention that on your intake form."

I didn't have to fake an anxious smile. "There really isn't a place to put it."

"Well, this is quite unusual." He rose from his chair and came around to the other side of the desk. He perched himself on the edge, my file folder still in his hands. I suspected he didn't forget much of what he saw, but even so, Doctor Gerard paged through the papers in front of him. "So, Penelope—"

"It's Pepper, please." I knew we had to get that out of the way, or I'd be so fixated on the whole Penelope thing, I'd get all turned around. Whenever someone uses my real name, I always figure we're talking about somebody else.

"Pepper." I could tell by the spark in his eyes that he wasn't a man who liked to be corrected. "Are you hearing any voices now or seeing anyone who isn't really here?"

"Not unless you're not really here." I tried for a smile that hit the wall of Doctor Gerard's stodgy expression. When it fell flat, I shook my head. "No voices."

"And you're not taking any medication for your condition."

I got out of my chair, too, and stationed myself behind it, my fingers clutched against the back. "It all just started, you see, and when it did..." This time, I didn't have to go far to look convincing. I'd been living with my special "Gift" for just about a year and even I didn't understand it. My shoulders slumped. "When it first happened, I thought I was crazy."

"Of course you did." He nodded in a way designed to comfort the glassy-eyed, blank-expressioned people out in the waiting room. "Would you like to tell me about it?"

I didn't, but I reminded myself that if I chickened out and kept my mouth shut, I wouldn't find out what I wanted to know. "It started back in Cleveland," I said. "That's where I live. I hit my head on the step of a mausoleum." And because I knew this was already sounding crazy, I added, "I work at a cemetery."

Doctor Gerard nodded. "Garden View Cemetery. I remember seeing that on your intake form. What happened to you at the cemetery, Pepper?"

I had never said the words out loud. Not to Ella, my boss who was also my friend. Or to Quinn Harrison, the cop who had saved my life a couple times and who I had nothing in common with except that he wanted my body and I wanted his. I hadn't even told Dan the whole story, and Dan was, after all, the main reason I was there.

"The guy buried in that mausoleum was Gus Scarpetti," I explained. "You've probably never heard of him here in Chicago, but in Cleveland, he's a legend. He was a mobster back in the 1970s, and after I hit my head on his tomb...well...I've seen Gus Scarpetti," I told the doctor. "I've talked to him. Plenty of times. And after he went away—"

"He disappeared? Just like that?"

Of course it wasn't that easy, but I didn't think this was the time to go into details. I got down to business, leaving out the part about how Gus didn't disappear until after I'd solved his murder. "The same thing happened with Didi Bowman. You may have heard of her. Her sister took credit for writing a famous book, but Didi really wrote it."

"And you talked to this Didi, too?"

"Sure." I dismissed this information as inconsequential. "And Damon Curtis, too."

"The rock star." Doctor Gerard made a note of this on the legal pad that sat out on his desk. "It's interesting, isn't it, that you've only seen and talked to famous people. What do you suppose it means?"

I didn't suppose anything. I knew what it meant: *famous* wasn't what mattered; *victim*, on the other hand, was. All three of them—Gus and Didi and Damon—had been murdered, and they couldn't rest in peace until someone brought their killers to justice. Since I'm the only one with this Gift mojo, the burden naturally falls on me. Did I want to get into this with Doctor Gerard? No way. He didn't need to know that I was a private investigator. All I wanted to do was make him believe I was crazy.

"I wish I knew what it meant." I tried to sound thoughtful, like it was something I spent a whole lot of time wondering about. "All I know is that I'd really like it to stop. That researcher, he says I've got issues."

"And do you?"

"Have issues?" I had to laugh. "Well, there's my father. He's in prison for Medicare fraud. And my mother. She took off for Florida to get away from all the bad publicity about my father. There's my ex-fiancé who's moved on with his life. He's getting married. And then of course…"

The *of course* part was all about Quinn and Dan—
who did I want, who didn't I want, and why. I might not
always be in touch with my logical self, but when it
comes to the subject of my love life, I know even a sea-
soned mental health professional isn't qualified to deal.
And I wasn't ready to talk about it. My sigh was genuine.
"Do you know anyone who doesn't have issues?"

"I don't know many people who openly admit to seeing and talking to people no one else can see or hear. It
takes a lot of courage to do what you're doing."

If he only knew!

On my way over to the clinic, I'd peered into the rear-
view mirror of the taxi while I practiced the trembling
lower lip I hoped to use to gain the doctor's trust. I used it
now and watched him melt. He was either a compassionate man or a sucker for vulnerable women.

"It isn't courage," I said. "It's desperation. Things
have gotten worse since I came here to Chicago. When I
heard about this place... When I heard about you and all
the wonderful work you're doing..." I hiccuped over a
sob that sounded like the real thing. "I knew you were
the only one who could help me."

Doctor Gerard tipped his head and studied me. "So
you're seeing and hearing people here, too? Tell me, did
this happen right away, as soon as you arrived in town?
Or maybe..." He eased off the desk and edged closer. I
stepped back. "Or did it happen after you'd visited someplace special. A church, for instance? Or a hospital? A
cemetery?"

Like this never would have occurred to me without
him pointing it out, I let my mouth drop open. "A cemetery! How did you know? I mean, you've just met me and

you already have that much of my psyche figured out. That's amazing. Really. Everything he said about you is true. And here I thought that Dan Callahan was—"

One blush gets a guy's attention. The second one reels him in. Anxious to gauge his reaction and while Doctor Gerard was still hooked, I stammered, "I guess I've let the cat out of the bag, huh? Do you...Have you ever heard of a researcher named Dan Callahan?"

He pretended to consider my question, but I knew a stall when I saw one. Doctor Gerard knew Dan Callahan, all right. This wasn't news, and I didn't need him to confirm or deny it. What was interesting, though, was the spark of anger that flashed in the doctor's eyes. He was pissed, and maybe this whole being psychic thing was beginning to sink in, because I knew exactly why. I'd witnessed a meeting between Dan and the doctor there in Chicago. It looked as if Pepper Martin's aberrant behavior had never been on the agenda. Otherwise Doctor Gerard wouldn't have been so miffed at finding out that Dan and I shared a connection.

The only question I had left was why he cared so much.

Still wondering what was up, I watched Doctor Gerard nod, chuckle, and play it cool. "Scruffy kid with bad taste in clothes? So, you've run into the famous Dan Callahan. I should have known as soon as you mentioned brain scans. As it turns out, I know Dan well. He was a student of mine at one time, and we've just gotten in touch again. He's helping me conduct some research here at the clinic. Dan is a brilliant man, but he believes that science—and only science—can find the answers to life's mysteries. That's too bad. He has yet to learn that he has to trust his gut, not his instruments. He tries to rely on science when he should rely on instinct." Doctor Gerard paused for a moment, thinking. "What did Dan tell you after he conducted those brain scan tests?" he finally asked. "About the voices you hear? And the people you see?"

"Well, that's the thing about Dan, isn't it? He pretty much doesn't tell anybody anything." This was one of the few true things I'd said since I walked in; my courage bolstered by it, I went on. "Dan's always lurking and watching and saying weird things that don't make any sense."

"Things about your aberrant behavior?"

I think Doctor Gerard was going for funny. I was so not in the mood. "Things about how dangerous the unknown is," I said. "Things about how I need to be careful and watch my back. It doesn't make any sense, and it worries me, Doctor. I'm scared." For effect, I wrapped my arms around myself. "Maybe Dan saw more on those brain scans than he's willing to tell me. Do you think..." I swallowed hard. "Do you think I'm crazy?"

My question spurred the doctor into action. He headed for the door, and on his way past, he patted my arm. "I don't know what to think. And I can't know what to think. Neither can you. Not until we do some tests of our own."

"But you said science doesn't have the answers. You said we can't rely on tests and—"

His hand on the office door, Doctor Gerard paused. "I said my old friend, Dan Callahan, relies too heavily on tests. That doesn't mean there aren't some tests that are legitimate. And appropriate. With your permission, I'll

run some brain scans of my own. The data we collect
will give us a good idea of where you are, and a baseline
to work from. You wait here. I'll be right back."

He stepped into the hallway, and when the door
snapped closed behind him, I let go of the breath I was
holding. It caught again in a gasp of surprise when I
heard a voice right behind me.

"That's your idea of acting crazy enough to get accepted into Hilton's study?"

I didn't have to turn around to know that I'd been
joined by the aforementioned Madeline Tremayne, but
since I didn't like the tone of her voice, I spun to face her
anyway. Except for the whole tripping over her spirit in a
cemetery thing and getting talked into taking on this case
because she'd convinced me that Dan was in trouble,
Madeline and I hardly knew each other. That was close
enough for me.

Madeline was one of those stiff-assed academic
types, and like brainiacs everywhere, she thought she
was better—and smarter—than everyone else. Most
particularly, me. Apparently, she also thought she knew
more about investigating than I did.

I stepped back, my weight on one foot and my hands
on my hips. "News flash, girlfriend. I'm the detective
here. I know what I'm doing. Besides, it worked, didn't
it?"

"Hilton's a sucker." With a little no-holds-barred
fashion analysis and an afternoon spent with the latest
issue of *Cosmo* and the determination to follow through
on the beauty advice found in its pages, Madeline might
actually have been pretty. She had filmy blue eyes and a
cloud of blond hair that framed the face of an angel. Her
nose was tiny and upturned, her chin was well shaped

without being too masculine, and her lips bowed just enough to make her look pouty but not petulant. Too bad the effect was spoiled by her choice of clothing. That afternoon Madeline was dressed—as she had been every time I'd seen her—in a shapeless black skirt that skimmed the tops of her black loafers, a utilitarian cotton blouse, and a white lab coat that made her skin look as pale as death.

Pun intended.

Her hair was pulled back into a severe bun (a style that added years to the thirty she'd lived here on earth), and her reading glasses hung around her neck on a black cord.

She strolled over and sat on the arm of the chair I'd just gotten out of. "Just because he's going to do some scans doesn't mean Hilton believes you. You can't trust your luck on this, Pepper. You've got to find some concrete evidence against him before he gets back."

The angel face and nicely curved body may have been enough for her to get her own way when she was alive, but I wasn't about to be pushed around. Not by a dead woman who needed my help to begin with.

"It's too soon to panic," I told her. "Everything's going to be all right. You heard him. He's already interested in what I had to say. You said—"

"I said I thought Hilton was singling out certain patients and I think whatever he's doing with them, it's nothing good. You should have played up the whole fact that you're crazy. You should have tried to get him to talk about Dan some more."

"Number one, I'm not crazy. So there really was no reason for me to play that up. As for Dan…" I heard a noise out in the hallway and looked over my shoulder toward the door, but whoever it was, the person passed by. "I'm being subtle."

"You're wasting a perfectly good opportunity." She glanced toward the door, too, and outside in the hallway, I heard Doctor Gerard instruct his receptionist to tell the folks in the waiting room that he would be busy for at least thirty more minutes. "He's got to get all the equipment ready," Madeline said. "You've got a couple minutes to look through his things."

I shot her a look that pretty much told her what I thought of this idea.

"Come on, Pepper." If she could have, she would have dragged me closer to Doctor Gerard's desk. As it is, ghosts are incorporeal and can't touch anyone or anything of this world. That's why so many of them need my help. Because they can't touch or feel or move things, they need someone who's alive to accomplish all that for them. This, of course, includes solving murders and explains how I got mixed up in the whole investigating-for-the-dead sideline in the first place. "There's a safe in his credenza. That's where he keeps his research results. I know the combination. Come on, before he gets back."

Just in case Madeline got the crazy idea to reach out a hand and grab me, I backed away. When a ghost comes in contact with a living person, that person gets chilled to the bone.

"Listen up," I told her. "I'm in charge of this investigation. And I'm not about to blow it by doing something stupid. If he walks in here and finds me looking through his stuff, Doctor Gerard will know I'm up to something."

"If he walks in here and tests you and finds out you're

lying, he's going to know you're up to something anyway."

"Except that I'm not lying." I shouldn't have had to point out the obvious. "Since I'm talking to you, that pretty much proves I talk to people no one else sees, doesn't it?"

"It doesn't prove you know what you're doing. I could—"

"What?" I didn't usually taunt the dead. It's bad form. But this was one dead chick who had spent the last couple days getting on my nerves. "What are you going to do if I don't cooperate, Madeline? Open the safe yourself?"

She flinched as if I'd slapped her. "You don't have to rub it in."

"Or maybe I do, because you seem to keep forgetting that without me, you're nowhere. Literally." I heard footsteps and the squeaking sounds of a rolling cart out in the hallway. I lowered my voice. "I'm going to handle this my own way. You'll see. He'll believe me. He'll ask me to be in his study. Then I can take a closer look around and talk to his other subjects. I can find out what happened to Ernie and I can see how deep Dan is into this whole thing."

Madeline crossed her arms over her chest. "I can't believe you've got the brains to pull this off."

I was about to point out that I had brains to spare, and most importantly, I had the corporeal body she no longer owned, when the door opened and Doctor Gerard walked in. He pushed a rolling cart ahead of him. There was a piece of medical equipment on it that looked like one of those lie detectors on the TV crime shows.

"Sit down, Pepper." Of course, he couldn't see Madeline roosting on the arm of the chair. He waved me toward it. "We'll get some electrodes hooked up, and in a couple minutes, we'll know a lot more about that occipital lobe of yours."

I motioned to Madeline to get lost and strode over to the chair. Once I was settled, Doctor Gerard stuck electrodes on my forehead. When he was done, he had me place my arms on the arms of the chair. I remembered the day Dan had done the brain scan test on me, and I knew that next, Doctor Gerard would hook up electrodes on my wrists.

Which explains why I was surprised when instead of electrodes, he pulled a leather strap out of his back pocket and tied my arm to the chair.

"Hey!" I squirmed, but with one arm already immobile, it was hard to keep him from tying my other arm, too. "What are you doing? I don't remember this from when I had my first scans done."

"I think we're going to be able to dispense with the scans." Doctor Gerard opened the drawer on the side of the rolling cart. He pulled out a syringe as long as a banana. The needle pricked my skin, and the next second, a sensation like fire rushed into my arm and spread up into my chest and down my spine. My breath caught. My head throbbed. My tongue felt huge and heavy. I couldn't close my eyes.

"Doctor—" My voice was thick. My words were slow. "What...are...you..."

Behind Doctor Gerard, I saw Madeline click her tongue and shake her head. "I knew you were too stupid to handle this," she said.

"Not...stupid." The voice was mine, but it sounded

like it came from a million miles away. "Told you...
told you he'd believe me. I told you he'd...put me in
his...study."

S o how did I get into this mess?
    It was exactly what I was asking myself as I
watched Doctor Gerard give me a satisfied smile, then
turn to leave the room. Trouble is, try as I might, I
couldn't answer my own question. My head spun, and
when I saw tight-lipped, sneering Madeline fade and
wink out, I wasn't sure if it was for real or if I was hallu-
cinating. I knew for certain that my stomach flipped, because there was a sour taste in my mouth. I tried to
swallow it down, but it was a losing cause. My mouth
was parched, my tongue felt as if it had been blown up
with a tire pump, and my limbs were as numb as if I'd
taken a dip in the icy waters of Lake Michigan.

    Which explains why I couldn't say a word when the
doctor came back with a wheelchair. Or why I didn't
even try to fight when he untied my arms, lifted me, and
dumped me into it. My head rolled back, and I had the
horrifying realization that I actually might be drooling.
It was so not pretty, and rather than consider it, I let my
mind wander.

    Was it any surprise that when it did, it landed right
back in Cleveland on the day all this started?

2

Quinn Harrison had a small, fan-shaped scar on his left shoulder blade. He said he got it when he made the mistake of turning his back on a bad guy who grabbed a tire iron and swung hard, but I wasn't so sure I believed him. To me, it looked more like the mark of a woman's stiletto heel.

Not that I was going to get picky.

For one thing, Quinn is not the type of guy to get picky with. I mean, because of the whole macho, I'm-a-cop thing. And the fact that he's just about as gorgeous a hunk as any I'd ever met. It's those green eyes of his, and the way they're shot through with amber and flecked with blue. It makes him look a little standoffish. Like he's better than everyone else.

I guess after a lifetime of seeing his own reflection looking back at him from the mirror, he's pretty much come to believe it.

That would explain why we've butted heads a time or two when we've tripped over each other during my investigations. Of course, I could be wrong. When it comes to solving murders, Quinn's attitude might stem from the fact that he's a professional and I'm a rank amateur who has no business sticking my nose where it doesn't belong. If that's true, then I guess I can forgive him: he doesn't know about the ghosts.

Not that I was going to get picky about that, either.

Not at a time like this.

I lightly traced the boundaries of the scar on his back with the tip of one finger. At the same time, I stifled a yawn.

"You're awake." On the pillow next to mine, Quinn turned his head and looked my way. His grin was as hot as it had been the night before when we found ourselves suddenly out of the restaurant where we'd been having dinner, in my apartment, in my bedroom, and yes, in my bed. "Sleep well?"

"I didn't sleep at all." As if he didn't know. He was, after all, the cause of my sleeplessness. I boosted myself up long enough to glance at the clock on my bedside table, fell back against the mattress, and groaned. "I've got to be at work in two hours."

"Me, too." Quinn rolled over on his back, pushed a strand of inky hair out of his eyes, and rested his head on one bent arm. "We could call in sick."

"The morning after my birthday? Ella might be a free-thinking ex-hippie, but she'd never fall for that. She's the mom of three teenaged girls, remember. Comes with the territory. Moms have that spooky radar thing going on. They can detect lies like *I'm sick the day after I went out to celebrate my birthday* from a mile away."

"It's just as well. I've got a mountain of paperwork to fill out for a new case I'm working on." He sighed. I liked the way the whisper of it rustled through my bedroom almost as much as I liked the feel of his body next to mine. Sure, it sounds like a page out of one of those romance novels my own mom loves so much, but just thinking about everything we did during the night...

Well, let's suffice it to say that I needed to push back the covers, that's how hot I got.

"You're not getting up." Quinn's hands were large and his fingers were long. He wrapped them around my wrist. "We've got two hours."

"We do." My smile was a response to his. "And no, I'm not getting up. I'm just hot."

"It's February." He lifted his head long enough to look toward the window. "And if I'm not mistaken, it's snowing like a son of a bitch."

"Which doesn't mean I can't be hot."

"Oh, you're hot, all right." He tickled a hand over my shoulders, down to my stomach, and back up again, and like it had so many times during the night, his touch made me tingle from head to toe. "Makes me glad you were almost going to have to spend your birthday alone."

"Ella had something to do with you calling me, didn't she?" I suspected it was true the moment my office phone rang the afternoon before and I heard Quinn's voice on the line. "She's such a softy! She felt terrible that she had to back out of my birthday dinner because one of the girls was coming down with the flu. She called you and told you to call me. Admit it." I poked him in the ribs. "You wouldn't have even known it was my birthday otherwise."

"How could I know when you never told me when your birthday was?"

"You know how many traffic tickets I've gotten. And how many parking tickets. You keep reminding me about those. You know how tall I am and—" I gulped. "And probably how much I weigh. Whether I tell you things or not, you find them out. You know everything about me."

Quinn flipped to his side and propped his head on one hand. "Not everything. I do know that you can't seem to mind your own business. But I don't know exactly how you got involved in those murder investigations last year. Or why."

It was an open invitation and the perfect opportunity for me to come clean. In a purely symbolic way, of course. And if ever there was a right time to do it, this was it. Yeah, the sex was that good.

None of which explained why I hesitated. Or why, after that moment's hesitation, I changed the subject. Or should I say I got the subject back on track? After all, I wasn't the one who changed it in the first place.

"Ella's a sucker for the underdog. She didn't want me to be alone on my birthday. That's why she told you to give me a call."

Quinn took the hint. Or maybe he knew what I knew: the morning after the night before is not the time to start an argument. Not when the night before was so good and the morning after was promising more of the same. "Ella's a nice lady. And she got her wish. You didn't spend your birthday alone."

I snuggled further into the mattress. "Something tells me this wasn't what she had in mind."

"Oh, come on! Give the lady some credit. She might

be middle-aged, but she's not dead. This was exactly what she had in mind."

It was so far from every concept I'd ever had about Ella, I gasped. "She'd be mortified."

"She'd be jealous."

He was right. This time, I was the one who grinned.

"So..." Quinn had tucked his cell phone under his pillow. Such are the demands of a homicide detective's job. He reached for it and checked the time. "Now we've got an hour and fifty minutes. How do you want to spend the time?"

Oh come on! I really don't have to say how I responded, do I?

G ood thing I live close to Garden View Cemetery. By the time we were done, I had less than an hour to get to work.

Freezing, I slipped into my flannel robe and stood in front of my open closet, wondering what to wear to the office, while Quinn took a shower, then offered to make coffee and toast. While he was at it, he called his lieutenant and, as casually as if it was an everyday thing, told her he'd been delayed and he'd be a little late.

Maybe it was an everyday thing.

In spite of myself, I wondered how many mornings he spent just like this. And where he spent them. And who he spent them with.

Just as quickly, I told myself to stop being small-minded, plucked a pair of creamy-colored wool pants off their hanger, and went in search of the brown mohair sweater my mom had given me for Christmas. By the time I found it in a pile of clothes I'd brought home from the dry cleaner and never put away, the coffee was ready, so before I headed into the shower, I poured a cup and took a gulp. Quinn made good coffee. Quinn, I can say with some authority, did a lot of things really well.

"Oh no." When I turned to slip past where he was sitting at my kitchen table, he grabbed my hand. He held out a piece of toast coated with strawberry jam. "You haven't eaten breakfast."

"I don't have time for breakfast."

"It's the most important meal of the day."

I could have argued. I would have—honest—if he hadn't pulled me onto his lap, wrapped his arms around me, and put the toast to my lips. I took a bite.

"See?" Quinn settled me and reached around me for his coffee cup. He must have been warm-blooded; he was wearing only boxers. His skin was still warm from the shower. I sunk back against him. He smelled like my mango bath gel. "Don't you feel better already?"

"I didn't feel bad to begin with."

He patted my butt. "I'll say."

"Not what I meant."

"But true, nonetheless." Though it was piping hot, he drank down his coffee. When he spoke again, I didn't have to look over my shoulder to know he was smiling. One night with Quinn and already, I could recognize the purr of satisfaction in his voice. "I was just thinking," he said. "You know, about last fall. About what might have happened if you never broke down and called me."

Did my shoulders automatically shoot back and my spine stiffen? I didn't like to think I was that touchy, but it was hard to deny facts. Before I said a word, I forced myself to relax. I took another bite of toast, too. Maybe the strawberry jam would sweeten the acid note in my voice. "Is that what you call it, breaking down? I didn't know this was some kind of competition."

"Not what I meant." He shooed me away long enough to get up and pour another cup of coffee, but when he sat back down and patted his lap, inviting me to get comfortable again, I pretended not to notice. "I meant I'm glad we've been seeing each other."

"And we might not be if I didn't make the first move."

His shrug said it all. "Last fall when you were messing around pretending to investigate the death of that ancient rock star—"

"I wasn't messing around. I found his killer, didn't I?"

"And nearly got yourself killed in the bargain." I would have been offended if it wasn't true. And if Quinn hadn't risked his own life to save mine when the killer got the best of me, tied me up, and tossed me in Lake Erie.

He washed away his comment with a sip of coffee. "I told you then that I wasn't going to be the one to come running after you. It's not the way I work."

"Oh, you work things like this, do you?" My voice was sharper than I would have liked, and I hoped Quinn didn't notice. He never flinched, so maybe he didn't. Or maybe that meant he did. In an effort to contain my frustration, I curled my hands into fists. "I don't think either one of us wants to fight."

"Who's fighting?" He finished the last of a piece of toast and brushed the crumbs from his hands. When he was done with his coffee, he took his cup to the sink. "I said I'm glad we're seeing each other. There, I'm being perfectly honest and aboveboard. I'm showing my softer side the way women say men never do. Big points for me." He did his best to smooth my ruffled feathers with a thousand-watt smile. "And hey, you have to admit, no matter what, I'm better than that dead guy you said you were dating last fall."

This time, I didn't smile back. I mean, how could I? Though Quinn thought I'd been kidding the autumn before when I told him I had to pass on a date with him because I was waiting at the cemetery for a dead guy, he didn't know I was as serious as a heart attack. In fact, the dead guy in question wasn't just any dead guy. He was rock legend Damon Curtis, and truth be told, we weren't just dating. We were in love. Of course, the whole dead thing has a way of ruining even the best of relationships. Damon was incorporeal. I was pining. Our romance was doomed from the start.

But come to think of it (and believe me, I'd thought about it plenty since the day I solved his murder and Damon crossed over and left me with nothing but questions about how I could live my empty life to its fullest), what I had with him was far more real—and far more profound—than anything I'd ever had with any other guy.

Present company included.

The thought caught me off guard, and I gave myself a mental slap. Quinn had never lied. He never pretended this was something more than it was. What it was, was great sex and a night to remember, and back before I met Damon, that had always been enough for me. It was enough for me now.

Wasn't it?

My coffee tasted bitter, and I went to the sink and spilled it out. "One too many sour-apple martinis and even the most levelheaded girl is apt to do crazy things," I grumbled.

Quinn frowned in return. "Are you saying you only went to bed with me because you were drunk?"

"Maybe not drunk enough."

"Which means, what? That you're sorry we—"

"I wasn't. Can't that be enough?"

"Does it have to be?"

Even I wasn't sure what we were arguing about; I only knew that there was some doubt niggling at my insides, chilling all the places that had been oh-so-hot just a short time before. Once upon a time, a night like the one I'd just had would have been the stuff of dreams. And now?

Now, I wondered where we were headed, me and Quinn. I questioned whether we were suited for each other and whether we could ever be compatible for more than one night, no matter how incredible it happened to be.

I found myself examining a conscience I never even knew I had until I started into this investigation-for-the-dead gig, and when I did, I had no choice but to face the stark truth: I could never be completely honest with Quinn—not about the ghosts or my Gift or the reason I investigated murders that most people had long forgotten—because if I was, he'd think I was a nut job. And if I couldn't be honest with him...Well, then we couldn't ever have anything that would pass for a relationship.

My shoulders slumped. "Sorry," I said, because let's face it, even though he and I were talking about different things, I was sorry, and it was what he wanted to hear anyway. "I can be cranky in the morning."

"That's good to know." When he moved toward me, I didn't back away. "I'll be careful from now on."

"Is there going to be a now on?"

He stopped in his tracks. "Is that what this is about? I didn't think you were the kind of girl who was picky about—"

"What? About wanting the guy she's with to respect her? To like her? About wanting to know that he realizes she's smart and savvy and capable of doing more than just keeping him happy in bed?"

When he closed in on me, a mischievous smile played around the corners of his mouth. "I like you," he said. He toyed with one end of the belt that cinched my robe around my waist. "I respect you. I think you're savvy and capable and—"

"Smart?" I looked him in the eye.

"Not if it means you getting tangled up in any more of my investigations."

"Oh, like I really have a choice!"

"Don't you?"

It was another opportunity to tell him about my Gift, and I so didn't want to go there. There were worse things than arguing with Quinn about...er...whatever it was we were arguing about. I might be willing to bare my body and my fantasies to him, but when it came to my soul, that was another thing altogether.

I back-stepped toward the bathroom. "I've got to get moving," I said.

"Right now?" He loosened the tie on my robe and slipped his hands inside. "You've got—"

"Thirty minutes." My suspicions were confirmed by the clock that hung above the sink.

Which didn't mean it was easy to ignore the thrill that raced up my spine when Quinn skimmed his hands over my hips.

And have I mentioned that Quinn's got a chest that looks as if it were chipped out of marble?

"Really, I've got to get going." I made a halfhearted attempt to pull away, and I wasn't sure if I was disappointed or relieved when he let me go.

Before I could decide—or change my mind—I hurried into the bathroom. When I turned on the shower, I made sure the water was cold.

E ven a ticking clock and the sense of obligation I felt to get to work reasonably on time wasn't enough to hurry me. Not too much, anyway. A girl has to have standards, after all, and I'm all about tradition. I wasn't about to start a new one by arriving at the office without makeup or with my hair a mess. By the time I walked out of the bathroom fit to be seen in public, Quinn was dressed. He was also just snapping closed my cell phone.

"It rang just as I was walking by," he said by way of explanation. "That was Dan."

I stopped mid-stride and gave him a look I can only imagine was incredulous.

"Dan? Dan Callahan?"

"That's what the guy said. And get this, he said he was returning your call from back in the fall. Nothing like waiting a few months to catch up on messages, huh?"

"Dan? Dan Callahan?"

Quinn is not known for his patience. Which explains

why he didn't bother answering a second time. He slanted me a look. "You're surprised."

"You think?" Sarcasm did not become me, and I avoided it on all occasions. Except, of course, when it was absolutely necessary. Too taken by surprise to do anything else, I flopped down on the couch. "Dan? Are you sure that's what he said?"

This time, he didn't even pretend he was listening. Quinn went over to the dining room table where he'd left his shoulder holster and gun the night before. He strapped the holster on and slipped his suit coat over it.

"You didn't call this Dan guy around the same time you called me last fall, did you? I mean, you weren't hedging your bets or anything, were you?"

This time, I got to be the one who avoided the question. "What did he want?" I asked instead.

Quinn shrugged. "Said he's been busy. Said he's sorry he hasn't had the chance to return your call. Something about being out of the country for the last couple months. He said he read about that rock-and-roll murder investigation in all the papers and he said to tell you he was glad he was able to help you solve your case." He looked at me hard. "You had a case? And he helped you solve it?"

I thought about the best way to answer and decided almost instantly there was no use even trying. What Dan had done was provide me with the EVP—that's electronic voice phenomenon, a term used by paranormal investigators to explain the ghostly sounds they sometimes record—that enabled me to get my investigation on the right track.

Quinn's Burberry raincoat was tossed on a living room chair. He picked it up, but he never took his eyes off me.

I may have been in shock from the news of Dan's call, but I'm not stupid. I knew Quinn was waiting for me to tell him who, exactly, Dan was. I might have done it, too. If only I could figure it out myself.

See, Dan Callahan was just another of the big question marks in my life, a brain researcher who wasn't, who knew more about ghosts than he should have even though he said he didn't. Get it? He'd been MIA for months, and now, out of nowhere, he was back. Just like that. And just like that, I was supposed to find the words that made sense of it all?

I shook my head, trying to clear my thoughts as I struggled for an explanation that would appease Quinn and help me sort through the tidal wave of emotions that swamped me. "Dan's this guy I know," I said.

"I'm this guy you know."

"I don't know Dan like I know you." I didn't say it to satisfy any caveman tendencies Quinn might have. Unfortunate or otherwise, it happened to be the truth. "Dan and I are just friends. Not even friends. We're acquaintances."

Was I imagining the spark of satisfaction that flared in Quinn's impossibly green eyes? I think not. He headed for the door. "Dan said he's going to be out of town for a couple weeks, but he'll give you a call when he gets back."

"OK." It seemed like a perfectly stupid thing to say considering the enormity of all Quinn had just told me. "Did he say anything else?"

"Well yeah, he did." With his hand on the doorknob, Quinn paused and turned to me. "He said that now that you've had a chance to think about everything he did for you, maybe you'll trust him and you two can finally be open and honest with each other. Call me nuts, but I don't think a guy who leaves another guy—me—a message about being open and honest with you is exactly ready to be open and honest with you. If you know what I mean."

So much for my trying to dodge the bullet with the ol' *we're just friends* story. I wasn't sure how I was going to explain what I didn't understand myself, but as it turned out, I didn't have to. My phone rang again.

Yeah, I was a little fast picking it up. And a little disappointed when I realized the voice on the other end was Ella's and not Dan's. I listened to her launch into what she had to say at the same time I watched Quinn watch me. He thought it might be Dan, too, and when I nodded and automatically responded to something my boss said with a "Yes, Ella," I saw some of the stiffness go out of his shoulders.

When Ella was done and I hung up, Quinn opened the door.

"I've got an FOP meeting tonight," he said, and explained with, "that's the Fraternal Order of Police. I'm giving a report about finances and...well, stuff you wouldn't be interested in. Tomorrow night?"

It took me a moment to realize what he was asking.

"Tomorrow night? You mean you want to—"

"See you again?" Quinn laughed. "You don't think I'm going to hold that being-cranky-in-the-morning thing against you, do you?"

"And Dan?"

His chin came up a fraction of an inch. "You said you were just friends."

"We are."

"Which means that if I show up here tomorrow night, say about seven, we could—"

"I won't be here." I looked at the phone in my hands. "That was Ella. Now all three of her girls have the flu and she thinks she's coming down with it, too. She's supposed to go to a cemetery conference, and there's no way. I have to go in her place."

"So no date tomorrow night?"

"No date tomorrow." My head was already reeling through the possibilities of what I'd need to pack and whether I needed a quick trip to Nordstrom for any last-minute outfits, and how I'd get to the airport in time. "By tomorrow night, I'll be in Chicago."

3

"Isn't it fabulous? I mean, just look around. It's...it's breathtaking!"

Didn't it figure? I was three-hundred-and-some miles from home and still, I'd managed to hook up with an Ella clone. The middle-aged, middle-sized woman had introduced herself earlier as Doris from Detroit. Now, I watched as she twirled like a ballerina in her sensible, low-heeled boots so she could take a good look all around the frozen landscape where we stood. "It's the most beautiful cemetery I've ever seen," she said, her words choked with emotion and her breath forming a cloud as it escaped from behind the red scarf she had wound all the way up to her chin. "Aren't you feeling like the luckiest girl alive to be here in Ella's place, Penelope?"

I glanced down at the conference name badge that hung around my neck and groaned, vowing that I would make the necessary adjustments to it as soon as I got ahold of a thick black Sharpie.

If I didn't freeze to death first.

Unlike the groups of people who had just gotten off the tour bus with us and whose conversations I could hear, I had little (more like nothing) to say about the concept of Victorian cemeteries, nineteenth-century funerary traditions, or the benefits of granite over marble for the building of monuments. All I could manage through my chattering teeth was, "It reminds me a lot of Garden View."

"Aren't you the fortunate one, to be working in a cemetery like that!" A man named Grant stepped close and muscled in on the small talk. Or maybe he was just trying to keep warm. "I'll tell you what..." He was either distracted by my name badge or my chest. Either way, when he finally looked up and into my eyes, his cheeks were pink. So were the tips of his ears where they showed below his stocking cap. "I'll tell you what, Penelope, back in Peoria, we're plenty jealous of that cemetery where you work. It's that famous."

I didn't so much smile in response to this announcement as I did grit my teeth. When my face froze in the expression, Grant took it as a good sign. He stepped closer. I stood my ground. Although it was only the first stop on our tour of Graceland Cemetery in the heart of Chicago, I was quickly learning that, leopard-print lining aside, my Dolce & Gabbana tall patent boots didn't provide much in the way of warmth. There was no use trying to move when I couldn't feel my feet.

"We'll have a lot to talk about at the conference dinner tonight." Grant winked. Or maybe the twitch was simply a reaction to the icy wind that howled through the cemetery. "Just imagine how exciting the week is going to be. Discussing cemetery business and nothing else! Like dying and going to heaven, huh?" Funny guy that he was, Grant emphasized this by poking an elbow into my ribs.

"And Penelope's even giving a talk." Although this tour was the first item on the week's agenda, Doris, it seemed, had already been through the conference program with a fine-tooth comb. *"Reactions to the Resurrectionists in the Planning and Design of the Urban Cemetery.* Isn't that right, Penelope?"

"It's Ella's talk. I'm just going to read it." I thought it wise to make this distinction before anyone actually thought I knew who—or what—these Resurrectionists were or why they cared how cemeteries were designed. "She couldn't be here. She's—"

"Sick. Yes, I know. I talked to her before I left home." Doris patted my arm. Her mittens were pink and thick and wooly. They looked warmer—but not nearly as pretty—as the black cashmere gloves that matched my black three-quarter-length wool jacket. "Ella and I are old friends. We see each other at conferences like this every year. I'm sorry she's not going to be here. We've had some good times, I'll tell you that." Doris chuckled. "Someday, you have to ask her about the time we got locked in the cemetery in Sheboygan. That story will make you howl!"

Fortunately, before I had any hope of responding, our tour guide called us to order. Her name was Stephanie and she was young, squat, and perky. She obviously loved her job. I had no doubt that someday, she would grow up to be just like Ella and Doris. "I promised a little history, so here goes," she said. "Graceland, as many of you probably already know, was established in 1860. It was originally outside the Chicago city limits in a town called Lake View. The old city cemetery was in what's now Lincoln Park. Bodies were removed from there when it was determined that cemetery was a health hazard because of overcrowding and waterborne diseases."

Doris leaned closer. "Such fascinating stuff!"

More politically correct than the *"Ew!"* I whispered.

"Those bodies were brought here and reburied, and eventually, the city swallowed Lake View and Graceland, too," Stephanie went on. "The cemetery now covers one hundred and nineteen acres and includes many famous monuments. We're going to see a lot of them this afternoon, but I thought we should start here, with the largest and one of the most famous—the burial site of Potter and Bertha Palmer." She waved a hand over her shoulder, directing our attention to what looked like a Greek temple.

I'd never been to Greece, and believe me, I don't remember much of what I learned as an art history major back at college. I'd never been to Chicago before, either, and even if I had, I sure wouldn't have hung around this place. There was no explanation for why I took one gander at the Palmer memorial and was smack in the middle of a déjà-vu experience.

The pillars that surrounded the open-sided platform...

The two huge sarcophagus (sarcophagi?) inside...

Even the way the anemic afternoon sunshine filtered through a layer of leaden clouds and outlined the bony branches of trees...

I could have sworn I'd seen it all before.

Or maybe my brain was playing tricks on me, shutting down right before I froze up like a margarita.

The shiver that snaked over my shoulders had less to do with the cold than it did with me coming to my senses. Just because I was flash-frozen didn't mean I had to look it, I reminded myself. Before the cold could wreak any more havoc and chap my lips, I opened my purse and felt around inside for my lip gloss.

What I pulled out instead was a postcard. One I'd forgotten I had.

My mind blinked back to the night the autumn before when I left my former fiancé's most recent engagement party and found the postcard on the street. Sure, I glanced at it then, but I had better things to think about, and the postcard wasn't important; I could have sworn I'd tossed it. Not so. It looked as if I'd transferred it out of my Jimmy Choo evening bag (a sweet little satin clutch with a short leather shoulder strap) to my everyday purse along with my lipstick and my mascara and such. Apparently, it had been hiding at the bottom of my purse ever since.

Now, I looked at the picture on the postcard, then over at the imposing Palmer monument.

Oh yeah, they were one and the same.

That's when I remembered the single word scrawled across the back of the card, "Help."

I may have groaned. I don't remember. I do know that a couple people turned away from Stephanie to glare at me for interrupting. I also remember that before I stuffed the postcard in my pocket, I looked over at the Palmer memorial one more time, and that when I did, I saw something I hadn't seen before. Or I should say, someone.

There was a woman standing just beyond the memorial, looking down at one of the gravestones near her feet. She wasn't wearing a coat.

I've been known to be slow on the uptake about any number of things (as I have proved with my engagement to Joel and perhaps even by taking so long to realize my night with Quinn was one of those maybe-it-never-should-have-happened events), but when it comes to my Gift, believe me, I was starting to get the message loud and clear: the woman at the grave was a ghost.

I groaned again. And grumbled, too. I actually thought about getting back on the tour bus where it was nice and warm and telling the driver I was sick and needed to return to the hotel, pronto.

I didn't. And here's why:

#1 - By this time in my career as investigator for the dead, I knew I couldn't just walk away. Believe me, I'd tried this before and it never worked. If I left now, I'd only find myself back here again. I wasn't going to take the chance that next time, it might actually be colder.

#2 - I'd already investigated three cases for those who rested but not in peace, and I knew the score. If I ignored them, they would bug me.

#3 - Ghosts mean trouble. Always. But even dealing with a ghost is better than facing the inevitability of a boring conference, and this conference had all the makings of being as dull as watching paint dry. I didn't want to be threatened, shot at, beat up, or followed by menacing hit-man types (all of which happens when I'm on a case), but at least being threatened and shot at and blah,

blah, blah keeps me awake and interested. *Reactions to the Resurrectionists in the Planning and Design of the Urban Cemetery* definitely does not.

#4 - Well…this one is the hardest to explain. It had to do with Damon Curtis, my most recent client, who, in addition to teaching me that love between the dead and the living is not the most feasible of arrangements, had made me realize that life was to be lived. Even among the dead. Sure, it sounded like some weird version of a Hallmark card, but what Damon said was true, and I had finally come to accept it: I had to take every opportunity and pursue every adventure (hence the encounter with Quinn). I had to grab the proverbial bull by the horns, and in my case, that meant accepting my Gift and making the most of it.

Did I like the conclusion I came to? Not one bit. But like it or not, the ability to talk to the dead was as much a part of me as my red hair and my unerring fashion sense. I had a skill no one else had. The flip side, of course, was the responsibility that came along with it.

Before I could convince myself otherwise, I slipped away from Doris and the rest of the cemeteries-are-great crowd, skirted the back of the group, arced around, and make a wide swing behind the Palmer memorial. I was nearly to the other side of it and closing in on my newest close encounter of the woo-woo kind when I hit a pocket of air so cold, it made the frosty Chicago weather feel like a summer day.

I stopped, frozen by the chill and strangely ill at ease. Fear prickled up my spine. It settled on my shoulders. I'd faced bad guys who were out to kill me, and rock-and-rollers with mayhem in their hearts. I'd once nearly gotten myself thrown off a very high bridge. And I'm not going to lie: every one of those times, I was scared shitless.

But not like this.

This was the kind of fear that lives in nightmares. It was gnawing and inescapable and even if I turned my back on it and ran for the tour bus, I knew it would follow me. I had no choice but to wait it out, and for what seemed like a long time, I stood stock-still and listened to the silence press against my ears while my heart slammed against my ribs. A creepy sensation crawled along my skin, leaving a trail of goose bumps behind. If it wasn't frozen solid, the hair on the back of my neck would have stood on end.

Too afraid to look and too afraid not to, I swallowed around the lump in my throat and dared a glance over my shoulder. I was just in time to see something slink behind a tree twenty feet away.

Man or woman, human or animal, I couldn't say. I did know it was big and black and it wasn't solid. It looked hazy, like a shadow, and like a shadow, it was gone in an instant.

Once it was gone, the air warmed to just below freezing, and before it could get colder again—and before that shadow could come back and totally freak me out—I hurried over to where the woman waited.

Maybe she didn't see the shadow. Or maybe, being ectoplasm and all, she simply didn't get frightened. She never flinched. She didn't say a word, either. All she did was watch me as I got nearer.

I saw right away that with a little fashion advice, a

complete makeover from the cosmetics counter at Saks, and a visit to a reputable aesthetician for some serious moisturizing, she actually might be pretty. She had fine porcelain skin, pale hair, and eyes that were blue and misty. The effect, sadly, was lost thanks to the fact that her hair was pulled back severely from her face. The shapeless black skirt did nothing for her slim figure and the white button-down shirt didn't help. Neither did the white lab coat that hung from her shoulders. The chunky black loafers were so eighties. And the Coke-bottle glasses ... well, maybe not everyone can afford Lasik, but, really, is there any excuse for pretending to be back in the Dark Ages before contacts were invented?

She looked me up and down, studying me as closely as I was watching her. I'm pretty sure I wasn't imagining it when her top lip curled.

"You're not what I expected," she said.

Not the best way to begin a conversation. Especially when I was already cold and bored. It was no wonder I snapped back. "What, you don't have some kind of ghostly Internet over on the Other Side? You weren't told to look for the best-dressed woman in the cemetery?"

She didn't smile. "I thought you would be older and ... you know ..."

"Not as pretty?"

A serious plucking would have done her eyebrows a world of good. They did a slow slide up her forehead. "I didn't want to be rude, but since you insist. I was going to say that I thought you'd look smarter."

"I'm plenty smart."

"Sure you are."

She said this in the same tone of voice I'd once heard

a clerk at Nordstrom use when a woman who shouldn't have been caught dead in a tankini sauntered out of the dressing room and asked how she looked.

Unlike that shopper, I was good at picking up on subtleties. I stepped back, shifting my weight to one foot. "You're the one who wanted to see me. At least I'm guessing you had something to do with the postcard and—hey!" An idea struck, and though I don't like exposing my ignorance or my weaknesses—not to anybody—I'd never been good at hiding my curiosity. I pulled the postcard out of my pocket and waved it in the air. "How'd you do that, anyway? Ghosts can't touch things. How did you write on this postcard? And how did you get it to me?"

"Ghosts can't touch things, is that what you think?" A smile touched her lips. Since she was already as cold as anybody can get, I doubt if she did it for warmth, but she tucked her hands into the pockets of her lab coat. "Looks like you don't know everything after all."

Like I said, I don't like admitting I'm not at the top of my game. Naturally, I prickled, and honestly, it wasn't such a bad thing. A little healthy anger went a long way toward warming me up. "I do know there's a reason you brought me here. And I'm pretty sure..." I pretended to think about this before I said, "No, I'm *very* sure I'm the only one who can see you and the only one who can help you. I suggest you cut the sarcasm."

"Oh, you are a feisty one! I hear that goes along with the red hair." She leaned nearer to give me a closer look. "If it's natural."

My smile was as brittle as the chill wind. "It's natural, all right. So's the curl. Which means I don't have to handle bad hair days by pulling my hair away from my face and tying it up in an old-lady bun."

"How clever of you to notice."

Two minutes with this spook and already she was getting on my nerves. I didn't walk away, though, not even when I saw out of the corner of my eye that the cemetery conference group had already moved on to another nearby monument. Remember what I said earlier. I knew that even if I left, this ghostly pain in the ass would find me again. I might as well get it over with. Though it was unlike me, I decided it was time to find some common middle ground. If I was going to get anywhere, a change of subject was in order.

I glanced toward where I'd last seen the hulking shadow and breathed a sigh of relief when I saw it was nowhere in sight. "What's with the spooky shadow?" I asked the woman.

Her shrug was barely noticeable. "I don't know what you're talking about."

"All rightee." Like I said, I was all about being non-confrontational. And smart enough to know arguing with this ghost would get me nowhere. I stepped closer and looked down at the gravestone nearest to where she stood. "Madeline Tremayne. Is that you?"

She didn't look at the gravestone but kept her head up. Her jaw was rigid. "It used to be."

I checked the dates carved into the rose granite. "You've only been dead for three years. And you didn't live all that long. Thirty? You don't look—"

"That old?" Her eyes flared.

"I was going to say that young. It's the lab coat. Sorry, but you must have realized the lab coat and the glasses and the shoes…" I couldn't make myself look at her black loafers again. "If you had any sense of style—"

"Women with brains don't need a sense of style. And

women who are psychologically healthy aren't fixated on looks and fashion."

"Fixated? Think so?" I glared at her. "Well, come to think of it, you must believe it. And you must have some pretty heavy psychological issues, too. Otherwise, you wouldn't be trying to prove how psychologically healthy you are by going out of your way to look so frumpy."

Madeline simply stared at me, her chin steady and her lips pulled into a thin line. Easy for her to do; she wasn't wearing any lipstick so she didn't have to worry about smudging it or biting it off. "It's far too early for a diagnosis, of course," she said, "but if push came to shove and I had to guess, I'd go with NPD. In case you don't know, and I'm certain you don't since I think it's clear you've never read the research of Heinz Kohut or the *Diagnostic and Statistical Manual of Mental Disorders*, that's narcissistic personality disorder. It's as clear as clear can be. You're preoccupied with your own physical and social image. You're wrapped up in your own thoughts and feelings without any concern for others at all. With your defensive attitude and your overblown sense of self-importance...Yes, I think we're looking at a classic case here. I do hope you're seeing a therapist, if not for yourself then out of consideration for all the people around you."

She wasn't funny and I wasn't laughing. "I don't need a therapist," I told her, even though I shouldn't have had to. "What I do need is to be left alone. What you need is to remember that if you're going to ask a living person for help, you need to show a little respect in return."

"Yes, yes, of course." I might have taken this as a form of apology if she wasn't nodding and mumbling and talking to herself. And if she didn't continue with her half-baked diagnosis. "Concern for your own affairs to the exclusion of all others, the inability to empathize with others who have clearly—being dead—gone through far more than you, interpersonal inflexibility, an insistence that you're the only one who's right and to take things far too personally..." Her mind apparently made up, she looked at me again. "You shouldn't be ashamed of it, you know. It's like any mental illness, and fortunately for you, I'm able to understand the root cause. You feel rejected. Humiliated. Threatened when you're criticized."

"And out of patience when I have to deal with stupid people, dead or alive." To prove it, I turned around and stalked away. "Sorry, lady, but you've offended the wrong Gifted person. Oh, wait!" I whirled back around; I didn't want to miss her expression when I delivered my parting shot. "I'm the only one with the Gift, aren't I? I guess that would sound narcissistic. Except that it's true. Just like it's true that I can choose to help whichever ghosts I want. News flash, the ones that piss me off don't get the time of day. Whatever you wanted my help with, you can just forget it."

"Fine." She folded her arms over her chest. "Go back to your cemetery conference and forget this ever happened. It doesn't make one bit of difference to me. After all, I wasn't going to ask for your help for myself. And if you don't want to help Dan—"

"Dan? Dan Callahan?" Without hesitating, I turned right back around and marched over to where Madeline waited. "You know Dan Callahan?"

Her slow smile was the only answer I needed, and I

cursed myself and this Gift of mine, which had a way of getting me in over my head every time.

While I was at it, I cursed Madeline, too. She had me at the first mention of Dan's name. And damn it, she knew it, too.

I was cool, calm, and collected. For about three and a half seconds. Then I closed in on Madeline.

"How do you know Dan?"

She slanted me a look. "Is that more than professional curiosity I hear in your voice?"

I wasn't about to confess my very personal interest in Dan. Not this early in the conversation. And not to this particular spook. I raised my chin, but since I was about a foot taller than Madeline to begin with, this didn't exactly have the imposing effect I was hoping for. I had to look down again to look her in the eye.

"Dan wants to study my brain," I told her. "And my aberrant behavior. He recorded the EVP that helped solve my last case. I can be plenty curious. Dan and me, we've got history."

"Is that all you have?"

It took me a second to figure out what she was getting

at. "No way!" I didn't so much wave away the very idea with one cashmere-enshrouded hand as I dismissed the subject as none of Madeline's business. "You can't be serious. Dan and I have never—"

"But it's not like you don't want to."

Did I?

OK, Dan was cute. He was more than cute. Dan was sexy. In a dorky sort of way. It never ceased to amaze me that I thought of him that way, since dorks have never been my thing and geeky scientists aren't exactly on the top of my list when it comes to guys I want to get up close and personal with.

Like I'd been up close and personal with Quinn.

The thought brought me up short, and I curled my hands into fists and held my arms close to my sides, keeping my secrets as carefully as I chose my words. This was not the time. And Madeline was not the person who needed to hear any of this.

I deflected her question with one of my own. "How do you know Dan?" I asked her again.

She expected more in the way of me owning up to Dan's deliciousness. When she didn't get it, her eyes narrowed. "I worked with him," she said. "Here in Chicago. At the Gerard Clinic."

"Dan worked in Chicago?"

"Ah, something else you didn't know." Madeline's smile was sleek. "Looks like the great detective needs a little help now and then after all. Danny…" Though it wasn't mussed or rumpled, she smoothed a hand over her lab coat. "He was a graduate student at Northwestern at the time. He was completing his dissertation and working with Doctor Hilton Gerard." She paused, waiting for me to respond, and when I didn't, Madeline shook her head sadly. "You've never heard of Doctor Gerard, have you?"

"I've heard of Doctor Doolittle. And Doctor Who. Is this Doctor Gerard guy related to either of them?"

"Ah yes, hiding your inadequacies behind jokes that aren't funny." Madeline seemed to make a mental note of this before she turned her attention back to our conversation. "Hilton Gerard is one of the most distinguished psychiatrists in the country. He runs the Gerard Clinic."

"Where Dan used to work."

"I worked there, too." This was obviously a matter of some pride to Madeline. Her chin came up. Her eyes sparkled as much as a dead person's can. "I was Hilton's chief research assistant."

"Which explains how you knew Dan."

This was not the gushy response she was expecting. I knew this when she pouted. On Madeline, it was not a pretty expression. "I conducted all Hilton's clinical studies," she said, in answer to the questions I was supposed to ask but didn't. "I interviewed and selected our test subjects, and I was in charge of collecting, compiling, and synthesizing our research data. The day-to-day operations of the clinic, that's Hilton's bailiwick. So are the grant proposals. And the fundraising . . . well, nobody can get the city's movers and shakers to open their wallets the way Hilton can. He's a genius."

"And he knows Dan."

Madeline let go of an annoyed sigh. I couldn't help but notice that when she did, there was no puff of cloudy air around her mouth. "Yes, Hilton knows Danny. That's the problem, don't you see?"

"Kind of hard to see something when you're not making anything clear." My fingers were numb; I shoved my hands in my pockets. "You want to explain what a job Dan had in grad school has to do with him being in trouble now?"

"I would. If you'd stop jabbering." Madeline stepped away from her grave. While she collected her thoughts, she paced back and forth, and when she was finally ready to speak, she stopped directly in front of me. "Three years ago, I left the clinic late one night and I got mugged. The mugger panicked when I didn't produce my wallet as quickly as he would have liked. He shot me. I died in the alley outside the clinic's back door."

"No way Dan had anything to do with that."

Madeline's eyes glistened. "So, though you pretend you're not interested in a personal sort of way, you do think highly enough of Danny to know he'd never do anything wrong. From a psychological standpoint, that's very interesting. You try not to reveal your true emotions, but—"

"Get back on track, will you, before I shoot you myself."

Madeline got the message. "Danny wasn't involved in my murder. You're correct in thinking that. He wasn't even at the clinic that night, though he was supposed to be. He had some statistics to tabulate and a few reports he should have been going over. But—"

"But he wasn't there and that's why you were alone and that's how you got mugged. Now you're pissed and you want justice." I'd heard this song and dance before, or at least ones similar to it. It didn't take more than a nanosecond for me to make up my mind. "If Dan wasn't there when he was supposed to be, then he must have had a good reason. So, nice try, but I'm not going to help you get your revenge from beyond the grave. Not against Dan."

"You're defending him. Even though you don't know the whole story. I like that!" Madeline smiled. When a skeleton finger of sun poked through the clouds, her eyes glittered. "That's nice. It proves you have feelings for him." Before I could respond with a lie, she went on. "Good thing I'm not asking for revenge."

"Not against Dan. OK, I get that since it wasn't his fault. But how about against the guy who shot you?"

The sun ducked back behind the clouds and Madeline's face was thrown into shadow. "The man who killed me . . . John Wilson . . . he was one of our clients and mentally unstable, poor soul. There's nothing to be gained from wanting revenge against him. When he snapped out of the dissociative state he was in when he shot me and realized what he'd done, the guilt was too much for him to bear. He took an overdose. He's been dead nearly as long as I have."

"So you're not mad at Dan. And you're not mad at this John guy. But you want my help anyway. Why?"

"Like I said, it's all because of Danny."

It was a sound bite, not an explanation. I stepped back, my arms crossed over my chest and my hands tucked under my arms and close to my body in a futile effort to generate some heat.

Madeline didn't have to worry about trying to maintain 98.6; she could afford to take her time. While I shifted from foot to foot and stamped my feet, she eased into her explanation.

"You know Danny is brilliant. I mean, you must. Anyone who meets him instantly knows he's unique. I knew it, too, as soon as Doctor Gerard introduced us. Once I started working with Danny . . . well, it didn't take me long to realize that in addition to his razor-sharp mind, he has something a lot of scientists lack—a special spark of creativity. Sure, he has an encyclopedic knowledge of psychology and biochemistry, but he can take that knowledge and combine it with experience and . . . well, it's hard to explain to a layperson, but his results are always surprising. He has a way of looking at old information in new ways. That's something special." Madeline raised her chin.

"I admired Danny's methods and his thought processes. I appreciated the fact that though I was his superior, he was open to asking for my advice. Many men won't do that, you know. Especially when it comes to research. Not when they're working with women who are more professionally and academically advanced and—" If I didn't know better, I would have said her smile was sweet. "Well, I guess you've probably never been in that position, have you?"

The smile I shot back was just as sugary. "You sound like you're writing Dan's retirement speech."

"I just want to be sure you understand. Danny was a real asset to the clinic. He was—"

"Terrific. Yeah, I get it. Dan was terrific, this Doctor Gerard guy is perfection, and you were the ace number one go-to person who kept the place running like clockwork. So?"

"So, even after Danny left Chicago, he kept in touch with Doctor Gerard. They're working together now on a special study."

A single snowflake drifted in front of my eyes, and the heavy clouds above us promised more. If I stood there much longer, I'd harden up and be mistaken for one of the statues. Like a bewildered spectator trying to decipher an especially baffling charade, I urged Madeline on with a wave of both hands. "And this study..."

She hesitated.

I grumbled.

Madeline drummed her fingers against her chin. "I hate to say anything denigrating against Doctor Gerard," she said. "He's a great man. A brilliant man. Without him and the Gerard Clinic, thousands of the indigent would never have adequate mental health care. It's just..." She drew in a breath. Without taking in any air, of course. "Some of Doctor Gerard's business practices aren't exactly on the up-and-up."

"And you know this, how?"

She shrugged. "Like I said, I was his research assistant. His right-hand man, so to speak. After taking a look at the clinic's operating budget and balancing it against what I knew we were bringing in with our fundraising efforts... well, I had my suspicions. Of course I dismissed them as flights of fancy. Doctor Gerard wouldn't... He couldn't... But then I found out it was true. Doctor Gerard was... he is—"

"A crook."

Madeline made a face. "You make it sound so tawdry. And Doctor Gerard is anything but. He's a wonderful, warm individual. And a great humanitarian. He's from old money, you know. His father and his grandfather and his great-grandfather, they were all distinguished psychiatrists, too. Back in the late 1800s, his great-grandfather founded the Gerard Hospital for the Insane and Mentally Feeble up near Winnetka. The name of the hospital makes it sound so incredibly antiquated and cruel, but back then, the place was cutting-edge and the therapies they used were humane and helpful. That Doctor Gerard... well, everyone who knows anything about psychiatry knows about his work."

Ancient history. It was getting us nowhere, and nowhere meant we'd never get through this and get inside someplace where it was warm. I wouldn't have had to point this out if she wasn't dead and oblivious to the cold. Instead, I pinned her with a look that told her to get a move on.

Thinking, Madeline chafed her hands together. "Hilton never would have done what he did if I was still around. Like I said, I made sure the clinic was—"

"Shipshape. Yeah, I know."

She didn't appreciate the interruption so she pretended it hadn't happened. "He also never would have gotten involved in what he's involved in if he didn't give so much of his own personal fortune to the clinic to make sure it stayed solvent. Government funding cuts, you know, and Hilton, he can't bear to see his patients suffer because of ridiculous government bureaucracy. He—"

"He cooked the books. Is that what you're trying to tell me?"

Madeline blinked rapidly. "He knew it was the only way, and then... well, like I said, I wasn't around and... and then things got out of hand."

"How out of hand?"

I doubt if ghosts can blush, but I swear her cheeks got dusky. "There's the house in the Bahamas," she said. "And the offshore accounts. Hilton isn't flamboyant, but he does appreciate the finer things in life. Clothes, cars, food, wine. I mean, it's just about impossible to hold any of it against him. If he's going to convince the city's elite to support the clinic, he needs to mingle with them. And if he's going to mingle with them, he needs to live like one of them. Besides, a man in his position has a great deal of stress and he deserves the little luxuries of life."

"Some people wouldn't consider a house in the Bahamas a little luxury."

"Of course not. Please don't get me wrong." Madeline's voice was almost pleading. "I don't want you to think badly of Hilton. That's not why I'm telling you any of this. He's misguided, that's all. And the quality of patient care at the clinic hasn't deteriorated in the least because of what he's doing. I know this for certain. I go over there now and again just to reassure myself. I've told myself that as long as the clinic is running efficiently and patients aren't affected, it's really none of my business, but—"

"But you're in love with this Hilton character. Or at least you were when you were alive. And you don't want to see him get in trouble." It didn't take a genius to read that much into Madeline's words, so really, she shouldn't have greeted my statement with a snort of contempt.

"In love? With Hilton? You really haven't been paying attention to a word I've said, have you? Hilton is a big boy, he can take care of himself. And he will. Believe me, you don't become as successful or as powerful as Hilton Gerard without learning to fine-tune your self-preservation skills. When the net closes around the Gerard Clinic, Hilton isn't the one who's going to be caught in it."

"Dan?" The name escaped past the sudden knot of anxiety that blocked my throat. "You mean he's mixed up in all this, too? No. Wait!" I swallowed down my panic. "No way. There's no way Dan would ever do anything dishonest. Whatever your Doctor Gerard is up to, Dan isn't a part of it."

This time, my loyalty to Dan didn't impress Madeline. Her sour expression pretty much summed up what she thought of me. "Don't you get it? It doesn't matter if Danny knows what's going on or not. He's getting funding from the clinic for that study he's conducting. Funding cuts or not, a whole lot of that money still comes from the government, from Medicare and such. When the federal authorities close in—"

Two little words—*federal authorities*—and my panic was back in full force. The psychology-minded might have called it conditioning. I attributed it to good old-fashioned been there, done that. I was backing away even before I was aware that I was moving.

"Oh no. No feds for me. I've had enough of those guys for one lifetime."

It wasn't until Madeline gave me a blank look that I realized that like it or not, I owed her an explanation.

"My dad," I said, and damn, but I hated telling this story. "He was a plastic surgeon. There was a little matter of Medicare fraud. Dad will be in federal prison for at least another eight years."

It was the Reader's Digest Condensed version, of course. I'd purposely left out all the stuff about how, thanks to Dad's illegal doings, our family had lost everything: the upscale house in the upscale suburb, his bank accounts and investments, the people who'd always said they were our friends. Mom didn't wait around to watch the Martin family go down in flames; she hightailed it to Florida to hide from the shame. And me? Well, I'd been dumped by the fiancé who had claimed he loved me more than my family's money, and instead of becoming a CCW (that's country-club wife) and working on my tan, on my backhand, or on completing what had been shaping up to be a superior collection of Marc Jacobs handbags, I was working as a tour guide in a cemetery.

Enough said.

Fortunately, Madeline didn't bother with any sympathy. Fine by me, since I wasn't looking for any. Ever the logical scientist, she breezed right on. "Then you understand the problem completely. I've heard rumor that the FBI is nosing around the clinic, and if that's true, you know they're going to uncover Hilton's wrongdoings. They're not going to care that the money Danny is using was filtered through Hilton. They're going to see that he's spending government funds on a study that was never approved. And then—"

"Dan's going to join my dad as a guest of the government."

I didn't like the thought or the picture that popped into my mind—the one of Dan behind bars. I swallowed hard and told my imagination to sit down and shut up.

"We're getting ahead of ourselves here," I told Madeline, forcing myself to think like a detective, because that was better than giving in to the panic. "We've got to look at the facts before we jump to conclusions. What kind of study is Dan working on with Doctor Gerard, anyway?"

Madeline shrugged. She didn't like being out of the loop, and three years of being dead pretty much assured that. "I don't know all the details. I do know it has something to do with brain waves. Whatever it is, it's not worth Danny risking his reputation. Or his freedom."

I was so not going to go there. That's why I glommed

on to the brain-wave part. "So Dan really is a research scientist, right? I mean, the whole thing about studying my brain and my aberrant behavior, that's legit?"

She cocked her head. "You didn't think it was?"

"I wasn't sure. I mean, I believed him at first because I met him in a hospital and all, but then when he saved my life—"

"Did he?" Madeline looked interested in spite of herself. "Danny's a man of many talents."

"And he believes in ghosts." I wasn't sure if this was news to Madeline, but I thought it only fair I share it. "He's never come right out and said it, but he's hinted, you know? He knows what he's talking about. He knows you guys exist."

Her smile was nothing short of beatific. "I told you, Danny thinks outside the box. And you..." When she looked at me, the expression faded. "You're glad he was telling the truth, aren't you? About the brain studies?"

I was, and I wasn't ashamed to admit it.

"Then you want to help him?"

I groaned. "Of course I don't want to see anything bad happen to Dan. But I can't believe he's mixed up in Doctor Gerard's fraud scheme. Really. Dan isn't the type."

"You haven't been listening." Madeline stalked away, whirled around, and came back at me. "It doesn't matter if he knows what's going on. Hilton's going to get caught, and when he does, Danny's going down with him. His career will be over. His life will be ruined. You're the only one who can stop it, Pepper. You've got to help him."

"But—"

Madeline's voice simmered with anger. "You just told

me Danny saved your life, and now you're going to let him spend the best years of his life in jail?"

"No. I mean, I don't want to. It's just that..." I collected my thoughts. "I just can't believe—"

"You don't believe Danny's involved? Well, I can prove it. He and Doctor Gerard are having dinner tonight at Piece, the brewery over on West North Avenue." Madeline shimmered around the edges. She faded like a bad TV picture. "Go there." Her voice faded, too, until it didn't sound as if it was coming from her at all. It was in the air all around me. And in the icy wind that ducked under my collar and shivered down my back. "You'll see."

"But..." By the time I made a move to close in on her, she was already gone. "What am I going to say to him?" I asked anyway. "How am I going to explain that I know that Doctor Gerard is skimming the clinic's money?"

My only answer was the sound of the wind that blew across the headstones around me.

"Damn," I grumbled, and I turned back toward the Palmer memorial.

That's when I realized the tour group—and the tour bus—had already moved on to another part of the cemetery.

And didn't it just figure? It started to snow.

5

Sure, Madeline told me that Dan and this Doctor Gerard character were having dinner that night at a place called Piece. But she'd failed to mention the time, and I'd been so worried about Dan (not to mention my noticeable lack of circulation and how I was certain it was just the first of the many ugly signs of hypothermia), I'd forgotten to ask. I wasn't about to give her the satisfaction of watching me stand in the middle of Graceland to try and call her back from wherever it was ghosts went when they weren't bugging me. It would brand me as unprofessional, and something told me she would enjoy that far too much.

There might have been tiny drifts of snow on my shoulders, and yes, I was frozen to the bone, but I knew what I had to do. Instead of worrying about Madeline or about Dan's dinner time, I came to grips with the fact that my tour group was long gone, found my way out of the cemetery, and hailed a cab.

Never let it be said that Pepper Martin is not committed to her investigations. Even the ones she doesn't want to be involved with in the first place. I got back to the conference hotel and took a very long, very hot shower. Even before I could feel my hands and feet again, I was bundled in jeans, a wool sweater, and the chunkiest, flattest-heeled, most utilitarian shoes I owned (which were not all that chunky, flat-heeled, or utilitarian, of course, but would have to do). Thus prepared, I decided to go to the restaurant early and stay late if I had to. It was the only way I could hope to catch Dan and Doctor Gerard together, and maybe in the bargain, find out if Madeline knew what she was talking about.

With that in mind, I arrived at Piece Brewery and Pizzeria a little before five. There was already a waiting list, and the tiny entryway was packed. Luckily, it was no longer snowing, but the wind was still as icy as it had been at the cemetery. When I stepped back onto the sidewalk to wait, it hit me in the face, and I cursed whoever it was who'd planned a February conference in Chicago rather than one in some nice, civilized place like West Palm. My teeth were knocking together and so were my knees. I hunkered down, stuffed my hands deep into my pockets, and nestled my chin into the scarf I'd bought at the hotel gift shop.

I know, I know . . . gray is not my color and acrylic is definitely not my fabric of choice. I was hardly making a fashion statement, but at that point, I didn't much care. The scarf cut some of the chill, and, more importantly, like the matching gray felted bucket hat I had pulled over my ears, it provided a bit of camouflage. I wasn't ready to let Dan know I was in Chicago, or that I had my eye on him. Not yet. Not until I had a better understanding of what was really going on.

"It's cold."

"No kidding." I'd already answered before I pulled my gaze away from the warm paradise that lay just on the other side of the front door of the restaurant, and saw that the person standing on the snow-pocked sidewalk next to me was a guy with a scrawny beard and hair that stuck out in weird spikes from beneath his battered baseball cap. The first thing I noticed was that he looked too young to be homeless. He did not, however, look too clean. His standard-issue green Army jacket hadn't been washed in forever, and his jeans were torn. His face was streaked with dirt. Even so, he had nice eyes. They were as brown as a teddy bear, and just as warm and friendly looking.

Nice eyes or not, no way this guy was waiting for a table. Even before he spoke, I knew what was coming.

"You got any extra cash?" he asked.

As it happened, I did. I also had enough experience in the downtown shopping districts of cities far and wide to know that like ghosts, panhandlers are persistent. I couldn't afford to be pestered while I was trying to go unnoticed and keep an eye on the people filing into and out of the restaurant. I felt around in my pocket for one of the dollars the cab driver who brought me to Piece gave me as change. I pulled it out.

Homeless Guy almost looked embarrassed. "Most people just give me quarters," he said.

"Sorry, no quarters." I held out the dollar, and I swear, he hesitated for so long, I actually thought he wasn't going to take it.

He gave in; I knew he would. With an embarrassed smile and a mumbled word that might have been "Thanks," he reached for the dollar. That's when something spooked him.

I can't say what it was, because as far as I could see, nothing had changed. Or had it? There were still tight knots of people standing on the sidewalk on either side of us. There was still traffic crawling by on the narrow street just to the other side of the cars parked nearby. I was still as cold as hell, and I wished he would just take the money and get it over with so I could put my hand back in my pocket.

Call it a hunch, or maybe it was detective's instinct, but I knew something was suddenly wrong with the picture when Mr. Homeless snatched the money out of my hand, tugged his jacket sleeves down around his bare hands, and took off for parts unknown. At that moment, a cab rolled up to the curb. A thin middle-aged man with high cheekbones and salt-and-pepper hair got out first, and a couple seconds later, Dan Callahan emerged from the backseat of the cab. While the older man paid the driver, Dan waited on the sidewalk not twenty feet from me.

I wasn't going to take the chance that he'd see me. Not this early in the game. I thanked those detective instincts for the scarf I was hiding behind, and spun around to face the front window of the restaurant. For once, I didn't focus on how warm the people inside looked. I was too busy watching Dan's reflection.

Here's the quick skinny on Dan: he's cute (I may have mentioned that before). He's got nice blue eyes and brown hair that's sometimes a little too shaggy, and he wears wire-rimmed glasses. They must have fogged when he stepped out of the warm cab, because he took his glasses off and rubbed the lenses with one corner of the houndstooth scarf he was wearing with a black leather jacket and jeans that were nicely worn and even more nicely tight.

"Well, are you just going to stand there like a lump? Or are you going to do something? Like follow them, maybe?"

There was no reflection in the window next to mine, but when I glanced to my side, there was Madeline in her boxy skirt and her lab coat.

My scarf covered my mouth, so in the great scheme of things, I was glad I'd plunked down my MasterCard and bought it. At least I could talk to her without looking too loony. "I am doing something," I pointed out, though I shouldn't have had to. "I've been standing out here freezing, waiting for Dan. Now he's here and—"

"They're going inside." Even before the door closed behind Dan and the man who must have been Hilton Gerard, Madeline was headed that way. "You've got to follow them, Pepper. It's the only way you'll find out what's going on."

She was right, and shit, but I hated when ghosts did that! Keeping an eye on Dan and the doctor, I sidestepped my way through the crowd and was nearly to the door when I realized I wasn't alone. Not ten feet away, Homeless Guy stood with his hands in his pockets. He was looking exactly where I'd been looking.

And I'd been looking at Dan.

Surprised, I stopped in my tracks and glanced from Mr. Homeless to Dan and back again.

By the time I did, Homeless Guy was gone.

Peculiar, yes? But I didn't find it nearly as curious as

the fact that Dan and Doctor Gerard were already being seated by the time I walked into the lobby. While the rest of us were still waiting? I was not a happy camper, and Madeline's sudden appearance atop the hostess stand didn't help.

With her fists on hips that were curvier than mine and must have made it hell to buy jeans that actually fit, she looked down her nose at me, the better to convey her opinion at the same time she found me in the thick of the crowd. "Now what?" she asked. "You're not just going to let them walk away, are you? Just like that? What kind of detective are you, anyway?"

"A damned good one." I'd already snarled back at her before I realized the people standing closest to me would not appreciate odd pronouncements from a woman whose teeth were chattering. "A damned good thing there's just enough room in here for all of us," I added quickly, and sent a sparkling smile toward the man standing closest to me. I was glad to see the old magic still worked. He was so busy smiling back, he didn't look worried about my sanity. He did, however, back up a few paces to give me a better look, so when the door opened again and a stream of people filed in, there was just enough room for all of us.

"Penelope!" Doris from Detroit pulled me into a hug almost before I had a chance to recognize the people who'd walked in as the folks who'd been on the cemetery tour with me. When she divested herself of the red scarf and the pink mittens and pulled off her hat, I saw that she had a head full of springy curls that were too dark to be natural. "We were so worried about you, honey. What happened? You didn't get back on the tour bus!"

"Er...I—"

"We were all set to call the police. I mean, you can just imagine how frightened out of our minds we were. And worried, too. But then somebody...it may have been Myra. You know, the one from Dayton, not the Myra from Albuquerque...Myra suggested we call the hotel first and good thing we did. The front desk clerk told us he'd just seen you walk through the lobby and go up to your room. Thank goodness!" Doris pressed one hand to her heart. "I wouldn't want to be the one to tell Ella that we'd lost her star employee."

"That's good. I—"

"And it looks like while you were back at the hotel, you took the time to read over the conference program schedule. That's good work, honey." She patted my shoulder. "That's how you knew we were meeting here for dinner. Good thinking, Penelope!"

"It is nice to see you again." Grant was right behind Doris, and practically before she was done talking, he stepped forward and pulled off his stocking cap. It was the first I realized he had a comb-over. I stood transfixed, fascinated and appalled all at the same time, and I guess he misunderstood. He stepped closer. "We can sit to-gether at dinner," he said.

"We can. We will." I tried for the sparkling smile again. This time, it fell flat.

Doris came to my rescue. "We've got tables reserved upstairs," she told me at the same time she tugged at my sleeve to drag me along.

With no choice, I dutifully followed, wondering the whole time how I'd slip away so that I could go in search of Dan. As it turned out, for the first time in my investi-gation, which wasn't much of an investigation at all, my luck changed for the better. Our table overlooked the main floor exactly at the spot where Dan and the doctor were sitting.

As soon as I caught sight of them, I jockeyed for position near the railing that surrounded the loft area. I guess I couldn't blame Grant for thinking I was scrambling to sit next to him. That would explain his smile when I sat down and stripped off my wintry outerwear.

"So, you ordering beer?" The way Grant wiggled his eyebrows when he said it, I got the impression that beer drinking was something he saved for his wilder moments, like cemetery conferences.

"I'm not much of a beer drinker," I told him, at the same time a chipper waitress came by. I ordered coffee, and fortunately, there was a pot nearby. She handed me a steaming mug, and I wrapped my hands around it and soaked up the warmth. Of course, the whole time, I kept an eye on Dan.

Or at least I tried.

It was pretty hard to do surveillance on anyone or anything when the cemetery crowd kept interrupting.

"Resurrectionists. Oh!" The aforementioned Myra from Dayton sat on Grant's right, and in her excitement, she nearly swooned. "I can't wait to hear your talk, Penelope. The Resurrectionists are part of the reason I got into the cemetery field. I read about them when I was a teenager, and I thought...well, some people would say it was morbid, but I thought the whole thing was absolutely fascinating."

I was supposed to reply to this. I took a drink, instead, and pretended I didn't want to be rude and talk and drink at the same time. Not that it mattered. A round middle-aged man at the other end of the table took up the subject, and my companions were off and running. They drank their beers and ordered pizza. While they did, I watched Dan and Hilton Gerard chat and wished to hell my Gift included bionic hearing. Then I'd know what they were talking about. What I got instead was an earful of cemetery chatter.

"So, are you finally ready to admit I was right?" Madeline popped up from out of nowhere. She was definitely not responding to Grant's most recent comment, which as far as I could tell (since I wasn't really listening) had something to do with the benefits of sod over grass seed at new burial sites. Madeline perched on the railing. "I told you they knew each other."

My menu in hand (just in case I needed to duck behind it), I turned slightly in my seat, the better to look down to the floor below. Doctor Gerard had just put down his menu. As if he'd decided not to order, he waved away the waitress and then sat back in his chair, sipping a glass of white wine. Dan sat across from him. He had a dark beer in front of him.

"Having a drink together doesn't mean anything. Not anything illegal, anyway." I mumbled this while I took another sip of coffee.

She shot me a look. "You need to get closer so you can hear what they're talking about."

"Not a chance."

I didn't know how loudly I'd said this until I realized everyone at the table had stopped talking. I swiveled in my seat and found them all looking my way. My smile was sheepish. "Sod," I said, and scrambled to remember everything I'd ever heard about the subject back at Garden View. It wasn't much. At least not much that I'd paid any attention to. "In our climate, there's not a chance we'd use sod. It's a lot more difficult to grow. It's grass seed for us. Every time."

"Just what I thought!" Doris grinned as if I'd revealed the combination to a Federal Reserve vault. "I always wondered how you folks at Garden View keep the grounds so pristine. Grass seed, eh? What variety?"

I took another drink, stalling. And in the next second, it really didn't matter, because a woman way down at the end of the table said something about fescue and they were lost again in discussing the fascinating intricacies of grass varieties as they applied to hillside burials, old tombs, and mowing around headstones.

"You're wasting time." Madeline was not happy. Like a sure-footed tightrope walker, she paced back and forth on the railing, looking down at me as she stepped past. "Who knows what's happening between Danny and Hilton! And instead of finding out, you're too busy sitting on your butt, talking about all the silly things you're interested in."

"Just for the record, I am not interested in fescue." I delivered this information just as the waitress brought our pizza and everybody was so busy oohing and aahing over it, no one heard me. "Landscaping has never been my thing."

Madeline plunked down on the table in front of me. Right on top of one of the three pepperoni and mushroom pizzas that had been ordered for the table. "Look, Danny is nodding in response to something Hilton said. What do you suppose they're talking about?"

I looked where she was looking and shrugged.

Not the response Madeline wanted. Her already sour expression turned positively tart. "Commitment-phobia," she said, the word so sure and precise, it was more a pronouncement than a simple comment. "You're feeling it now, aren't you? You're breathless, dizzy. I'll bet you're nauseous, too." She leaned nearer and looked at me hard. "Are you sweating excessively?"

"No." I sat back and tucked my arms against my sides, defending myself and my personal hygiene just as Grant asked if I wanted a glass of beer. I wondered if he noticed that I turned down his offer with more force than it called for. Or that I was glaring at the pizza. Just as quickly, I decided I didn't care.

I slipped my napkin off my lap and then bent to pick it up. While I was down there, I looked up and made sure to tell Madeline, "I don't have issues with commitment. I'm not afraid of a relationship with Dan. We're not even talking about a relationship with Dan. We're talking about—"

"Commitment phobics—CPs—don't just focus on interpersonal relationships. Their fears . . . your fears, Pepper . . . are rooted in the possibility of lost options and the dread of making poor decisions. Most CPs show signs of commitment fears across many areas of their lives. You probably don't even recognize these indicators in yourself, but remember, I'm a trained professional. I can see it as clearly as I can see you now. That's why you're avoiding Dan. And this investigation. You're feeling sick, aren't you? Your mouth is dry, your hands are shaking. How about heart palpitations? Are you having those? It's all a natural response to your condition, so don't be afraid to admit it."

I came up holding my napkin as tightly as my temper. "I'm not—"

"Sure, that's what they all say. At first. Until they

learn to come to terms with their problem. Counseling would help. You know that, don't you? With the right therapist, you'll feel safe, and it's the perfect place for you to finally confront your fear of being hurt, and your fear of trusting another person. There's the fear of sacrifice, too. Is that why you're willing to stand back and watch Danny go to jail? You think getting involved will inconvenience your little life too much?"

I tossed my napkin on the table, and cemetery conference goers or not, I was about to give Madeline a piece of my non-commitment-phobic mind. My words stopped short when I saw Hilton Gerard reach into the inside pocket of his suit coat. He came out with a fat envelope that he slid across the table to Dan.

I sat up a little straighter. I leaned farther forward.

Just in time to see Dan open the envelope and peek inside.

And I was in just the right spot to see what no one else in the restaurant could see.

That envelope was stuffed with money.

"See. I told you so." Madeline leaned over the railing. "There must be a couple thousand dollars in that envelope. No way you can pretend that's innocent, Pepper. I'm right, and you know it. Danny's getting caught up in something illegal. He's not going to be able to get himself out of it, either. Not unless you help."

"I don't know what to do!"

"Just sit back, sweetie!" Doris had been anointed official pizza-hander-outer, and she waved a wedge-shaped spatula in my direction. "You don't have to do anything at all, just hold out your plate and let me at that pizza!"

Doris closed in on the pizza, and I aimed a dirty look in Madeline's direction. She got the message and slid off the table—and our pizza. There was no tomato sauce on her butt.

"They finished their drinks. They're getting their coats on." Madeline's back was to me, but I couldn't miss the urgency that edged her voice. "You're going to miss your chance. They're going to leave, and you're not going to—"

"Excuse me." I pushed back my chair and was out of it and slipping behind Grant's chair in an instant. "I'll be right back."

I was almost over to the stairway and on my way down to the first floor when I heard Doris call to our waitress, "Miss! We've got a problem. This pizza…" I turned in time to see her lay a hand on the pizza on the table in front of where I'd been sitting. "This pizza is ice cold!"

Outside, I made sure to stay well out of Dan's line of vision as he and Hilton Gerard waited for a cab. Madeline had no such constraints. As soon as we were back out on the sidewalk, she drifted over to where they were waiting. She was back in a minute, and she didn't look happy.

"This is even worse than I thought." She chewed her lower lip and glanced over her shoulder to where Dan and the doctor stood. "That money Dan accepted is for the special study he's helping Hilton with. I heard Hilton say so. It's for supplies and expenses."

"And that's bad because it's money they shouldn't be

spending." I nodded, confirming the worst to myself, and I would have thought Madeline would have at least been happy that I was finally getting on board.

Instead, she stomped down the street, far from where the bright restaurant lights colored the snow. "You're just not getting this, are you?" Her words were as desperate as the look in her eyes. "Danny's getting himself in big, big trouble, and all you're worried about is money?"

I was glad to be away from the restaurant crowd and in the shadows. I didn't have to talk between my teeth. Or keep my voice down. "What else am I supposed to be worried about? It's all you've told me." And when she looked away, I added, "Come clean, Madeline. Something else is going on, and you better understand right here and now, if I don't know the whole story, I'm not going to help."

When she turned back around, she had the decency to look guilty. "I thought if I told you about the money...I thought that would be enough to get you involved. But I see that you need more. The truth is..." She twisted her hands together. "Hilton has been interested in brain activity for years. He picks certain patients at the clinic...those who show abnormal brain function or those whose aberrant behavior can't be fully explained. Those patients are funneled into a special study. That's what Danny's been helping Hilton with all this time, and now, I just heard him say that he's going to come onto the clinic staff as a full-time associate."

"And this is a bad thing because...?"

Again, Madeline hesitated. I guess the fact that I took a step toward her, fire in my eyes, helped her make up her mind. "That special study?" Her voice was small.

"Hilton's been working on it for quite some time. I know the particulars, Pepper. And I know that some of the people he recruits to be part of it...some of the people who go into the study are never seen or heard from again."

6

"The people who are recruited into Dan's study are missing and you never bothered to mention it...because...? Don't you think that's kind of important?"

I didn't stop to look at Madeline as I asked this. It was the morning after I'd been to Piece. I was in my hotel room, and I was busy gathering my coat and my dorky hat and scarf. Once I had it all bundled in my arms, I turned to face her. "Huh? Did I hear you say something? Because maybe you didn't say it loud enough. Maybe that's why I didn't hear your explanation."

If she had any class at all, Madeline would have looked at least a little embarrassed. Or a little guilty. Instead, she sniffed in an I'm-better-than-you-and-you-wouldn't-understand-anyway sort of way. "Exactly why I disappeared last night after Danny and Hilton left in their cab," she said. "I knew you'd have this attitude."

"What attitude would that be, exactly? The one that says a detective who's investigating needs all the facts? Shit, Madeline, if people are really going into that study and never coming out again—"

"They are."

Ice filled my stomach and poured through my veins. In spite of the fact that I was hugging my wool coat, I was chilled to the bone. "No way Dan could be involved."

She made that annoying sniffing sound again. "That's what you said about the money."

"But the money—"

"Is for the study. Weren't you listening to a thing I said last night? Danny has come on board at the clinic. He's going to be Hilton's assistant. If people are missing—and they are, Pepper, believe me when I tell you this—if people are missing, then he's going to have a lot more to answer for than just some government money that's been misspent."

I knew this. It was one of the reasons I hadn't slept a wink the night before. Believe me, I could prove this, because it had taken a major coat of Guerlain Happylogy to hide the dark circles under my eyes. Unfortunately, not even high-priced cosmetics could calm the chaos inside me. My heart pounded a mile a minute and my knees were weak. "Why didn't you tell me?" This time when I asked the question, I looked Madeline in the eye, the better to pin her down. "It's not exactly a little detail."

"No, it isn't." She glanced away.

Was that a bit of a conscience I detected? My temper ratcheted back a bit, and for the first time since I'd bumped into this ectoplasmic nuisance, I found myself thinking that beneath all that academic horseshit, there actually might be a compassionate person—in a very dead way, of course.

"I didn't think you'd believe me," she said. "It's clear to me that you have feelings for Danny, and..." She brushed aside the comment, and it was just as well. I was in no mood to go another couple rounds with her while I tried to make her understand all the things about my relationship with Dan that I didn't understand myself.

"You had to see them together," Madeline said. "It was the only way I could prove to you that they know each other, that they're working together. I hoped that when you did—"

"You could tell me the rest of the story."

She nodded. "So what are you going to do now?" she asked.

I marched across the room and grabbed the Chicago Transit map I'd picked up at the concierge desk in the middle of the night when pacing around the nearly deserted hotel struck me as a better idea than lying in bed and staring at the ceiling.

"Do? I don't know what you're going to do, but I'm going to use public transportation," I told her.

I didn't bother trying to explain. There was no way I could make her understand that the very notion struck more terror in my heart than any ghost ever had.

My plan hit its first speed bump the minute I was off the elevator and into the lobby. That's when Doris spotted me and closed in.

"Aren't you the eager beaver!" She said this like Ella would have. Like it was a good thing. "But you don't need your coat yet, honey. The tour of Rosehill Cemetery isn't until this afternoon. We've got the welcoming speech from the conference chair first, and then the morning break-out sessions start. What are you going to?" She flipped through the conference program she had clutched in one hand. It was already well-worn, and a number of the pages had their corners bent to mark them. "*Legislative Update on Land Management* sounds terrific, of course, but I can buy the tape of that session. I'm thinking I'll do either *Burial Rights* or *Flag Etiquette*. How about you?"

"*Flag Etiquette*." I answered without thinking, and when she chirped in with, "Then I'll come along," I amended it to, "*Burial Rights*."

"It's hard to make up your mind when all the sessions sound so good, isn't it?" Doris waved to someone across the lobby, and though I hoped that meant our little meeting was officially at an end, she never left my side. "I know what I'll be going to later in the week." She grinned when she said this and opened her booklet to a page where she had the talk on Resurrectionists circled in red. "Wouldn't miss it for the world. Partly because I know it's Ella's topic. Ella's research is always impeccable and her sources...well...they just blow me away! But I'll tell you, kiddo, I'm anxious to hear you speak, too. I've got a feeling that with a couple more years under your belt, you're going to be a powerful force in the cemetery business."

I wasn't sure what made me queasier, her prediction or the thought of standing up in front of a room filled with people and reading the inch-high report Ella had sent to Chicago with me. Rather than worry about either,

I sidestepped toward the revolving door that led out to the street. "I'll be back in time for *Burial Rights*," I said, lying through my teeth with an ease that can only come from long practice. "I've just got to run out for a bit and..."

Lucky for me, I wasn't obliged to finish. Grant showed up with Myra and the rest of the bunch we'd had dinner with the night before, and while they were busy chatting, I slipped out of the hotel.

My luck held. The nearest L station was close, and the transit system was far easier to navigate than I imagined any big city's public transportation could be. Without too much incident (and being careful not to get too close to any of the folks on the train who looked as grimy as the guy who'd accosted me the night before), I got out at the right station and followed the directions I'd printed from the hotel's computer.

The closer I got to my destination, the more folks I saw who looked like Mr. Homeless. It wasn't hard to see why. The neighborhood was as shabby as the people who shambled by. I ignored a guy sleeping in a doorway and pretended not to notice the one taking a pee in an alleyway. Instead, I double-checked the address on that same computer printout and stopped directly across the street from the Gerard Clinic.

What was I planning to do now that I was there?

It was exactly what I'd been asking myself, and the answer was pretty much that I wasn't sure, but I thought I might—maybe—go inside and see if Dan was around, and if he was, that I might—maybe—find a way to warn him that he might—maybe—be in trouble. If I could accomplish all that, then I might—maybe—try to talk some sense into him without confessing that I had the inside scoop on the dirty dealings going on there from a person who worked at the clinic before she was dead.

Just thinking about it all made my head hurt.

Before I had a chance to give in to the pain or the nervousness that drummed through me when I wondered how I was going to pull it all off, I stepped off the curb to cross the street. When I did, something caught my eye. Or I should say more accurately, someone. He was standing in the alleyway between the clinic and the building next door, and I recognized the dirty Army jacket and the weird, spiky hair in an instant. Yeah, that's right—it was the same panhandler I'd run into outside of Piece.

Not so unusual, since as ragged as he was, he fit right into the neighborhood. But considering how far I was from where I'd been the night before, it struck me as a tad odd to find him loitering. So did the fact that he took one look at me and took off like a bat out of hell.

I tried to follow, but let's face it, athletics is not my strong suit. By the time I dodged traffic and got to the other side of the street, I was out of breath and Homeless Guy had already rounded the nearest corner. There was no way I was going to catch him, so there was no use even trying.

"You know that guy?"

The question came from behind me in a deep baritone voice, and I turned just as a man emerged from the alley. He was tall and thin, wearing a gray raincoat that had seen better days and one of those flat-topped, brimmed tweed caps that looks like it should be on the head of some guy drinking in an Irish pub. His skin was the color of strong coffee, his eyes were dark, and when he looked where I was looking, his eyes lit with a spark of curiosity. "He a friend of yours?"

I nearly said something along the lines of "Not a chance, considering the guy who ran is a homeless panhandler and I do not associate with the likes of him." I stopped myself just in time when I realized the man who stepped out of the alley was a homeless panhandler, too. The hell with being politically correct; I was not about to get myself in trouble in a neighborhood where I clearly did not belong.

"A friend? Nope." I tucked my hands into my pockets and took a step back and away from the mouth of the alleyway. There were smells coming out of it that were less than pleasant, and I was no fool. Though the guy in the raincoat seemed friendly enough, I wasn't going to take the chance of getting mugged. "He looks plenty familiar, though. Do you know him?"

"Seen him hanging around." The man in the raincoat shifted his gaze and gave me a careful once-over. "Haven't seen you here before."

"No. It's my first time." I took another step back. "I'm here to see one of Doctor Gerard's assistants."

"You applying for a job?"

It seemed as good an excuse as any. "Maybe," I told him. "Are there any openings?"

He rocked back on his heels. "Can't say for sure, but when you get inside, maybe you could put in a good word for me. The name's Ernie." For the first time, I noticed he was carrying something tucked under his right arm. He shifted it and stuck out his hand. He wasn't wearing gloves.

Eager for information and with no options, I shook

his hand. "A good word? Are you looking for work here, too?"

Ernie's laugh was full-bodied. "Don't think I'm qualified," he said. "Alberta, now she would fit in perfect at the clinic." He reached for what was now tucked under his left arm and turned it toward me, and I saw that it was a photograph in a beat-up frame. It showed a smiling African American woman wearing a neat suit and a string of pearls. I'm not much for history, but from her clothing and her hairdo, I guessed the picture was taken back in the seventies. "She's an educated woman, my Alberta. Works at the library, over at the Scottsdale branch." He paused, and when he gave the photo a long look, his eyes misted. "A real educated woman," he said.

The way his voice faded, I could tell I was going to lose him if I didn't act fast. "So, you want me to put in a good word for you, huh? Sure, I can do that."

Ernie tucked the picture back where it came from. "You think? That would be real nice. I tried to talk to Doctor Gerard myself about it, but he's a busy man, you know. He said maybe next time I've got an appointment we could discuss it, but... well... like I said, he's a busy man and I'm not due to get my medications filled for at least another week. By that time... well..." He chafed his hands together. "It sure isn't getting any warmer out here, if you know what I mean. If you could talk to him about it today, that would be real nice."

I scrambled to put together the pieces of what Ernie was talking about and got nowhere fast. With a sigh that sent a cloud of heated air around me, I gave up. "I'd be happy to," I told Ernie. "Only you have to tell me what you want me to talk to him about."

"Why, that study of his, of course." Something told

me that had he been less polite, Ernie would have pointed out that I was lamebrained for not knowing this. "Doctor Gerard, he's got that special study of his, and I hear he's accepting new patients. Oscar, my friend who lives in the alley here just next to where I've got my stuff, he went into it just last week. And Becka, that nasty crack whore who used to hang out around here looking to score, I haven't seen her in a while. I hear she got into the study, too."

The excitement in Ernie's voice did not jibe with what I'd heard from Madeline. "So it's a good thing to be part of the study?"

Ernie looked at me as if I was the dumbest woman he'd ever met, and for all I knew, I was. "The patients in the study, they get three squares a day. And a place to live. Hell, even if it's just a room there in the clinic, it's got to be warmer than my box here in the alley."

I probed carefully. "Is that what they say? The folks in the study? They told you they're getting meals and a place to live?"

Ernie thought about this for a moment. "Well, not in so many words," he finally said. He scratched a hand along his chin. "Seeing as how once they're in that study, they don't come around here anymore. Why would they? I mean, if they've got beds to sleep in and food in their stomachs, why would they bother with us anymore?"

I didn't want to put words into his mouth, but I had to know the truth. "So they go into the study and then..."

"Lucky devils." Ernie did not follow where I was hoping to lead him, which was to a confirmation—or denial—of what Madeline had told me. Instead, he shook his head. "That's why I'm hoping you could mention my name to Doctor Gerard. You know, as a kind of favor.

Don't know how much longer I can last in that box of mine."

I was getting nowhere except colder. I took another step toward the clinic. "Got it!" I gave Ernie the thumbs-up. "I'll be sure to tell him all about you and how you're qualified and all." A thought struck, and I stopped in my tracks. "How are people accepted into the study, any-way?" I asked Ernie. "What do you have to do?"

"Don't have to do anything. Just have to be special." Ernie nodded. "The way I see it, I'm pretty special."

"You are." I nodded in return. "But special, how?"

"Aberrant behavior. That's what I heard one of the nurses there in the clinic call it." He tipped his head to-ward the building. "They're looking for folks with aber-rant behavior, and when they find them, they put them into that study. Alberta, she would know what they're talking about, but it makes no sense to me. You got any idea what that might mean, that talk of aberrant behav-ior?"

I did, but I wasn't about to go into details. Back when I first met Dan, he had mentioned any number of times that my brain scans revealed that my behavior should be aberrant. As far as I was concerned, I had never demon-strated this (at least not to him), so he wasn't justified in pointing it out. I guess I was still a little touchy on the subject. That would explain why my spine stiffened.

"Aberrant. That might mean people who hear things. And see things. Things that other people can't see or hear," I told Ernie.

"Well, that would explain Becka, that's for sure. Though I think she only saw things when she was high. Hardly counts, does it?"

I couldn't deny this.

Ernie turned away. "Aberrant." His grumble echoed back at me from the gloomy alley where he disappeared into the shadows. "As soon as I figure out what they're looking for, I'm going to act aberrant, too. If it will get me a good home-cooked meal, hell, it just might be worth it."

I wasn't about to follow Ernie into that alley. Instead, I turned and headed up the steps to the clinic door. I was almost there when I heard someone call my name.

I turned just in time to see Dan Callahan step out of a cab and wave to me, and though I'd been obsessing about what to say to him and how to explain what I was doing there, Dan, apparently, had no such worries. He raced up the steps to greet me, his smile a mile wide.

"This is terrific! It's so good to see you again." He grabbed both my hands and squeezed them, then he held on to me. I was glad. His black leather gloves provided an extra layer of warmth. Or maybe the heat was generated by the simple fact that Dan was standing so close to me. "I knew you'd come around," he said, honest relief in his voice. "Tell me, how did you find Doctor Gerard?"

Have I mentioned that I was getting very good at lying? When I looked into Dan's eyes, I smiled. "Oh, you know how it is." Hoping to catch him off guard, I made sure I giggled a bit, too. I know for a fact that when a woman giggles, a guy doesn't always pay close attention to what she's saying. "Doctor Gerard is famous. It's only natural that I heard—"

"About the study. Of course." Dan let go of my hands. Too bad. Even when he backed up a step, his smile never wavered. "I'm glad you're finally ready to admit you're special," he said.

This should have cheered me. It would have if he had said *special* the way I'd always imagined he'd say it when he was looking deep into my eyes. I was hoping for *special* as in *wow, Pepper, you're the most special woman I know*. What I got instead was more like *wow, Pepper, those are some special brain scans you have*.

I guess I'm not very good at hiding my disappointment, because he picked up on my mood instantly.

"Doctor Gerard is one of the world's foremost authorities on abnormal brain function." Dan said this like he knew it would make me feel better. "This is the best place for you."

My smile was tight. "And what are you doing here?" I asked.

"I'm working with Doctor Gerard," Dan said, and he was so excited, I don't think he noticed that my shoulders drooped. So, Madeline was right. A claw of uneasiness made my insides as cold as my outsides. "It's the chance of a lifetime," Dan said. "And your timing couldn't be more perfect. You know I called you the other day?"

I remembered the phone call Quinn had fielded while I was in the shower. "You didn't say what you wanted."

"I didn't expect a man to answer the phone. Not that early in the morning. What, was he there fixing your cable or something?" Leave it to Dan not to consider there might be any other possibility. Before I could point this out, he went right on. "I was planning to call again as soon as I was settled in here. I was going to try and convince you to come to the clinic and be evaluated, but it looks like you beat me to it. This is great, Pepper. We'll have the chance to work together. You've done all your initial screening tests?"

Who was I to tell him he was way off base? Or to ruin a perfectly good chance to find out more about what was going on? I nodded.

"Great. Then I'll look over the results as soon as I have a chance, and we can plan the next phase of your assessment from there. Right now . . ." He glanced toward the clinic door. "I've got a meeting with Doctor Gerard in just a couple minutes, and he doesn't like to be kept waiting. Dinner?"

Poor Dan, he took my smiling agreement at face value. If only he knew the truth. Dinner was my chance to get closer to him, sure.

It was also the perfect opportunity to figure out what was happening.

And to find out once and for all how deeply he was involved with the disappearances at the Gerard Clinic.

When Dan arrived at my hotel late that afternoon, he found me pacing my room. Quick study that he is, he knew right away that something was wrong.

Or maybe he picked up on that because I was grumbling.

And the pages of Ella's presentation were scattered all over the floor.

"What?" Leave it to Dan to be Mr. Neatnik. No sooner was he inside the door than he bent to retrieve the pages closest to him. "You had a hurricane in here or something?"

I barely contained a screech. "I can't stand the thought of giving that stupid talk." I wasn't a clean freak, but even I knew I wouldn't sleep that night with the room in that state. While I cursed myself for losing my temper and chucking the pages, I scooped up the papers that had landed near the bathroom door. "It's boring," I said, plunking the pages down on the coffee table. "It's dull. Ella's the one who wrote this stupid speech and nobody's going to want to hear me give it and I'm—"

"You're giving a talk here at the conference?" Dan glanced at the pages briefly before he set them down. He glanced at me, too, and I couldn't help but notice that something almost like admiration shone in his eyes. "You're nervous."

I could have argued with him, but there didn't seem to be much point. I dropped into the nearest chair, pulled in a deep breath, and confessed to him what I'd been afraid to admit even to myself. "I'm scared to death."

His laugh didn't make me feel better. "Hey!" He hurried over and patted my shoulder. "It's not so bad. Believe me, I've given plenty of talks in my day." He flipped through the pages still in his hands. "Resurrectionists, huh? They'll eat this stuff up."

"Easy for you to say. You're not the one who's going to be standing in front of a room full of cemetery geeks." Because I didn't want to think about it, I got up, and without being too obvious about it, checked my hair and my makeup in the nearest mirror. I'd dressed carefully in jeans and a dark, bulky sweater. I didn't know where we were going for dinner, but I wasn't going to take any chances with the cold. I added a coat of gloss over the lipstick I was wearing.

By the time I was done, Dan had all the pages picked up and stacked neatly. "Good thing they're numbered," he said. "Maybe Ella knew you'd lose it and end up tossing her talk."

He was going for funny. I wasn't laughing.

"I'll tell you what." Dan did his best to appease me. "We'll take the pages along and you can practice on me. What do you say?"

"Really?" Not one to pass on an opportunity, I grabbed Ella's talk and stuffed the pages into my purse. "You'll let me read it? It'll put you to sleep."

"Pepper." I don't know if his eyes twinkled or if it was a reflection off his glasses. I only know that when he looked at me that way, even reading a dull talk about a dull subject suddenly didn't sound so dull anymore. "I could never get bored when I'm with you," he said.

I got so warm, I almost forgot to grab my jacket before we left the room.

We were in the elevator and headed downstairs when Dan looked at his watch.

"I hope you don't mind that I asked to meet you so early," he said. "There's still something I have to take care of before we can head off to dinner, and I want to get there before they close. I thought maybe you'd like to come along."

Our elevator stopped, and a couple people I recognized as conference goers got in. Fortunately, they weren't with the Doris crowd. They didn't know me and I didn't know them. I was free to continue my conversation with Dan, and I ignored them and turned my attention back to him.

Dan's smile was sincere. "When I'm in Chicago I never let a day go by without doing what I thought we could do now. I've been busy all day and there hasn't been a chance and—"

I hated to see him feel bad. Especially since he'd volunteered to listen to Ella's talk. "No problem." The elevator bumped to a stop at the lobby, and since we were in the back, we waited while the people up front got off. He stepped aside so I could get off before him. "Where are we headed, anyway?" I asked.

Dan's comment was casual enough. "I thought we'd stop and visit my wife."

Did I say casual? My reaction to this bombshell was anything but. As a matter of fact, I stood there so long, the elevator doors were already closing before I realized I was headed back upstairs. I bumped the door with my hip and saw that while I was frozen with shock, Dan had already gotten off the elevator. Maybe he realized he'd blindsided me when he saw that my mouth was hanging open.

"I'm sorry, Pepper. I should have told you sooner." His words teetered between being an apology and a simple statement of fact. "I would have, of course, but the subject just never came up. Now that you're in Doctor Gerard's study and we're going to be seeing each other more, it makes sense for us to be honest and open with each other." The smile Dan offered had warmed me through and through only a short time before. Now it did nothing but ignite my temper. "I guess it's time we know everything there is about each other, right?"

"And you're telling me..." Was that my voice? It sounded high and tight. I coughed and tried again, and it took more willpower than I knew I had to control my anger. "You're going to stand here like it's nothing at all and tell me that you have a wife? Don't you think you could have mentioned that before?"

"I could have. I would have, but..." Dan shrugged. "It didn't seem important at the time."

Maybe I'd been getting the wrong signals from Dan all this time, but I thought not. A woman knows these things, and this woman knew that the signals Dan was sending weren't the signals of a married man. Not when it came to me. OK, a married man who just wants to be friends might have saved my life the way Dan did back at the cemetery the spring before. But that same married man never would have kissed me the way he kissed me after. Not unless he had something more than just friendship in mind.

I swallowed down the lump of outrage in my throat. "You're telling me you're married and that's not important?"

His smile was instantly apologetic. "Not married. *Was* married. I'm not explaining this well, am I?" Dan ran a hand through his a-little-more-than-shaggy hair before he reached into his back pocket, pulled out his wallet, and flipped it open. "Here," he said, holding a picture out for me to see. "Here's a picture of my wife. My late wife. You see, she's dead."

Oh, I saw, all right. I saw plenty.

Because right then and there, I found myself face-to-face with a photograph of Madeline Tremayne.

7

For the second time in as many days, I found myself standing in the freezing cold at Graceland Cemetery. Side by side with Dan, I stared at the grave of Madeline Tremayne.

"Sorry it's so awful out here." Dan pulled his scarf closer around his neck. "When it comes to Maddy, I never think about the weather. Rain or shine, I don't much care. Every day I'm in Chicago—"

"You come here. Of course."

Sure, my voice was a little snippy. Like anyone could blame me? I'd just been blindsided by the living and the dead, it was as cold as hell, my feet were numb, and my teeth were chattering. Add to all that the fact that I was still trying to work through what had me flummoxed in the cab on the way over, and my current funky mood was not only excusable but understandable. There I was, shivering, and I was no closer to figuring out what, exactly, was going on, why I hadn't caught on sooner, and how I was supposed to proceed now that I knew that the ghost who had engaged my services was connected (in more ways than I wanted to consider) to a guy I thought was going to be a guy in my life, only maybe now he wasn't, and maybe I didn't want him to be, anyway, seeing as how he'd never bothered to mention this incredibly important oh-by-the-way-I-used-to-be-married detail.

It was enough to make my head pound and my blood whoosh through my veins with all the clatter of an L train, and before it could upend me, I sucked in a breath of frigid air and told myself to get a grip. If nothing else, I now understood why Madeline was so worried about Dan. She was his wife, after all. Or at least she used to be. Of course she cared about him. She loved him.

From the way he looked at her grave, his expression grim and his eyes brimming with grief that was practically palpable, I knew that even after three years, Dan still loved her, too.

It was actually pretty sweet.

My feet were as numb as ever, but my heart warmed.

"She didn't use your name." There was a light dusting of snow on the pink granite headstone. I bent to sweep it away then brushed my gloves against my coat to get rid of the snow that stuck to them. "It says Madeline Tremayne, not Madeline Callahan."

Dan never took his eyes off the grave. "Maddy earned her degrees before I ever met her," he said. "She taught under that name. She lectured under that name. She was published under that name. I felt it was only right that she be remembered for what she accomplished, not for just being my wife."

My heart warmed a little more, even when an icy wind kicked up. I glanced around. That day, like every day, the cemetery closed at four thirty, and though we still had a half hour or so, it was an overcast afternoon in the dead of winter; the light was already beginning to fade. The Palmer memorial, not all that far away, was wrapped in gray. I shivered and stepped closer to Dan. Don't get the wrong idea; I am not insensitive or callous. I knew this wasn't the time—and it certainly wasn't the place—to try and put the moves on him. I was hoping for nothing more than to share a smidgen of body heat.

"She died young." It was a way to keep the conversation going; I didn't need to mention it. Something told me that not a day went by when Dan didn't think about Madeline. In a strange way, it explained a lot.

He barely nodded. "Too young. She was Doctor Gerard's assistant at the clinic. Well, really, she was more than his assistant. Maddy was indispensable. She practically ran the place. She worked there when I met her. I was a graduate student and I needed some hours of fieldwork. I guess there are some people who might say our relationship was inappropriate, seeing that she was my supervisor, but it wasn't like that at all! She was just a couple years older than me, and we struck up an instant friendship. Exactly one month and three days after we met, I proposed. I didn't think I could ever be lucky enough to have her feel about me the way I felt about her, so I wasn't just thrilled when she said yes, I was on top of the world. I was willing to wait if I had to, but she wanted to get married fast. Good thing Maddy wasn't a woman who believed in all that razzle-dazzle wedding nonsense."

It wasn't my imagination. Dan really did pause right

there. It was as if he actually knew that the wedding I had once planned was complete with a videographer, a sound tech, and a computer geek whose job it was to make sure every guest left with a DVD of the day's events. Of course, there were also the two swans that were set to be released from their pen to float by on the country-club lake just as Joel and I cut our wedding cake. And the bevy of pink-gowned little girls (children of cousins and friends) whose sole function at the festivities was to blow soap bubbles as we emerged from the stretch limo that just happened to be the same shade of ivory as my brides-maids' gowns.

Of course Dan's pointed silence reminded me of all this, but I didn't take offense. Not too much, anyway. He was so lost in thought, his expression so dreamy, I for-gave him.

"We were married at city hall that week," he said, and thinking about it, a smile touched his lips. "That was just a few months before..." He cleared his throat. "Maddy was leaving the clinic one night when she ran into one of her clients. He was off his meds. He asked for money; she didn't have any to give him, she needed it for cab fare. He claimed he didn't remember exactly what hap-pened after that, but—"

"He killed her."

When Dan's eyes snapped to mine, I knew I had to explain.

I shrugged, but I doubted he noticed, since the light was fading fast and I was cocooned in my wool coat. "What else could it have been? I mean, a woman that young, and you said she was mugged. It only makes sense that she was—"

"Yeah." Dan's voice was no louder than the whisper

of frosty wind that raised the hair on the back of my neck. "What a waste of such a promising life! And it's even sadder when you think she only had a couple bucks with her. I know that for a fact, because she called earlier in the day and asked me to bring some extra cash when I came down to the clinic. She needed to stop on the way home and pick up some things from the grocery store, and she hated to write a check for food. Said it wasn't worth the effort. Maybe if I'd been there like I was supposed to be..."

There was nothing I could say, so I didn't even try, and good thing. Dan was so caught up in the past and the guilt that was eating him from the inside out, he never would have heard me.

"She was brilliant," he said. "She was clever. Maddy was beautiful."

"Huh?" I slapped one gloved hand over my mouth, but by then, it was already too late. I couldn't take back my skeptical question, and I sure couldn't tell Dan that the Madeline I knew wasn't just irritating and self-important, she was as plain as a mud fence and had the fashion sense of a cloistered nun. With no other choice, I scrambled for an excuse. "That picture you showed me, it wasn't the best. It didn't do her justice. I bet she was plenty pretty."

Dan smiled in a way I always imagined some guy—somewhere, someday—would smile when he talked about me. "Pretty? That's putting it mildly! Maddy was blond and blue-eyed and she had the cutest little dimple that showed up on her right cheek when she smiled."

I'd never noticed the dimple, but then, I wasn't sure I'd ever seen Madeline smile. No matter, hearing the affection that colored Dan's voice made me think of that old saying about beauty being in the eye of the beholder. No doubt, in Dan's eyes, Madeline was the belle of the ball.

I hate getting all sloppy and sentimental, but facts are facts; my heart softened even more.

"I'm sorry I never told you about her." To try and gauge my reaction, Dan gave me a sidelong glance. "It just never seemed to be the right time. But then this afternoon, when I saw you coming out of the clinic and realized you were going to be part of Doctor Gerard's study..." He pulled in a breath and let it out in a puff. When he turned to me, his expression wasn't nearly as solemn anymore. Something very much like hope shone in Dan's blue eyes. "This is great, Pepper. Really. I'm convinced that you're our best bet. If we ever have any hope of contacting those on the Other Side—"

I didn't have to say a word to stop Dan cold. That's because I latched onto his arm so hard and so fast, he was too startled to go on.

Confused, he blinked at me in wonder, and I stammered over questions I could barely put into words. "You mean, the ghost thing? Your interest in the paranormal? All that talk about...about warnings of danger and...and things that go bump in the night and...and how you took that picture of me once and you must have used some kind of crazy camera because it showed me and two blobs of mist and...and you never really came right out and said it, of course, because that would have been too easy and...and you just sort of skirted around the issue and...and you talked about my aberrant behavior instead and...and my brain scans and all and...and how weird they were since I hit my head on that mausoleum back at Garden View and...and now this study with

Doctor Gerard and...and are you telling me this is all because of—"

"Because of Maddy. Of course."

Dan was so calm, his voice so matter-of-fact, it made my ramblings sound crazier than ever. And they already sounded pretty crazy.

I steadied myself with a calming breath, and though it wasn't easy, I refused to say another word until I was sure I wouldn't come across sounding like a lunatic. When I finally spoke, my words were as calm and as measured as the look I gave Dan.

"You're interested in the paranormal because you want to contact Madeline."

Buying some time to organize his thoughts, he took a couple steps away. "I've always been interested in the paranormal," he said. "You know, the way a lot of people are. As a kid, I loved ghost stories and scary movies, and sometimes even these days, I watch those ghost-hunting shows on TV. But I never really believed any of it. Back when I was in school, I mean. I was a scientist, after all, and I took my research work very seriously. Then I met Maddy."

Dan was still looking my way, but I could tell he wasn't seeing me. His eyes were misted. He was clearly thinking about the past.

"She was the love of my life. My soul mate. When she died..." His shoulders slumped as if a weight had been dropped from the leaden clouds above us. "I have to find her again, Pepper. I'll never rest until I do. After Maddy died, that's when I got seriously involved in paranormal research. I was making progress, too. But not enough. Not fast enough. That's when I took the chance and mentioned my interest to Doctor Gerard. He didn't laugh.

Not like I expected him to. In fact, he understood perfectly. He knew Maddy as well as anyone. He missed her, too. He agreed to fund my research on one condition: I had to share my findings with him. Since then, I've made great strides. It's amazing what can happen when you've got financing behind you. I've got the best equipment in the world and—"

"Then it's true? Doctor Gerard is giving you the money for your research?"

If Dan thought my question was odd or impertinent, he didn't say. He simply nodded. "Hilton Gerard is a man who can really make things happen."

Be that as it may, I was still stuck on the bit about Doctor Gerard and the money. "Where does it come from?"

"The money?" This time, the whole *odd* part of the equation was evident in the look Dan gave me. "Hilton's got a huge family fortune."

That, apparently, was supposed to be explanation enough.

It might actually have been if I wasn't hell-bent on finding out more.

"You're sure?"

Dan made a face. "Of course I'm sure. Where else would it come from? You can't possibly think that Doctor Gerard is—"

"Of course not." It was too soon to point fingers, but not too soon to probe. Just a little more. "What about the people in your study?" I asked Dan. "Where do they come from? How do you find them?"

And what happens to them when you're done poking around in their brains?

That was the question I was dying to ask, but like I

said, it was too soon. Better to play it cool than take the chance that Dan would get offended and leave me high and dry. And I wasn't just talking about being left at the cemetery alone again. I could deal with that. But if Dan shut me out…well, then I'd lose any hope of helping him.

His answer to my question about his test subjects was a shrug. "I find subjects the way any researcher does," he said. "Questionnaires, feelers, requests to other researchers, referrals. I find them the way I found you. You know, by working in hospitals, watching who comes in, checking out their records. I have to tell you, Pepper, by the time I met you, I was losing faith. I'd looked into lead after lead. Doctor Gerard had studied patient after patient. Even the promising ones…well, they never panned out. Then when I saw your brain scans, I knew you were different. Special. I thought—"

"You thought I could help your study along."

"It's not like I was trying to take advantage of you. It's just that—"

"You were trying to take advantage of me."

Dan didn't look any happier admitting this than I did saying it. He didn't meet my eyes when he said, "You're a terrific girl, Pepper. Really, I like you a lot. It's just that—"

"You'll always be in love with Madeline."

Maybe he didn't hear the disappointment that dripped from my every word. That would explain why he responded to my statement as if it was a good thing. "I'm glad you understand," he said. His smile was brief, and I got the feeling it was more for my sake than anything else. "I knew you would. It just shows what a kind and sensitive person you are. I know it's not a very scientific thing to say—after all, it can't really be measured, can it?—but your understanding and your compassion...I think that has something to do with your ability to communicate with the dead."

He didn't say it like it was a question. Dan was way more up front than that. And me? Well, if ever there was a time for me to come clean, I knew this was it.

My sigh rippled the icy air between us. "It's not something I'm thrilled about."

"You should be! Think of all you can accomplish with this wonderful Gift of yours. You can give grieving people hope. You can be a messenger between the here and now and the Other Side. You can find her for me, Pepper." At this point, Dan's eyes weren't just bright, they were fiery. I'd never seen him look that way before, and it made me a little uncomfortable. "I'll do anything—anything—to talk to Maddy again. I need to see her and I need to tell her how very much I love her."

"And you think I can help?"

"I know you can." Before I even had a chance to react, Dan had his hands on my shoulders. His look was pleading. "With Doctor Gerard's guidance, we can make this thing happen. I know we can, Pepper. And when we do, we're going to change the world!"

If I was as understanding and compassionate as Dan thought I was, I would have responded to this statement with some genuine enthusiasm. I actually might have if I wasn't thinking about what I'd learned from Ernie outside the clinic that afternoon. My detective tendencies kicked into high gear. "Doctor Gerard isn't just looking for folks with aberrant behavior, is he? He's looking for people who see things. And people who hear things. Because—"

"Because..." Dan reined in his wild enthusiasm to answer. "Because though most of the people who exhibit those behaviors are mentally ill, he suspects what you and I both already know. Not all of them are."

I let this news sink in before I responded. "So Doctor Gerard thinks that some of the people who hear things and see things really do hear things and see things. And that the people who do—"

"Are lucky enough to be in contact with the Other Side. Yes." Dan nodded. "Now that you're on board, well, things can really start to come together, can't they? All our other subjects...they might hear and see things, but they're not things from the Other Side. But I know you're different, Pepper. I just know it. We're going to accomplish wonderful things. This is cutting-edge science, and not something the mainstream scientific community would endorse. But hey, they made fun of Galileo, too, right?"

I wasn't sure about that, so it seemed best not to answer. Instead, I forced myself to hold off on all the questions I was burning to ask. Why bother when I knew I wouldn't get a straight answer. Not from a man who had chucked his conventional scientific ways to devote his life to exploring the possibility of communicating with his dead wife. If I was going to find out what was really going on in that study, I would have to bide my time. As I'd already learned in the course of three previous investigations, biding my time meant playing along. At least until I figured out who was who, what was what, and what the hell was really going on.

Looking back on it, I guess that's why I didn't mention that I'd already been in touch with Madeline. If I gave away that secret, Dan would want details, and there was no way I was ready to tell him that the Maddy I met didn't exactly jibe with his memories, colored as they were with guilt, sentiment, and loneliness. In point of fact, she was a snooty, bigheaded pain in the—

"Did you see that?" A movement in the shadows on my left caught my eye and interrupted my train of thought. I spun around that way, and when I did, Dan dropped his hands from my shoulders and looked around, too.

"See what?"

I squinted into the gloom, but if there had been something there before, it sure wasn't there now. Or was it?

An arctic blast of air curled around my feet and slithered up my legs, penetrating my layers of clothing. It left me feeling icy and so scared, my knees knocked together and I couldn't breathe.

Believe me, this was one frosty feeling I recognized on contact. I thought back to my visit to the cemetery the day before and to the shadow that had followed me for a while, then slipped away and disappeared. Yeah, that one. The spooky shadow that scared me to death.

As frightened out of my gourd now as I was then, I hugged my arms around myself and looked hard in the direction the attack of cold had come from.

I was just in time to see a shadow—thicker and darker than the ones around it—pass behind a standing headstone. It didn't come out on the other side.

"That." I pointed, but by the time Dan caught on and looked in the right direction, the heavyweight shadow was already gone.

And if I told him how just looking at it made me want

to run off screaming into the night, I'd sound like a nutcase.

"Must have been a bird." My smile wasn't any more convincing than my feeble explanation, but let's face it, Dan was too busy thinking about his beloved Madeline to worry about anything else. He twitched his shoulders before he turned back to me, and if he noticed that while he spoke my gaze kept darting to the place I'd seen the shadow disappear, he was polite enough not to say anything about it.

"I'm glad we had this chance to talk." From behind the lenses of his wire-rimmed glasses, Dan's eyes shone with emotion. "I just wish..."

He didn't have to fill in the blanks. I knew exactly what he was wishing for.

I wondered what he'd say if he realized that the next second, she was standing right behind him.

"What is it?" Dan must have seen the flash of awareness in my eyes, because he spun around and looked where I was looking. Of course, he didn't have my Gift (lucky guy). All he saw was a vast stretch of cemetery and row upon row of headstones and monuments, as cold as the wintry air. "You're looking at something. At someone. Is she..." Dan was so excited, he could barely get the words out. I watched anticipation wash across his face. "Is Maddy here?"

It was either lie to him or tell him the truth and watch him melt into a puddle of mush. I wasn't prepared for that. Or for revealing the whole truth and nothing but about my Gift. At least not until I learned more about Dan's study and those people who'd gone into it and never come out again.

None of that explains the words that came out of my

mouth. Then again, the look of longing in Dan's eyes probably does.

"Madeline is here," I said, and always the rational scientist—even when we were talking about something completely irrational—he tried hard to control his smile. "She's standing there." I put a hand on his arm and nudged him around so that he was facing the right way.

"He's anxious to see me, poor darling." Madeline drifted back and forth in front of Dan. "Tell him, Pepper. Tell him I say hello."

"She says hello."

Dan blinked away tears. "How does she look? What is she wearing? Is she happy? Does she..." He swallowed so hard, I saw his Adam's apple jump. "Does she miss me?"

"He's a sweetheart." Madeline's voice was as soft as the look she gave her husband. "I don't want to see him suffer."

"She doesn't want to see you suffer." I relayed the message to Dan, of course, because I didn't want to see him suffer, either.

"I want him to be happy."

"She says that she wants you to be happy."

He nodded, but pardon me for not being convinced. There was so much pain in Dan's eyes, I could tell that happiness was the farthest thing from his mind. "I can never be happy," he said, echoing my thoughts. "Not without you, Maddy. I'm sorry about what happened at the clinic that day. If only I—"

"Shhhh." Madeline drifted closer. Her clunky shoes never touched the ground. "Tell him there was nothing he could do. Our fates are sealed, he couldn't change mine."

"She said you shouldn't feel guilty."

"It's time for him to get on with his life. Tell him, Pepper."

"She wants you to move on with your life."

"It's time for him to put the past behind."

"It's time for you to put the past behind."

"It's time for him to open his heart to new possibilities."

"It's time for you to..." Madeline's message was just too lame. I wrinkled my nose and decided a little poetic license was in order. "It's time for you to start fresh."

"She wouldn't understand if I did. How could she?" Dan barely looked my way before he stepped toward where I'd told him Madeline was standing. "I promised I'd love you forever, Maddy. I meant that. With all my heart."

"He was the man of my dreams." Madeline stepped away, fading as she did. "He was the perfect husband. If only... if only there was someone who could make him as happy as I did. I want him to be happy."

I decided not to relay this part of the message. Talking to a dead wife about finding her husband a live wife... well, that was a little too weird, even for me.

When I didn't say anything, Dan spun toward me. "Is she gone?" he asked.

I looked to where Madeline was standing. There was nothing and no one there now. "She's gone."

"But she'll be back, right?"

I didn't have the answer, but it didn't stop me from saying, "Of course she will be."

A bittersweet smile touched Dan's lips. He patted my arm. "You're a good friend, Pepper," he said. "I'm glad you're the one who's giving me the messages from

Maddy. It means..." His voice clogged with tears. "It means so much to me. You understand, don't you? When Maddy talks about me being happy again...I know she means it, and believe me, I'd really like to. But you understand that it isn't possible, right? It's just not that easy to turn off grief."

8

By the time it was all over, I had lost my taste for dinner. I don't think I was imagining that Dan didn't even notice. When I said I wanted to go right back to the hotel, he never questioned it. He didn't say much in the cab, either, except, "Thank you," and "Thank you," and "Thank you" again. He was so ecstatic that I'd finally admitted to my ability to commune with the Other Side and with his own close encounter with the late Mrs. Callahan, he barely bothered to say good night.

I didn't have much of a chance to be offended. We weren't on the road for more than ten minutes when it started snowing like crazy, and by the time I stepped out of the cab at the conference hotel, I had to tiptoe over the mounds of slush on the street and the piles of snow on the sidewalks. The wind nearly blasted me off my feet, and it was either hold my dorky felt hat in place or lose it.

Oh yeah, and Madeline was waiting outside the hotel door, too.

"That's a cute trick."

The valet thought I was talking to him, and before he could wonder what he'd done to warrant such an acerbic statement, I gave him a tight smile and darted into the revolving door.

"I don't know what you're talking about." Madeline was right next to me, and when it comes to ghosts, *right next to* is too close for comfort. I scooted as far away from her as I could in the confined space.

"I'm talking about first, you not telling me about the patients who are MIA. Then forgetting . . . forgetting—"

The door spit us out in the lobby, and since there were knots of conference goers standing around and talking about whether they wanted to venture out in the nasty weather, I swallowed my words. There was an alcove nearby with a chintz-covered settee and a potted palm. I darted inside, slid the palm in front of me so no one could see me, and flopped down on the couch. I stripped off my hat and my gloves and slapped them down on the couch beside me to emphasize my words.

"You forgot to mention that you and Dan were married."

Madeline sniffed. "You're the detective," she said. "You should have figured it out."

"What I'm figuring out is that you have a problem with the truth."

Sitting down had been a tactical mistake. When Madeline replied, she was looking down at me. Literally and figuratively.

"And what would you have done if I told you about me and Danny?" she asked. "Would you have believed me? And if you did... well, I don't think I'm imagining things here, Pepper. If I told you Danny and I were married, you never would have concentrated on the case. You would have been too busy being jealous."

"Of you?" The words practically choked me. Maybe because they were so preposterous. Maybe because they were true. I decided to stick with the preposterous theory because it was, after all, more likely. It was also far less humbling than considering that I might harbor the tiniest inkling of jealousy for a woman as plain and as boring and as downright annoying as Madeline. To stress my point and how much I so didn't care, I rolled my eyes. "Please! I'm way more professional than that. And in case you haven't noticed, I'm not exactly the jealous type. I don't need to be."

"Because you think you're better than everyone else." Madeline nodded, as if she'd just been waiting for me to say this. "It's your narcissism rearing its ugly head again. I knew it would eventually. No one with as many serious mental health issues as you have can possibly hold it together for too long. It's statistically impossible. And before you get all defensive—" She held out a hand to shut me up because let's face it, I was already getting all defensive. "Let me tell you that I do understand. Narcissistic personality disorder is insulating, disenfranchising, terribly painful, and thus, overwhelming for those who deal with it. Believe me, Pepper, I feel your pain."

At that moment, I really wished she could.

When I stood, my teeth were clenched and my jaw was tight. "The only pain around here is you. You're a royal pain in the—"

"Of course that's how you would respond." All-knowing, she pressed her lips together and nodded. "It's

practically impossible for you to rise above your childish, defensive personality structure. Not without inten-
sive psychotherapy. Have you thought about getting it,
Pepper? You really would be doing yourself a favor. And
making the world a better place."

"Actually, I think I'd be doing myself a favor if I forgot all about you and this stupid case of yours." I grabbed
my hat and gloves and stepped around the potted palm,
prepared to leave the alcove. "I don't need this aggrava-
tion."

"And Danny doesn't need to go to jail."

"Then I'll tell you what. I'll give him the skinny on
what's going on. Now that Dan knows I can talk to you,
I'll tell him how you told me that Doctor Gerard is a
crook. Then he can tell Doctor Gerard that he knows
what's going on and—"

"Oh please don't!" Suddenly as upset as she had been
self-important only moments before, her mouth fell open
and her voice wobbled. "We can't risk that, Pepper. If
Hilton knows…" She swallowed hard. "If he finds out,
Danny could be in danger."

"Come off it!" I wheeled away and then turned back
to her. It was warm in the tiny room off the lobby, and I
unbuttoned my coat. "You're making this Hilton guy
sound like some kind of criminal mastermind. Is there
more you haven't told me about him?"

Madeline shook her head. "I swear, Pepper. You know
everything now. Everything. I just…" She wrung her
hands, and her cheeks were as pale as her lab coat. "I just
don't know what I'd do if something happened to Danny.
I love him so much. I only want what's best for him. You
understand that, don't you? You must have been in love
at least once in your life."

I thought about the string of boyfriends I'd had back in my high school and college days. The ones I'd loved as only a young girl can—with all my heart and all my soul. At least until the next boyfriend came along.

I thought about Joel, who had once professed his to-my-dying-day love for me, and who I'd once been stupid enough to believe.

I thought about Quinn, because believe me, even though my trip to Chicago was turning out to be way more than I bargained for, I hadn't forgotten Quinn or the incredible night we spent together. That didn't mean I didn't know what was what as far as my favorite cop was concerned. Quinn might be more than willing to share my bed, but I wasn't kidding myself. He'd never let a dangerous four-letter word like L-O-V-E cross his lips or his mind.

And of course, I thought about Dan. Only it wasn't as easy, since when it came to him, I didn't know what to think. Especially now that I knew about Madeline. Not to mention the shady money that funded his research and the missing patients.

But of course, I wasn't willing to talk about my personal life. Not with Madeline, anyway. Any woman who could pull off a wedding within one week of her fiancé proposing—and at city hall, no less—would never understand the intricacies of my love life.

And I wouldn't want her to.

"Is that why you haven't crossed over?" I asked her instead. "Because you're worried about Dan?"

"Worried about him? Yes, of course." Madeline turned away, but she wasn't fooling me; I heard her sniffle. When she turned back to me, there were tears on her cheeks. "I don't want to see him in trouble, but I don't want to see him alone, either. He's such a wonderful man. I can't bear to think of him being lonely for the rest of his life. I can't leave. Not until I know he's happy."

"And you don't think he'll be happy until—"

"Well, not if he's in jail, of course." This was a given, so Madeline did not elaborate. "But once I'm satisfied that Danny won't be entangled in any messy legal problems... well..." A rush of color stained her cheeks. "I'd like to see him find another woman. One who loves him as much as I did. I'd like him to love another woman as much as he loved me. It's only fair. I know you don't understand, but on this Side, jealousy and petty feelings, they don't mean a thing. So you see, if he did find someone to love, I wouldn't mind at all. All I want is what's best for my Danny, and I'm anxious to see him get it. I can't rest unless I know he's happy. Maybe..." When she looked at me, her eyes were pleading. "Maybe you could help him find someone?"

I don't think my reaction had anything to do with narcissism, because a person doesn't have to be officially narcissistic to get insulted.

Insulted, I raised my chin and glared at Madeline. "What you're saying is that I should go out and look for a woman for him because... what? You don't think Dan and I could ever be a couple?"

"It's not that."

It was. I could tell from the way Madeline said the words.

"He needs someone who loves him deeply. Do you love him deeply, Pepper?"

I didn't know him well enough for that kind of feeling, and I told Madeline so. That didn't mean we couldn't try to be friends and see where things went from there. I told her that, too.

She merely shook her head in disappointment.

By this time, I wasn't just offended, I was royally pissed. Madeline wasn't just questioning if I was compatible with Dan. Hell, I'd questioned that, too. Dozens of times. I'd be a fool not to go on questioning it. At least until I knew him better.

Oh no. Madeline was way more thorough than that. She was questioning my motives. And my worth. Without so much as saying a word about it, she was questioning my character and my intentions and damn it, my sex appeal, too. This was not something I was going to take sitting down.

Even though I was already standing up.

I went toe-to-toe with her. "What? You think I'm not pretty enough? Or funny enough? Or—"

"Let's face it, Pepper." Madeline's expression was downright pained. "A man like Danny has so many interests and such wide-ranging reading habits. He bores easily, of course, because with a mind like his, it's just natural that he needs stimulation and mental challenges. I doubt if you can understand, seeing as how you're just a detective."

Did I catch a whiff of condescension in that last word?

You bet I did, but before I could say anything about it, Madeline went right on. "I'm sorry, Pepper. Though we can always try to improve ourselves through study and reading and, in some cases like yours, with the help of trained professionals who understand our challenges and our limitations, we can't change our basic natures. Or

our mental abilities and capabilities. My Danny...he
needs someone who's his intellectual equal."

"And you're saying I'm not smart enough." Gloves
clutched in one hand, hat in the other, I propped my fists
on my hips and tapped the toe of one boot against the
carpeting while I waited for her answer, or at least her
apology. I guess I could have gone on tapping and waiting until hell was as frozen as the Chicago streets outside, because instead of taking back her insulting words
the way any self-respecting ghost would, Madeline just
smiled sadly and faded away.

Even when her ectoplasm had disappeared, her voice
floated in the air around me. Which was too bad, because
I wasn't sure where to aim my glare. "I understand that
this is a real blow to your psyche, Pepper. Facing reality
always is for a person as enmeshed in her own narcissism as you are. But it's time to face facts. You can try all
you want, but you can't change the truth. You simply
aren't good enough for my Danny."

Of course, I knew better.
        I was plenty smart. And plenty good enough for
Dan. I also happened to be the only one who could save
him.

It was time to start proving it, and with that in mind, I
went to the hotel coffee shop and ordered a to-go container of beef barley soup and a cheeseburger with everything on it. I already had the paper bag with the food in it
clutched in one hand and was heading for the front doors
when something in a hallway off the lobby caught my
eye.

It was a laundry cart stacked with fresh bedding. I

looked over my shoulder to make sure no one was watching, ducked into the hallway, and got to work.

Just for the record (and in case any of my old friends get wind of this and start asking questions), I have never before made a social call on anyone who lives in a box.

My hands tucked into my sleeves, my scarf wound up to my nose, I hunkered down on an old milk crate newly covered with a blanket that had the hotel's name embroidered in one corner and did my best to make myself comfortable. Since Ernie had been lucky enough to get his hands on a box that must once have contained some large piece of commercial equipment, this was not as hard as it sounds. What he didn't have was a source of heat, and I shivered and watched him adjust the new blanket draped over his shoulders (a twin of the one I was sitting on). He drew in a long breath.

"This is the best meal I've had in as long as I can remember." In the light of a battery-operated lantern, Ernie's smile shone bright. "Way better than that mushy stew they give us over at St. Katherine's. Thank you." The photograph of his wife was next to him, and he looked at it briefly and smiled. "Alberta says thanks, too. I mean, she would if she were here."

"She's dead?" I wasn't usually so forward, but there was something about sitting close in the semidarkness while the snow swirled through the alley just on the other side of the tarp draped over the opening to the box that made me feel as if Ernie and I were old friends. "How long?"

"Dead?" There were a couple globs of gooey cheese on the paper the burger had been wrapped in and Ernie scraped them off and licked them from his finger. "Alberta's as right as rain. Still working at the Scottsdale library as far as I know. Not that I'd ever dare stop in to see her. I wouldn't want to upset her. You understand."

I didn't, but for reasons I couldn't explain, I wanted to. "If she's got a job—"

"Why am I sleeping out here in the cold?" I was glad he'd finished the question for me, because I wasn't sure how to word it. "Seems better, don't you think?" Ernie crumpled the burger wrapper and stuffed it in the paper bag along with the empty soup container. "Alberta, she's better off without me in her life."

"And you're better off here? That doesn't seem possible. How long have you lived on the street, Ernie?"

He thought about it for a moment. "Twelve years. At least as far as I can remember. It was the winter right after little Morgan was born. My youngest grandson. Doctor said I wouldn't get better and I could see how my way of acting and doing things was affecting Alberta." His eyes glittered. "I'm crazy, you know. At least that's what they say."

I waved off this announcement as inconsequential. "Believe me, I've met people who are way crazier than you. Besides, if you took your medication—"

"I feel better when I take it, sure. But then I figure I don't need to take it anymore. That's when I get all crazy again. Alberta, she don't deserve to live with a crazy man." He touched a finger to the photograph. "She's a good woman."

"I'll bet she misses you."

"You think?" Ernie's smile was bittersweet. "Not a day goes by that I don't think about her. That's for certain." His sigh rippled the air between us, and I reminded myself that next time I stopped in, I'd bring Crest, a toothbrush, and a lifetime supply of Listerine. "So, you were just passing by? Is that what you said?"

It was clear that Ernie didn't believe it, even though that was exactly how I'd explained stopping by with the food. I shrugged. "Actually, I was going to take a look around the clinic and maybe talk to whoever is on duty. It's open late tonight, right?"

"Open until ten every night. Doctor Gerard, I've heard him say there's no time clock for people who need help. He's a good man, don't you think?"

I stood, and when I hit my head on the roof of Ernie's box, I hunched my shoulders and sidled toward the doorway. "I haven't met him yet," I told Ernie. "But I'd like to. Does Doctor Gerard..." I eased into the subject because, let's face it, just because Ernie was mentally ill didn't mean he was dumb. "Does Doctor Gerard ever talk about ghosts?"

His eyebrows rose. "Is that what it's all about? Hell, wish I knew that years ago. I would have been happy to tell Doctor Gerard I believed in ghosts if I knew it was going to get me inside." He thought I was kidding, so he laughed.

I knew I wasn't, so I laughed, too, and headed back into the alley where it was only slightly colder than it was in Ernie's box. I had already rounded the corner to the street and climbed the steps up to the clinic's front door when it banged open and Dan Callahan slammed into me.

Dan being Dan, he acted instinctively and honorably. He made a grab for me and latched onto my sleeve to keep me from falling backward and down the steps.

Of course, that was before he did a double take and realized it was me.

There was enough light coming from the security lamp over the doorway for me to see his face, so I knew I wasn't imagining things. From the look that darted across Dan's face, I saw that given a second chance, he wouldn't have grabbed me to keep me from breaking my neck. In fact, I had the uneasy feeling that he might have given me a push to help me on my way.

"I thought we finally trusted each other, Pepper."

His look, his words, and the anger that simmered in his voice were all so far removed from the "Thank you, thank you, thank you" I'd heard from him only a couple hours earlier, I was too stunned to speak. Which was probably a good thing since he rushed right on.

"How could you?" Dan dropped his hand and backed away. "How could anyone be as cold and as cruel as you?"

Since not much of what he said made sense, I glommed on to what did. I stomped my feet and shoved my hands into my pockets. "I'll say I'm cold. As for being cruel…" I looked at Dan hard. "What the hell *are* you talking about?"

"As if you didn't know." Dan marched down the steps.

Too curious to let it go, I followed. "Pardon me for not being all cryptic along with you, but it's late and I'm freezing and I just spent the better part of the last hour in a cardboard box." I didn't explain because I didn't want to, and besides, I liked the idea of making that too-big brain of Dan's work overtime on trying to figure out what I was talking about. "The way I remember things, the last time I saw you, you pretty much thought I walked on water. As far as I know, I haven't done anything since to change that."

"Really?" He looked at me hard. "How about lying to me? Does that count? You said you were a patient of Doctor Gerard's."

"Oh."

Nothing like a reality check to take the wind out of a girl's sails.

But only for a second. "I never said that." If Dan was as smart as Madeline claimed he was, I shouldn't have had to tell him this. He would have remembered on his own. "You saw me here and you assumed I was a patient of Doctor Gerard's. You said—"

"I said I was glad you were finally seeing an expert and you—" He emphasized his point by poking a finger toward me, a gesture I did not appreciate in the least. "You never contradicted me. But you know what? I was just in the clinic and while I was there, I looked through the files. There's no record of you ever being a patient here, Pepper. There's no file with your name on it, and there's no notation of your appointment on Doctor Gerard's calendar. You lied. About all of it."

"Like you lied to me about being a brain researcher at a hospital."

He grunted. "That's hardly the same."

"It's exactly the same." My words echoed back at me in the deserted street, but who could blame me for sounding angry? I wasn't used to being ambushed. I didn't appreciate it, and as long as I was justifying my sudden burst of temper, I figured I might as well add that I didn't deserve it, either. "That study you said you were doing for the hospital . . . That weird equipment you hooked me up to, to test my brain . . . It was all a bunch of nonsense, because you never cared about my brain. All you cared about was my ability to talk to the dead."

"And that . . ." Dan drew in a breath. When he let it out slowly, it clouded in the snowy air. "That's the worst part of it. You told me you talked to her, Pepper. You said you'd seen her." His anger dissolved beneath his pain, and he choked over the words. "All that stuff about me moving on with my life . . . how can any woman be as shallow as you? You pretended you'd heard it from Maddy. You said all that . . . why? Just to get me to date you? That's pathetic."

"It's the truth."

"It's bull."

"I really do talk to the dead, Dan." Even I couldn't believe that I was defending myself on this, the one topic I'd sworn never to discuss with anybody—ever. "I've talked to plenty of dead people. Gus Scarpetti and Didi Bowman and—"

"But not Madeline. Never Madeline." His shoulders slumped. "You know what, Pepper? I always thought that when I finally met someone who could actually communicate with the Other Side . . . I thought I'd be thrilled. I thought I'd see this whole new world of research and scientific breakthroughs opening up in front of me. But now it's happened, and I'm not feeling anything. Anything at all. And I don't even care." He turned and walked away from me. "You lied to me, Pepper. You said you know Maddy, but truth is, you don't know anything."

"Oh yeah?" As comebacks went, it was pretty lame,

but not to worry, I had more ammunition and I wasn't shy about using it. I raised my voice so Dan couldn't fail to hear me. "I know the patients who are admitted into that study of yours don't come out again."

Big points for me, I knew how to deliver a parting shot; Dan stopped dead in his snowy tracks. When he turned back around, his eyes were narrowed.

"What are you talking about?"

"I'm talking about the people Doctor Gerard and you recruit for your study. They go in, Dan, but they don't come out again. Where are you keeping them? What are you doing to them?"

He wasn't the sputtering type, so while it would have been satisfying to see him scramble for an explanation, I shouldn't have been surprised that his words were well measured. "What makes you think that? How do you . . . ? Where did you get that idea?"

Like I was going to bring up Madeline's name and get him all hot and bothered again? I thought not. "What I know and how I know it is my business." Dan and I were just about the same height, and I used that to my advantage. I closed in on him and looked him in the eye. "I'll tell you one thing for certain, though. I'm going to get to the bottom of this. And you—" Yeah, it was childish of me to point a finger at his nose the way he had done to me. That didn't stop me from doing it. "You better hope that whatever's going on, you're clear of it. Because if there's something fishy happening at this place, somebody's going down for it."

Since this was a great closing line, I was glad when a cab rolled by as if on cue. I flagged it down, but before I climbed inside, I decided an encore was in order. "If that happens to be you, Dan, so be it. Then maybe you'll believe me when I tell you I talk to the dead. All the dead. Even Madeline."

When I closed the door, I saw that the cab driver was staring.

That was fine with me. Snow or no snow, he got me back to my hotel in no time flat.

G hosts have a way of disappearing. People don't. Not permanently and not without leaving some trace of themselves, anyway. I knew this in my heart and in my head, just as I knew (both in my heart and in my head) that as much as I didn't want to, I was going to have to prove it.

It was the only way I could get Dan to see that I was telling the truth.

I know, I know...I couldn't believe it, either. I'd spent so much time trying to hide my Gift from Dan and everybody else in the known universe, and now I was going to go out of my way—and in the cold, too—to investigate, just so I could dig up all the right evidence to convince him I was the genuine article and that I did talk to Madeline. Hell, the whole *I see dead people* schtick was exactly what he wanted to hear from me since the day we met, wasn't it? And now that I'd finally confessed...

It was the next morning, and too irritated to keep still, I got up from the standard-issue hotel room settee where I'd been sitting and thinking (OK, obsessing) and walked to the room's single window and back again. My room wasn't much bigger than my office back at Garden View, and it didn't take long to walk its length. Too bad. By the time I was done, I was no less aggravated.

Did I send signals that I was that desperate?

Did I come across as truly pitiful?

Was it possible—I mean really possible—for Dan to think I'd made up the whole thing about how I was able to talk to Madeline and how she told me that she wanted him to be happy just because I was jonesing for a date?

It was embarrassing. Not to mention annoying. It was unfair, too, and for a couple crazed moments, I was actually tempted to call the Cleveland Police Department and conference Dan in, just so Quinn could vouch for the fact that I had a healthy sex life, thank you very much. Without any help from Dan Callahan at all.

Cooler heads prevailed, and I decided sticking to my original plan was a better option. Follow my logic here. It is—as always—impeccable.

Dan didn't believe I could see and talk to Madeline.

Madeline was the one who told me about the shady dealings at the clinic.

Since I had no other connection there and since somebody besides Dan and Doctor Gerard must have known about the missing patients but no one was talking, I could only have heard it from Madeline.

So if I proved that patients really were missing, I could therefore prove that I talked to Madeline.

Then Dan would know, once and for all, that I wasn't

just some desperate-for-a-date chickie with hope in her heart and sex on her mind.

This was all good, yes? But wait—as they say in those commercials—there really was more.

If everything panned out the way I hoped, I'd also help Dan see that as Hilton Gerard's sidekick, he was headed nowhere fast. Except maybe toward being my dad's roomie in the federal pen.

Was I being magnanimous?

Well, yes. And no.

Sure, Dan had pissed me off. Majorly. He'd wounded my ego in a big way. But as much fun as it was to think that he deserved every nasty form of revenge I could concoct (and believe me, after what Joel had pulled on me, I was an expert at fantasizing about revenge), I knew better. Dan didn't belong in prison. This, too, I knew in my heart and in my head. Deep down inside, I firmly believed that Dan was one of the good guys. And besides, he was way too cute; he'd look terrible in an orange jumpsuit.

Then, of course, there were those missing patients to consider. Whether Dan was part of the equation or not, that was something I couldn't forget.

There were folks out there who might be in trouble. Homeless, mentally ill folks.

And, damn it, it looked like I was the only one who could help them.

Reasonable person that I am, I started my investigation in the most reasonable place—the Gerard Clinic.

The moment the front door swished closed behind

me, I realized that reasonable or not, I was a fish out of water. I glanced around the waiting room with its institutional beige walls brightened only by the framed posters that offered advice like *Every Day is a Gift* and *Today is the First Day of the Rest of Your Life*.

Call me cynical, but I did not think this was necessarily good news to the weather-beaten, ragtag clientele who sat around, stoop-shouldered with blank expressions, on plastic chairs. Though it went against the grain (not to mention every piece of advice I'd ever gotten from the experts over at *Cosmo*), I knew this was one instance when being conspicuous was not a virtue.

I stripped off my cashmere gloves and stuffed them in my pockets, but even sans luxury fiber, I stuck out like a sore thumb. If I needed the reminder, it came from the looks I got as I made my way to the reception desk.

I was almost there when a woman wearing a pink parka that was too small for her hopped up and stepped into my path. She put a hand on my arm before I could establish personal space boundaries, and let me go on the record here as saying this was not a good thing. If ever there was a time for firm limits, this was it. Especially considering that the woman's hands were grimy and she smelled like old socks.

"Are you my attorney?" She was so glassy-eyed that even if I had been so inclined, it would have been hard to take the question seriously. "I'm waiting for my attorney."

"Sorry. I'm not an attorney." I did not want to continue contact in any way, shape, or form, so rather than pluck her fingers from my sleeve, I backed up and out of her reach.

Silly me to think that would deter her. She closed in

on me and grabbed my sleeve again. "Are you my proba-
tion officer?"

"Nope." I tried for a smile. I doubt she noticed. She
was too busy looking confused.

"Then, are you—"

"Not that, either." I got a move on. "Can't help you."

I covered the distance to the reception desk in record
time.

The heavyset gray-haired woman behind the desk
didn't look convinced that I belonged there, either. I
didn't get it. I'd gone out of my way to dress like a social
worker in black pants and a black turtleneck. Maybe it
was the gold hoop earrings that gave me away. Or my
boots with their stiletto heels.

What, a social worker can't be fashionable?

Whatever the reasons, the receptionist slid open the
glass that separated the staff from the patients they were
supposed to be there to serve, and looked me up and
down—twice—before she said, "Can I help you?"

On the way over to the clinic on the L, I'd carefully
practiced everything I was going to do and say, and I reminded myself to take it slow. I had a pseudo-leather
portfolio under one arm and, carefully keeping it turned
over so that the receptionist couldn't see the flowing
script on the other side that clearly branded it as a freebie
from the cemetery conference, I set it down on the ledge
so there was no way the receptionist could close the
glass. My smile was bright, but not too sunshiny. I had
no proof, but I suspected social workers weren't sunshiny.

"Health Department," I said, a little hurriedly and under my breath so I could deny it if push came to shove.
"I'm checking on two of your patients. A man named

Oscar and a woman named…" I opened the portfolio and ran my finger down a list of names as phony as the leather. "Becka, I think it is." I snapped the portfolio shut. "I presume her name is really Rebecca. Sad case, that one." I leaned in close and lowered my voice, keeping in mind what I'd learned from Ernie about the only two people he'd ever named who, he said, had gone into Doctor Gerard's program and never come out again. "Drugs, you know."

"Uh huh." The woman gave me another careful look, one so long and probing, I was all set to mumble something about how I must have been mistaken and hightail it out of there. Until she touched one hand to a nearby computer keyboard. "Last names?" she asked.

I breathed a sigh of relief. "Last names? Their last names?" I wasn't a complete moron, I knew she'd ask, and being prepared, I was ready to equivocate with the best of them. "That's the problem. I'm filling in for somebody, you see. The woman who usually takes care of this sort of thing. She left me the information, of course, but she's not very organized." I lifted the portfolio and thumbed through the pages of a legal pad I'd tucked in it. "She forgot to leave me that information, and it's exactly what I'm looking for. Oscar and Becka's last names."

"Uh huh."

It was exactly what the receptionist said the first time, right before she caved. Encouraged, I leaned forward. It was a good thing I didn't lean too far or I might have sustained a permanent injury when she slid the glass window shut.

I tapped on it.

She ignored me.

I waved my hands.

She turned her back.

I'm not a quitter, but even I could see I was getting nowhere fast.

It was time to try Plan B. As soon as I thought of one. I'd already gotten back to the door and was heading outside to regroup when I felt a tug on my sleeve.

I turned to find Pink Parka Woman shuffling her tattered sneakers against the pitted linoleum. "I know Oscar," she said. "He's my friend. Do you want to talk about Oscar?"

I had barely gotten out my "I do," though, when she wrinkled her nose, narrowed her eyes, and looked at me like she'd never seen me before.

"Are you my attorney?" she asked.

I put a hand on her arm and ushered her to the door. I might have sounded a little eager, but she was so out of it, I don't think she noticed when I told her, "Your attorney? You bet I am, sweetie."

I offered to buy Pink Parka Woman a cup of coffee, but once we were outside, that didn't look like it was going to happen. There were no bistros—charming or otherwise—in the area. No dingy diners, either. Pink Parka Woman didn't let that stop her. Like a limpet on a rock, she took my arm and led the way, and before another ten minutes had passed, we found ourselves in the basement of St. Katherine's Church, where a long line of people as shabby looking as the ones I'd seen at the Gerard Clinic were waiting patiently for lunch to be put out on the buffet tables.

Pink Parka Woman (I'll just call her PPW, it's easier) had obviously been there before; she knew the lay of the land. She skirted the line and went right for the coffee carafes set up on a table against the far wall. She filled a cup, added about a half a pound of sugar, and sat down at the nearest table where plastic cutlery had already been set out on paper place mats.

I, of course, was not about to take any chances with the food or the coffee. There was no point in beating around the bush, and I wanted to get this over with as soon as possible. I sat down across the table from her and launched into my investigation. "Oscar," I said, because I had a funny feeling she might need the reminder. "We're here to talk about Oscar. You said he was a friend of yours."

PPW nodded. She took a long drink of coffee and nodded some more. When she finally spoke, it was so quietly, I had to strain to hear, so it's no wonder I responded with, "Huh?"

"That's right." Her nodding made my head hurt. She finished her coffee and got up to refill her cup. When she came back to the table, she pulled the chair next to mine way too close and sat down. "They came and *whoosh*! Just like that, he was gone." She emphasized the speed of whatever she was talking about by touching her palms together then throwing out her hands in opposite directions. When she did, she knocked into her coffee cup. It went spinning and coffee splattered the table and the tile floor.

I told myself I'd worry about the mess after I got the rest of the story out of her and before she went off on the attorney tangent again. "Oscar's gone?" I didn't wait for her to answer. I just didn't want her to forget what we were talking about. "Who took him? Was it after he went to see Doctor Gerard?"

"Came in the middle of the night. They always do."

"And you saw him go?"

She looked me in the eye, and one corner of her mouth pulled into what was almost a smile. "For an attorney," she said, "you're not very bright."

"They don't teach us everything in law school."

"I'll say." She chewed her lower lip. It was dry and cracked, and when it split, a drop of blood oozed out and stained the corner of her mouth. I couldn't stand to watch, and I couldn't afford to walk away, so I reached into my purse, found my Trish McEvoy lip gloss, and passed it to her.

PPW slathered her lips, but when she handed the tube back to me, I kept my hands firmly on my lap.

"It's cold out. You'll need it later," I told her. Better than *not on your life*, which, of course, was exactly what I was thinking.

"Need it later." She gave me a toothless grin and added another coat.

The beauty regimen taken care of, I got back to the matter at hand. "So you were saying...about Oscar. What did you say his last name was?"

"Oscar's my friend." PPW smacked her lips together. She used so much gloss, it oozed, spread, and stuck, like stalagmites (or was it *tites*?). "He's gone."

"That's right." I flipped open my portfolio and got ready to write. "And you said his last name is...?"

PPW rubbed her lips together. By this time, they were nice and slippery, and enjoying the sensation, she smiled and did it again. "Don't know his last name."

I stifled a groan, but before I could lose heart, I reminded myself that all was not as lost as the twenty-five
bucks I'd spent for my lip gloss. PPW was the closest I'd
gotten to corroboration of the story I'd heard only from
Madeline. If she stayed lucid long enough, she might be
able to tell me even more. "So you don't know Oscar's
last name. But you do know that he left. Did you see him
leave?"

She rolled her eyes. "Like I said, for an attorney—"

"I'm not very bright. Yeah, I know. Because when I
asked about you seeing Oscar leave—"

"They always come at night. How am I supposed to
see when the lights are off?"

"Exactly." My smile might have been smoother if I
had any gloss on my own lips. "So you didn't see him
leave, but you know he's gone. Is that because he hasn't
come back? Or has he? Did Oscar come back and talk
about where he's been?"

Apparently, even the gift of my lip gloss wasn't
enough to endear me to her; not when I asked questions
that dumb.

PPW made a face. The left sleeve of her parka was
torn at the elbow, and she added one more coat of gloss,
then tucked the tube up between the pink outer layer of
her jacket and the lining that peeked out from the hole.

"They never come back," she said. "How can they? It
would be such a long way and how would they do it?"

"They? Are other people missing?"

PPW scraped back her chair. "Plenty. But they can't
come back. It's millions and millions of miles."

"To—"

"The mother ship, of course." I was apparently stupid
enough to rate a click of her tongue. "They can't come

back unless they have ships of their own. You know, UFOs."

It isn't often that I find myself at a loss for words. This, however, was one of those times. I stared at PPW in wonder, trying to come up with a way to keep her talking that didn't include telling her that I knew for certain now that she was a nutcase.

While I stared, PPW shook her head, sadly disappointed.

"They need new classes in lawyer school," she said. She didn't take her coffee cup with her when she walked away. "Don't they teach you anything about alien abductions?"

I guess I was so busy watching her with my mouth open, I didn't even notice I had company until I heard a quiet "Excuse me" from over on my left.

I turned to find a slim, fifty-something woman in jeans and a navy blue pullover sweater. Her dark hair was shot with gray. It was cut short and stylish, and though she wasn't wearing any makeup, her skin was flawless. Her face was sprinkled with freckles that were just starting to get lost in the wrinkles at the corners of her eyes and on her cheeks.

"Are you here to help?" the woman asked.

I would have laughed, but let's face it, even I knew that probably wasn't the best response. Instead, I pushed back my chair and stood, distancing myself from her and the question that sounded a little too hopeful to me. "I'm not exactly the helpful type."

She looked at the spilled coffee before she gave me a quick once-over. Instead of turning up her nose the way the receptionist over at the clinic had done, this woman grinned. "Well," she said, "you sure don't look like you're here for lunch."

"No. I was just talking to…" I motioned toward where PPW had disappeared through a doorway on the other side of the room. "I was just looking for information, that's all."

The woman's expression grew thoughtful. She, too, looked toward where PPW had gone. "Information? From Stella? That's certainly an interesting choice of sources. I hope you weren't counting on her help too much, because I can pretty much guarantee, whatever she told you, it isn't true. Not that it's her fault or anything," she added quickly. "It's just that she's a little—"

"Yeah, so I noticed."

The woman smiled, but not in a mean way. More like she actually understood what was going on in Stella's head. "What's today's delusion? Monsters in Lake Michigan? Leprechauns?"

"Aliens." I tried to smile, too, but I couldn't. The whole thing creeped me out. "I guess I should have known since she was hanging around the clinic—"

"The Gerard Clinic?" I don't think I imagined it; the woman actually looked over her shoulder after she said this. She lowered her voice. "You're looking for information about someone at the Gerard Clinic? I can't say for sure, but I might be able to help you."

Did I look skeptical? I must have, because the next second, she held out a hand. "I'm Sister Maggie," she said. "For better or worse, I'm in charge of this place. And you're…"

"Just trying to satisfy my curiosity."

Sister Maggie's eyebrows rose. "Reporter?"

I shook my head. "Just...interested, I guess. I heard from a friend that some of the people who used to hang around at the clinic..." I shrugged, because I wasn't exactly in a position to explain about Madeline. "I'm looking for a couple of them. A man named Oscar and a woman named Becka. Unfortunately, I don't have last names and that makes it pretty difficult."

Sister Maggie nodded her understanding. "The folks who go to that clinic—most days, they stop here when they're done. We serve lunch every day and dinner on Mondays and Wednesdays. A lot of them are regulars."

"So you know them? Oscar and Becka?"

Sister Maggie looked toward where a volunteer in a white apron was carrying a huge pot of stew to the table. "We're shorthanded," she said. "It's going to take forever to feed them all today. As for cleanup..." Again, her gaze traveled to the coffee that Stella had spilled.

She didn't say another word. She didn't have to.

And me? I stifled a groan. I might not believe in divine intervention, but I knew an opportunity when I saw one, just like I knew when I was being offered a deal.

My jaw was clenched when I spoke. That was because my gut was telling me that I was going to regret this.

I told it to shut up, right before I asked Sister Maggie for an apron and a mop.

10

Some people are meant to serve others. After three hours of watching her, I knew Sister Maggie was one of these. The woman was the Energizer Bunny with sacred vows, plus she didn't have an uncharitable bone in her body. No matter how dirty or nasty or grubby they looked, she chatted with the soup kitchen visitors like they were old friends. She helped the ones who couldn't carry their own food trays, and got coffee for them if they'd already sat down and forgotten to get their own. When we ran out of bread and there was still a line for lunch, she headed over to the local corner store for more and came back with a whole box. She wasn't shy about announcing that she'd used her powers of persuasion (and who knows what heavenly connections) to get it donated.

I, on the other hand, was not made of the same stuff. Believe me, I'm not saying this because I felt inadequate, or because I had second thoughts or any regrets about how I'd spent my life up until that very day without ever setting foot in a soup kitchen. I point it out only because it is relevant to the understanding of my suffering. See, helping people, Sister Maggie was in her glory.

Me?

Not so much.

By the time the last of the lunch eaters disappeared into the cold and gloomy afternoon and the other volunteers sat down to finish what was left of the stew (do I need to point out that I declined the invitation to join them?), my apron was dotted with gravy and so were the cuffs of my black turtleneck. It should come as no surprise that I wasn't used to swabbing floors; thanks to the Stella's-spilled-coffee cleanup effort, my jeans were soggy. I had a first-degree burn on my right hand from trying (and failing) to change the Sterno under a chafing dish of potatoes, and I was so tired of giving unto others and so grossed out by much of what I'd seen, I couldn't wait to get out of there and back to my hotel where I could take a nice hot shower, in which I planned to use up all of the Bliss lemon and sage bath gel I'd brought to Chicago with me. On my way back to the hotel, maybe I'd stop at Bloomingdale's for an extra bottle. Just in case.

Cleanliness aside, though, I hadn't forgotten why I was there.

That would explain why even after the homeless had disappeared and the kitchen was cleaned up, the tables were set for the next day's lunch and the last of the volunteers was gone, I was out in the hallway waiting for Sister Maggie.

She locked the door to the cafeteria and pocketed the

key. "I hate having to do this," she said. "I wish they could all just stay here and stay warm. Rules and regulations, you know. And we're not approved for live-ins. I've tried to skirt the authorities. One time, I *forgot* to lock the door, Lord forgive me." She made the sign of the cross. "I learned my lesson. As soon as word went out that we weren't locked up tight, the locals came in and stripped our copper pipes." She led the way to the stairs that would take us up and back out to the street. "You coming back? We sure could use the help."

It didn't seem like the right place to say *no way in hell*, so I skirted the issue. "You said we'd talk after lunch. You know, about Oscar and Becka."

We were at the bottom of the stairway. On the landing above us, a bare lightbulb illuminated the nooks and crannies of the church entrance. There was nothing up there but a door and a pamphlet rack that contained everything from transit maps to information on free HIV testing. There was nothing down on the level where we stood, either, except the long, dark hallway that led back to the kitchen and a doorway over on our right with a sign above it that showed it was the way to the restrooms.

We were the only ones left in the building. Still, Sister Maggie looked around before she spoke. "Oscar, Becka, and the Gerard Clinic?"

Dealing with the dead has a way of heightening a person's awareness when it comes to things like fear. Oh yeah, I could tell Sister Maggie was scared, all right. Since she didn't seem the type, I was anxious to find out why. I searched for something neutral to say.

"You don't approve of the clinic."

She slipped into the black coat she'd carried out of the

kitchen. "The clinic serves an important mission in our neighborhood. There are plenty of people who wouldn't get the mental health care they need or the counseling or their medication without Doctor Gerard."

"But you're not a fan."

"Did I say that?" With a look, Sister Maggie dared me to contradict her. I had a funny feeling she was also trying to do a Vulcan mind-meld move on me so she'd know what I was thinking. For all I knew, she could do that, too.

"Why do you care so much?" she asked. "I practically had to twist your arm to get you to stay to help. That tells me you don't have a political agenda. You're not one of those bleeding-heart liberal do-gooders who come by once in a while. You know, just so they can brag to their friends in the burbs about their good deeds.

"You don't have a personal stake, either. Don't ask me how I know, I just do. After all the years I've been doing this, I can tell just from looking. It happens once in a while. Families come searching for relatives they know are out on the streets. They hardly ever find them." Superwoman or not, this bothered her. I could tell because she looked away. But if years of long practice had taught her nothing else, it was how to grin and bear it. Even in the face of grinding poverty. The next second, she had her act together and was all business again.

"You're asking about Oscar and Becka, and you were talking to Stella. No way you're related to any of them. Your world and theirs, they don't overlap. They never have. So it's not social conscience and it's not guilt and it's not to fulfill some promise you made to a dying relative about how you'd find so-and-so and put things right.

Still..." She spent a few moments thinking. "You care about this enough to trade your time for my information. And you would rather be shopping or at a spa than here in the hood. You would have rather spent your afternoon anywhere else. Maybe even at that cemetery conference?" She glanced briefly at my giveaway portfolio. "Why are you so anxious to find these people?"

Sure, we were in the basement, but it still qualified as being in church. In a rare moment, I opted for the truth. "I hear that both Oscar and Becka haven't been seen in a while, and I'd like to find out if that's fact or rumor. It would be easier for me to check if I could get some actual information. Like last names."

"You're a cop."

"Do we need the cops?"

She didn't answer, and I knew why. She was waiting for me to fess up.

I wasn't a Catholic. I didn't have to be to know that nuns had the whole tell-the-truth-or-else mojo going for them. I gave up with a sigh. "I'm not a cop," I said. "I'm a sort of... well, sort of a private investigator."

"And you want to know if it's true, about the folks who are accepted into that special study Doctor Gerard is conducting."

This time when I sighed, it was with relief. Finally, I had corroboration. From somebody who was a somebody whose body wasn't six feet under. "It's true then? They really are missing?"

Sister Maggie bought some time, slowly buttoning her coat. "I've never found any proof."

"You've looked."

"I've heard stories."

I really didn't need to ask. I'd seen the way she oper-
ated, and I couldn't imagine her not going to the mat if
she thought something wasn't on the up-and-up. I asked
anyway. "You've gone to the authorities with these stories?"

She tucked her hands in her pockets. "I tried. Once.
About eighteen months ago. But without any proof..."
Another shrug. This one pretty much told me all I needed
to know. "They told me to come back if I ever had any
more information, and unfortunately, I haven't been able
to dig up a thing. If there's anything happening at that
clinic, they've been able to keep it pretty quiet."

"Until now."

This seemed like a no-brainer to me, but I didn't like
the way Sister Maggie looked in response. Like she'd
just bitten into a lemon.

"What?" I shifted my portfolio from one hand to the
other. "I'm only stating facts. Nobody's looked into the
matter. Not seriously, anyway. I mean, not that I don't
think you were serious about it, but hey, you've got plenty
of other things to worry about. Now, I'm on the case."

There was that look again. The one that practically
threatened eternal damnation if I wasn't truthful. "Are
you that good?"

There was no use being modest, so I didn't even try.
"I've solved a few cases that had the cops stumped."

I thought she would have been more impressed. I
mean, even if she didn't mean it, she owed me that much
for the soggy jeans and the stained sweater and the fact
that I was standing in a stone-cold church on a gloomy
afternoon when I could have been anywhere else. Even
that cemetery conference, where it was sure to be boring,
but a heck of a lot warmer.

Sister Maggie's brows dropped low over her eyes. "You know you'd better be careful, right?"

I would have laughed if she didn't sound so doggone serious. "Those cases that I solved, some of them were pretty dangerous. Nobody's gotten to me yet."

"It's not you I'm worried about."

Since she said this just as she started up the steps, I scrambled up after her.

"What do you mean?" I asked when we got to the top.

She stopped, her hand on the door that led outside. "I can see that you can take care of yourself. Even if you don't know how to change the Sterno in a chafing dish!" Her smile came and went. "The people over at the clinic, though, most of them aren't so lucky."

I shouldn't have felt guilty, but I must have. That would explain why I scrambled to explain myself. "I didn't do anything to Stella. Anything but—"

"You talked to her. And let me guess, you left the clinic with her, right? That means somebody probably saw you two together."

"Sure, but—"

Briefly, she put a hand on my sleeve. "I'm not trying to make you feel bad. Please, don't think I am. I'm just pointing out that if there is something shady going on at the clinic, and if whoever is behind it thinks you're snooping around, and if that someone saw you talking to Stella—"

"No. No way." My denial sounded a little too quick, even to me. That didn't keep me from trying to talk myself out of thinking I might have put Stella in jeopardy.

Too bad it didn't work. My shoulders slumped. "Shit."

Sister Maggie laughed. "That's one way of putting it." She kept her smile in place, and I would have been encouraged if I didn't suspect she was just trying to make me feel better. "You can't change what's already happened," she said, and I would have bet anything it was a line she'd used a couple million times before on the people who came through the soup kitchen and got a side dish of counseling with their meals. "And chances are, nobody even paid any attention to you and Stella. You just might want to be a little more careful in the future."

I nodded my understanding. "You know, I can do something to make sure none of the people over at the clinic ever have to worry again about who they talk to. Or what they say."

"Because you're going to keep investigating until you find out what's really going on."

We were finally on the same page. I knew this for a fact because, call me narcissistic, but I could see the way Sister Maggie's eyes shone with admiration. And maybe a little bit of envy, too. Something told me that given half the chance and time away from the responsibilities of feeding the homeless of Chicago, she'd be all over this case herself.

Shopping opportunities aside (not to mention religion and the whole celibacy thing), it looked like me and Sister Maggie, we had a lot more in common than I ever would have imagined.

"I'm going to make sure no one else goes missing," I told her.

"If they're missing." It was her turn to sigh. "It's not the same world you live in," she said, and if we'd known each other long enough, I might have pointed out that nobody lived in the same world I lived in.

She took a black wool scarf out of her pocket and wound it on. "The homeless here in Chicago are like the homeless everywhere. They come and they go. Some of them get lucky and find their way to warmer places. Some of them die out on the streets. A precious few turn their lives around, find jobs, get places to live. Just because we don't see them again doesn't mean anything sinister has happened to them."

"Except you think that maybe it has. Otherwise you never would have gone to the cops."

Thinking, she tipped her head, and honestly, I wasn't sure what she was going to say next. When she blurted out, "Zmeskis, Oscar's last name is Zmeskis," I was so surprised that I fumbled to flip open the portfolio, asked her to spell the name, and wrote it down carefully.

"Becka isn't a Rebecca, just a Becka. Becka Chance." She looked over my shoulder to where I was writing. "You might as well add Alan Grankowski, Leon Harris, Lony Billberger, and Athalea Misborough." She waited while I wrote down these names, too. "I haven't seen them in a while, and I've been told they were seen at the clinic, that they talked about that study."

My thank-you came out along with a smile of gratitude.

Except I don't think Sister Maggie wanted any thanks. She didn't expect any, that's for sure. She pushed open the door and held it so I could step out into the church parking lot ahead of her. "Just promise me you'll be careful, OK?"

I was going to say something witty, like "Careful is my middle name" or "Nothing's going to happen if I'm too careful," only when I looked back, her expression was so thoughtful, I didn't have the heart.

"I promise," I told her. "No more talking to clinic patients where anybody can see us."

"And you won't take any foolish chances with your own safety, either, right?"

This, I didn't want to get into. Not with a nun, anyway. To date, my life had been filled with foolish chances. Some of them had panned out. Others, not so much. It wasn't fair to burden her with the story of Joel, and I didn't think telling her about Quinn was exactly appropriate, so I gave her a cocky smile instead. "I've dodged a few bullets in my day."

"I hope that's just a figure of speech."

It wasn't. Behind my back, I crossed the fingers of one hand and told her it was. I guess that made her happy. She closed the door to the church, locked it, and walked away. Last I saw her, she was handing a dollar to a guy hanging around at the corner.

I went in the opposite direction, feeling pretty proud of myself.

Sure it had cost me the price of dry cleaning for a sweater and a pair of jeans (not to mention the burn that would need some aloe lotion, *stat*), but I knew more than I had when I left the hotel that morning. I had last names to go with first names, and more first names and last names on the list. Armed with that information, I could do some digging. I could also provide Dan with some concrete evidence that he could use to check against the clinic files. Once he did, maybe then he'd believe that I (and my claim to fame as the Dr. Phil of the undead) was on the up-and-up.

I basked in the glow of my success all the way back to the L station. True to my word to Sister Maggie, in addition to being pretty darned satisfied with the way the day had panned out, I was also careful. I took a quick look around every chance I got, and I knew nobody was following me. Or even watching me. As far as I could remember, nobody had since I'd been in Chicago.

Except maybe for the homeless guy with the weird spiky hair who I'd seen at Piece and at the clinic.

And that spooky black shadow.

The thought sent a skitter of cold up my spine, and as I stood waiting to cross the street, then turn a corner to head to the L station, I shivered.

Or maybe that's because when I did turn that corner, I saw two police cars parked in front of the station. Their flashing lights clashed with the swirling red light on top of the ambulance parked nearby. As I got to the back of the crowd gathered around to watch, the paramedics were just carrying a stretcher down the steps. Whoever was on it, the prognosis wasn't good; the body was completely covered by a sheet.

"What happened?" I asked a woman standing and watching at my side.

"Can't say for sure. Just got here myself."

A man over on our right put in his two cents. "I heard the woman ended up under a train. That's her there." He looked over to where the paramedics wheeled the gurney toward the ambulance. "I'll bet there's not a whole lot left once that train's done with you."

Just thinking about it made my stomach jump. I gulped. "Accident?" I asked. "Or suicide?"

The woman at my side shrugged. "You never know around here."

There was a young guy standing in front of us, his hands pushed into the pockets of his winter jacket. He turned. "The way I heard it," he said, "somebody pushed her. Only I ain't telling nobody that. I was up there and I didn't see nothing myself and besides, I don't want to be the next one that gets pushed."

It was too awful to consider, and I'd just decided not to do it when a curious thing happened. The gurney that carried the body hit a bump, and that bump jarred the victim on the stretcher. Her arm slipped out from under the sheet and swung limply over the side of the stretcher.

Creepy enough.

Creepier still when I realized that the dead woman was wearing a pink parka.

And when something fell out of her hand and hit the pavement.

It was a tube of Trish McEvoy lip gloss.

11

A body snatcher could earn between three and six months' wages for a fresh corpse.

Less than twenty-four hours after I'd seen Stella's body being carted away, thinking about fresh corpses wasn't exactly what I needed to take my mind off my problems. Sure, I'm in the business of death. Sometimes more than I like. But give me some credit; that doesn't mean the whole notion doesn't gross me out.

Kind of like the memory of Stella's arm slipping out from under that sheet.

I shivered. Skimming over Ella's paper for the presentation I was scheduled to give on the final day of the conference was supposed to distract me. Too bad it wasn't working. Always a trooper, I tried again.

Unlawful exhumations and the sale of the bodies that were dug up were done by men known as Resurrec-

*tion men or Resurrectionists. Sometimes, they were
called sack-'em-ups, because they used sacks to
carry the corpses to the doctors and medical students
who would then dissect them.*

"Yetch!" I tossed the presentation down on the coffee
table in my hotel room and hugged my arms around myself. It was bad enough I was nervous about speaking in
front of who knew how many cemetery geeks. Worse
when the topic was so weird that even I (who had, after
all, seen, talked to, and investigated for the weirdest of
the weirdest) got the willies.

No. I take that back. The worst part was that even the
stack of papers Ella had sent to Chicago with me wasn't
enough to take my mind off what had happened to
Stella.

And make me wonder if it was my fault.

This time when I grumbled, it had nothing to do with
Resurrectionists, cemetery conferences, or Ella's mis-
placed faith that I could speak in front of a crowd without making a fool of myself. Oh no. The mixture of
disgust and guilt was all about me. All about whether I'd
made a mistake going to the clinic. And about poor dead
Stella, of course.

Was that guy in the crowd—the one who said Stella
had been pushed—right?

I hoped not, because believe me, I wasn't happy
thinking what it might mean. Maybe Stella knew more
than she let on. Maybe someone at the clinic had seen me
and Stella together and was afraid she'd say too much.
Maybe that same someone killed her to shut her up. Or
maybe Stella was as clueless as she appeared to be.
Maybe her untimely end was meant as a message—one

that told me MIND YOUR OWN BUSINESS in neon letters, six feet high.

Any way I looked at it, it took what had simply been the business of the maybe-missing patients and turned it way ugly.

Of course, I could have chosen to find comfort in the morning *Tribune*. The article about Stella's death had been relegated to a small column in an inside section. It used the word *accident* liberally. If that was true, I actually might be able to sleep better at night.

If it wasn't...

I grabbed my coat and went to the door. Now that I had a dead woman on my hands (so to speak) and the names of the missing patients, I also had a ton of questions. I'd been waiting all morning for Madeline to show so I could ask them, and I was getting sick and tired of it. Heading out seemed the perfect solution, both to finding her and to keeping myself so busy that maybe I could forget the picture that kept popping into my head—the one of that arm in the ripped pink parka when it slipped out from under the sheet and flapped back and forth.

Like Stella was waving to me.

I am not completely delusional. I didn't really think Madeline would accommodate me and show up at her gravesite to chat, but hey, whoever said that hope springs eternal knows the perils of investigating for the dead.

It was the only way I could think to contact her, so I waited in the cold, grateful that if nothing else, at least it wasn't snowing. In fact, the skies had been clear all that day, and the sun nearly blinded me as it sank toward the horizon and ricocheted off the couple inches of fresh snow that had fallen the night before. Unfortunately, the sun was no more than a tease. It was no warmer than it had been since I stepped foot in Chicago, and after thirty minutes of waiting and shivering, I convinced myself that enough was enough. Madeline wanted me to help Dan, but I couldn't do it until I talked to her. If she was MIA, for now, there was nothing I could do to convince Dan that I was the real deal.

And if Madeline never resurfaced?

See, that's the problem with the dead. No e-mail, no cell phones, and they only pop in when they want to. Or when they want something. If for whatever reason Madeline wasn't going to show hide nor ghostly hair and help me, then I'd simply have to find the answers to all my questions on my own.

It was the least I could do for Stella.

My determination renewed (even if it was a little frosty around the edges), I turned from Madeline's grave. That's the first time I realized I wasn't alone.

Maybe the cold was freezing more than just my feet, my fingers, and the tip of my nose. Maybe my self-preservation instincts were frostbitten, too.

Maybe that's why I hadn't realized that big, terrifying shadow was back.

For the space of a dozen heartbeats, too scared to move or to think, I stared at the black mass drifting a couple feet above the ground between me and the Palmer memorial. As I watched, it billowed like an angry thundercloud, then collapsed in on itself, growing denser and heavier and darker. It grew taller, too. Its middle slimmed out, and a bit of shadow on each side of it split off. Like arms.

It wasn't a person. Not exactly. It looked more like an animal, a monster, and when it took a couple steps in my direction, I swear, the ground shook.

Or maybe that was just my knees.

Funny thing about getting scared, though. Once I hit rock bottom, the only way to go was up. When I bounced back from that initial thud of panic, it should come as no surprise that I did it with a healthy dose of how-dare-you. Before I even knew what I was doing, my anger was in charge. It wasn't until I made a move to kick through the snow and move toward the thing that I realized something weird was going on. I mean, something weirder than the weird something that was already going on.

Because everywhere within ten feet of the shadow, there was no snow. It had all melted.

I refused to consider the implications. Physical, cosmic, or otherwise.

"OK, you want to tell me what's up?" I demanded of the thing. "Because I'm a little tired of this stupid game. I'm supposed to be scared?" I made sure I laughed when I said this, because if I allowed it, the scared part of me would swallow up the angry part and then I'd be back to quivering and sniveling. So not attractive, and counterproductive to boot. "Please! I'm the one with the Gift, remember? You non-dead types are old news. You're not scaring me at all. In fact, all you're doing is pissing me off. So why don't you quit it with the drama and the big, spooky shadow act and just tell me what you want. It will make your life simpler. Oh!" I slapped one gloved hand to the side of my face. "You don't have a life, do you? But I do, buddy, and I'm sick of having it interrupted."

The shadow's eyes were as red as blood. They glowed

and flared, and when the thing made a move, I thought for sure it was going to come at me. I tensed, all set to run, but before I could, it spoke.

"Don't want you." Its voice was like sandpaper on stone. "Go away, don't want you."

I thought about Dan and how he'd assumed I was desperate and dateless. "Yeah, there's a lot of that going around. But if you don't want me, why do you keep bugging me?"

"Don't want you."

I sighed my frustration. "I know that. But you keep showing up. Every time I'm here." I chanced a step closer.

"No!" It held up one hand. Or paw. Or whatever it was. When it did, something hit me like a punch. I staggered back and fought to catch my breath. "No closer."

"Not to worry." I held up a hand to signal that I was more than ready for a time-out, and bent at the waist, struggling to fight off the heaviness in my chest. "Apparently…" I hauled in a lungful of frigid air and stood straight again. "Apparently, that's not something I want to do."

I was talking to myself. The shadow was gone. The only indication that it had ever been there was the melted snow.

With no other choice, I figured it was time to get the hell out of there. I spun around, but the grass was wet, and my boots were muddy. When I felt myself slip, I put on the brakes, but by that time, there was no way I could keep on my feet.

There was a gravestone not two feet to my left. One look, and I knew it was déjà-vu all over again. Believe me, I wasn't taking chances.

I pivoted, skidded, and slid. Helpless, I felt my legs go out from under me at the same time I watched an especially muddy patch of grass get closer and closer to my nose. I would have landed with a splat if not for the fact that someone grabbed me from behind and yanked me to my feet.

My hat was down over my eyes, and I grabbed it and pulled it off at the same time I struggled to regain my composure. I turned toward my rescuer. "Thank—you?"

OK, so it wasn't exactly polite, and I'm not exactly Miss Manners. I had a perfect excuse, since I found myself looking at the homeless guy with the spiky hair.

He sloughed off my surprise as inconsequential. "You OK?"

"Are you kidding?" Since my coat was all twisted and tangled, I straightened it and stepped back and away from him. One of my gloves had fallen off and I bent to pick it up. Homeless Guy was faster. He grabbed the glove before I could and held it out to me.

I snatched it from him and tugged it on. "You want to explain what's going on?"

"That's funny, that's exactly what I was going to ask you." He acted like it was the most logical response in the world. "I heard you talking, though..." He glanced around at the expanse of very empty cemetery that surrounded us. "Who were you talking to?"

"Nobody." The perfect truth, since (at least in my book) a shadow does not qualify as a *who*.

"Then who were you here waiting for?"

The same logic applied. I wasn't about to start into an explanation. "What are you doing here?" I asked him instead.

"A better question might be what's a cemetery tour guide from Cleveland doing here?"

I backed up another step. "You know who I am. How?"

"Word gets around."

"Word from who?"

"Whom. The proper way to say it is *word from whom.*"

"I'm so not in the mood for this." To prove it, I turned to walk away. Homeless Guy fell in step beside me.

I made sure the sidelong glance I gave him was short on friendliness and heavy on suspicion. "I know you're not—" I was going to say *dead*, but seeing as how I was alone in a strange town and in a deserted cemetery with a guy I didn't know who was already acting plenty fishy, I didn't want to freak him out. Still, I was encouraged thinking that at least this time, I didn't have to contend with the whole undead scenario. I knew this because the man had grabbed me to keep me from falling down, and when he did, I didn't feel a bone-freezing chill (at least not one that was any colder than the air around us). Just to satisfy myself that I truly was dealing with flesh and bone, I pretended to brush his sleeve accidentally. He was real, all right, and satisfied, I drew back again.

When I did, the edge of my glove caught on one of the buttons on the sleeve of his jacket, pulling it up and re-vealing one grungy cuff of an equally grimy flannel shirt.

It was just enough to spark a memory of the day I'd first encountered him outside the restaurant. The scene played itself in my head—and in slow motion, to boot. I watched myself hand the man a dollar. I saw him stick

out his hand to accept it. When he did, the sleeve of his
jacket slid up, just like it did now.

And I realized what it was that had spooked him that
night and made him hurry away.

"You weren't wearing a flannel shirt that first night I
saw you outside Piece."

Big points for Mr. Homeless, he didn't contradict me.
He did look surprised, though—plenty surprised—and
while he was still processing what I said, I closed in (figuratively speaking, of course, since he wasn't all that
clean looking and I wasn't all that eager to make new
friends).

"You were wearing a dress shirt that night. A dress
shirt with French cuffs. And you forgot you had it on until your jacket sleeve sneaked up. You didn't want me to
see it. That's why you grabbed my money and hurried
away. What, you thought taking off your cuff links would
make you look more homeless?"

"You've got a good eye."

That went without saying, but it wasn't going to distract me. "You're a cop."

"You think?"

"I think homeless people don't wear business shirts,
heavy on the starch."

"How do you know it was heavy on the starch?"

"Give me some credit," I said, the better to let him
know that I wasn't just some moron with no fashion
sense who, number one, hadn't been engaged to a guy
who was just as fashion conscious as I was and number
two, didn't date (if what Quinn and I did could be called
dating) a guy who knew what was what when it came to
the right way to dress. (And to undress, for that matter,

but that wasn't something I wanted to consider at the moment.) "Why are you following me?"

"Why are you so interested in the Gerard Clinic?"

"Why are you?" Even as I asked the question, I knew the answer. "You've got your eye on Doctor Gerard. And Dan. You weren't just hanging around outside the restaurant that night, you were waiting for them. You were following them. That's why I've seen you outside the clinic, too. You're doing surveillance, though I've got to tell you, I don't think it qualifies as undercover. Not if you're careless enough to forget to change your office shirt to one that's a little more in keeping with the whole I'm-a-poor-homeless-person thing. And since you're not— homeless, that is . . . how about giving me back that buck I gave you?"

"You referred to Mr. Callahan by his first name. You must be friends."

"And you must be delusional if you think I'm going to give him up to some cop playing dress-up." This was one of those classic comebacks that was too good to waste. For emphasis and to show him I meant business, I quickened my pace.

He was apparently not as into great scene-ending lines. He hurried to catch up. "Do you know something you could give him up for?"

"Do you think if I did, I'd spill my guts to some guy I don't know?"

"What if I told you you'd be better off if you did?"

"Is that a threat?"

I hadn't realized I'd stopped and turned to him, my chin raised, until I already had. He was only a hair taller than me, and my guess was that he wasn't used to people confronting him so openly. His chin came up, too.

"I don't need to threaten," he said. "But if you're smart, you'll listen to a warning."

"Oh no!" Whether he knew it or not, he had spoken the magic word. Warnings were something I was sick to death of getting from Dan. I wasn't going to fall into that trap again. "Don't even start. No talk of things that go bump in the night, OK? Not unless the thing that's bumping is that creepy shadow that's been following me around, and you can explain what it is and what it wants and—" Since we were standing so close, I knew exactly when I spooked him. That would have been when what I was saying sank in and he backstepped away. And his expression went from stony, to curious, to just a little apprehensive.

I regrouped. "OK, so you're not going to warn me about ghosts and such. Good. That's not something I want to talk about. But that means you were going to warn me about real things, right? Things like—"

"How about things like breaking the law?" He regrouped, too, and now that I'd stopped talking crazy, he went back to stony in an instant.

"I wouldn't dream of breaking the law."

"Then how about what you know about your friend Mr. Callahan breaking the law?"

I threw my hands in the air. As far as I was concerned, there was no better way to demonstrate my feelings and distance myself from the half-truth I was about to fling as casually as if it was the bouquet I never got to throw at the wedding that never happened. "Can't say he has," I pointed out, because, let's face it, to date, I hadn't found a thing to prove or disprove Madeline's theory, either about Doctor Gerard or Dan. "And just for the record, I can't believe he ever would. Dan Callahan is a nice, regular, ethical guy, and even if I thought he was doing something wrong, I wouldn't tell you. Because you know what? Even if you're one of the good guys, I don't trust you. There's the whole scamming-a-buck-from-me thing, to begin with. And the fact that anybody who would try to get away with a disguise as hokey as yours can't be very good at what he does. So unless you've got an actual reason to talk to me—which you don't—and unless you've got some legitimate reason to follow me—which you don't—and unless you show up with a subpoena or a writ or whatever the hell you police types call it when you force people to talk even when they don't want to talk and they don't have anything to say anyway—which you never will since you don't have any of those other things to begin with and that means you could never get a subpoena or a writ or a whatever—"

"Are you done?"

I was, but only because I'd run out of air.

He didn't bother to say good-bye.

Something told me it didn't matter, since it wasn't the last I was going to see of him.

I watched him walk away, and before he was out of sight, I followed. He was headed for the front gate, and I was anxious to get out of the place.

"Told you I was right."

I didn't jump and squeal when Madeline popped up beside me.

Not too much, anyway.

My sneer told her what I thought of her tactics. "You mean, *I* was right. He's following Doctor Gerard. And Dan. He thinks I can tell him something about what they're up to. He's a cop."

"He's an FBI agent. And *I* was right." Madeline didn't

have to worry about the slick patch of ice in the middle of the road. I walked around it. She floated right above. "You see what this means, don't you?"

"It means—"

"It means the net is closing on Danny."

"That's what I was going to say."

"Sure you were." I'd never heard anybody agree about anything in a more condescending way. "It's time to stop messing around, Pepper, and do something. Fast. You have to help Danny, or something really, really bad is going to happen to him."

I could have said I didn't care.

I could have mentioned that whatever Dan had gotten himself into, he could get himself out of.

I could have brought up the not-so-small point that I still wasn't convinced I wasn't on a wild goose chase.

Except for the fact that the feds were onto Dan, and something told me they didn't like to waste their time.

And then, of course, there was that little voice inside of me. The one that told me that if my appearance at the clinic had anything to do with Stella going under that train . . .

Well, if it did, that meant I owed her.

That's why just an hour or so later—after I found a cab and headed to the other side of town—I found myself at the Gerard Clinic again. This time, I wasn't going to mess around. I was going to march in, demand to talk to Dan about each and every one of the people on that list Sister Maggie had given me, and get to the bottom of things once and for all.

And I would have done it, too, if I didn't see something odd just inside the alley that Ernie called home sweet home.

Something square and flat caught the light of a nearby streetlamp and sparkled at me from the murky shadows. Something that looked like it was covered with glass.

I took the chance, stepped into the alley, and bent for a closer look.

"Alberta?" I picked up the framed photo of Ernie's wife and automatically glanced around. Every other time I'd seen the picture, Ernie had been hanging on to it for dear life. I knew that once he realized the photo was missing, he'd panic, so I carefully picked my way through the garbage in the alley and headed for his box.

I knocked on the lid. "Ernie!"

"He ain't there."

The answer came from a doorway along with a man in a tattered jacket who was in the process of zipping his pants. "Ernie's gone."

"Gone? Where?"

"Lucky bastard. I hear he got himself accepted into that special study of Doctor Gerard's."

My heart thudded. "Are you..." I swallowed hard. Not easy considering that my mouth suddenly felt as dry as a sun-parched desert. "Are you sure?"

The man was pencil thin and hardly taller than the Dumpster he opened and began picking through. "Not sure, no," he said. When he fished out all that was left of a brown and battered apple and took a bite, I turned away. "But he said he had an appointment. Last night. He said he was going to talk to Doctor Gerard because he finally knew how to get into the study for sure. And since then, well, nobody's seen him. Hey!" When the man plucked at my sleeve, I turned back to him. "Since he ain't using it, think I can move into Ernie's box?"

"No." I shook him off, tucked the photo of Alberta into Ernie's box, and started for the clinic, my mind made up once and for all. "Ernie will be back," I told the man, and myself. "No matter what it takes, Ernie will be back. Because I'm going to go in there right now and find out what the hell is really going on."

I did, too. I went into the clinic, demanded an appointment, filled out the appropriate forms, and waited with the great unwashed.

And when the gray-haired receptionist finally called my name and told me Doctor Gerard would see me? Well, I have to admit, I was actually jazzed.

But then, I had no idea what I was getting myself into.

12

I dreamed about a ghost with bad taste in clothes, a box that was a house, and Dan in an orange jumpsuit. I think he was an FBI agent.

Oh yeah, and while it was on a roll, my drug-muddled subconscious tossed in a bit about a syringe as big as a banana. No surprise there.

The image was burned into my brain. So was the memory of Doctor Gerard leaning over me, grinning, as the needle pierced my skin. My head told me none of it was real, that it was all something I'd experienced hours (or was it days?) before. That didn't keep the rest of me from reliving every terrifying moment. Or from feeling exactly like I had back there in Doctor Gerard's office when that syringe penetrated my skin and the nasty, mind-numbing drug inside it coursed through my veins.

First, fire spread up and down my arm. Then it rushed

into my chest and made my heart feel as if it were pumping lava. Every muscle in my body contracted. My head felt as if it was going to explode. My tongue swelled. My eyes flew open.

I'm pretty sure that was the point where I sat up and screamed.

It was also when I realized there was no one around to hear me.

I was alone in a nearly pitch-dark place, and with nothing else to go on, I relied on instinct and instinct alone. My instincts told me I wasn't in my hotel room. It wasn't my apartment, either, or any part of the Gerard Clinic I'd ever seen. For one confused minute, as I fought to make sense of my surroundings and couldn't, panic washed over me. I hate to admit it, but for that one minute, I let it. Too tired to fight, too frightened to care, I gave in to the out-of-control sensations. My heartbeat raced and my breaths came in gasps and I curled up into a tight little ball on the mushy mattress where I found myself. I knew giving up and giving in like that was a sign of weakness, but honestly, I didn't give a damn. I only knew that I felt like hell, I didn't know where I was, and I was really, really scared.

Maybe I fell asleep. I can't say. I only know that by the time I stopped crying and opened my eyes again, my head wasn't pounding nearly as hard, and there were thin slices of gray morning sneaking in through the mini-blinds. In the anemic light, I saw that I was in a hospital room. There was a white, standard-issue dresser across from the bed where I lay in a snarl of sweat-clammy sheets. There was a metal chair to the left of the dresser. On the other side of it was a bigger, darker rectangle that

I knew must be a doorway. The door was closed. Another door on the wall to my right was open, and from where I lay, I could see into a tiny bathroom.

None of it looked the least bit familiar.

"Not to worry." The comforting words that scraped their way out of my parched throat didn't do their job. When I untangled myself from the blankets, my hands shook, and when I swung my legs over the side of the bed, I knew I had to take my time. My knees were weak, my legs were shaking, but that didn't stop me from standing. Or from collapsing right back on the bed.

"Not to worry," I said again, because at that point, lying to myself sure beat facing the truth. "Snap out of it, Pepper. There's nothing weird going on. There's a logical explanation for all of this. Something went wrong when Doctor Gerard gave you that shot. Yeah, yeah, that's what happened. Doctor Gerard called the paramedics. The way a nice, responsible, professional doctor would. They took you to a hospital. A nice, responsible, professional Chicago hospital. Like the one on *ER*."

That made me feel better, and feeling better, I figured I'd ring for the nurse, find out what was going on, and hightail it out of there as fast as I could. I wasn't made of money, and the health care benefits at Garden View left a lot to be desired. The sooner someone called a cab for me and I got back to my hotel, the happier I'd be.

Too bad I couldn't find one of those nurse call buttons.

Or a phone, for that matter.

And though my purse was on the chair across from the bed, my cell phone wasn't in it.

I grumbled my displeasure and decided on a more direct approach. I went to the door and turned the knob.

The door was locked.

This was not something I'd ever seen the nice, responsible, professional folks on *ER* do, but was I worried? Well, not too much. Just like there had to be a logical reason for me being in the hospital, there had to be a just-as-logical one for my door being locked. Maybe those nice paramedics who brought me there realized Doctor Gerard was acting weird. Maybe they locked the door to keep him away from me. Or maybe I had something contagious. I pushed up the sleeve of my peachy sweater and scratched my arm even though it didn't itch. Determined to make sense of the whole thing, I found a light switch and flicked it on.

Light on, light off, it didn't make a whole bunch of difference. The door was still locked, there still wasn't a phone in sight, and damn, I still didn't know where I was.

I grumbled my displeasure, considered my options, and chose the first one that came to mind. I cranked open the blinds.

I found myself looking over a sloping roofline and gingerbread woodwork where snow swirled and icicles hung from the gutters like dragon's teeth. A couple stories down was a wide expanse of windswept land. The grass was frosty and the landscape was dotted with trees, their branches bare at this time of year and their limbs waving madly in the wind. Beyond that, the waters of what must have been Lake Michigan churned into white-caps and sent sprays of ice crystals into the air. There wasn't another building in sight. Or another person, for that matter.

If this was Chicago, it was a rustic, desolate part of town that wasn't on any tourist map.

"Yeah, a part of Chicago that doesn't exist."

My words were no more enthusiastic than my mood, and my mood went from merely terrible to truly awful, because the second I looked out the window I realized something else. I mean, something other than the fact that I wasn't in Chicago anymore.

There were bars on the windows.

This, I told myself, could not be a good thing.

The next time I woke up, it was morning, though I couldn't say if it was the same morning or the next. The sun (at least what I could see of it from behind the bank of heavy clouds that hung close to the roiling lake outside my window) was higher in the sky than it had been last I looked. And I was as hungry as if I hadn't eaten in days.

"Hey!" I went to the door and pounded on it. "Anybody out there? I could use some breakfast in here."

I didn't get an answer. Not right away, anyway. I was all set to start pounding again when a buzzer sounded somewhere in the distance and my door popped open.

"Well, it's about time." I stepped into a long, bare hallway with a green tile floor, one of those fake panel ceilings, and walls that were painted institutional beige. I am no decorator (I mean, that's what those of us who can afford it—or at least those of us who used to be able to afford it—pay professionals for, right?), but even I knew that with the added pizzazz of some paintings, maybe a wall hanging or two, and the right upholstery on the furniture, the color combination might have worked. The way it was, there were no pictures on the walls at all. There was no furniture around, either. In fact, there was nothing to relieve the starkness of the hallway except a utilitarian metal desk all the way at the far end. Behind the desk was a burly guy with short-cropped hair and a neck as big as a linebacker's. He was wearing white scrubs and a solemn expression that clearly said he had better things to do than be bothered by me.

Like I was going to let that stop me?

My legs were still wobbly, but step by careful step, I closed in on him.

"What's the deal?" I asked. "Where am I? And what's going on? And while you're explaining all that, you can tell me where breakfast is, too. And the day spa. There is a day spa, isn't there?" I didn't think there was, but a girl can hope, right? Besides, I thought maybe the request would get a rise out of him.

I was wrong. His name tag said he was Henry. Which is more than Henry himself had to say. He hardly spared me a glance before he went back to looking over the medical chart in his hands.

"Hey! Earth to Henry!" I rapped on the desk to get his attention. "I asked what was going on here. And where's Doctor Gerard, anyway? The last time I saw him—"

"Thaddeus will take you down to breakfast." Henry delivered this news just as the doors to the elevator to the right of the desk swished open. Another white-clad guy stepped out. Aside from the fact that his name tag was different, Thaddeus could have been Henry's twin. He was just as big, just as burly, and he was wearing scrubs, too. He didn't greet me; he just stepped back into the elevator and stood aside. I knew an invitation when I saw one. I also knew that refusing was not an option.

Soon the elevator bumped to a stop and the doors slid open. Thaddeus motioned me to get out, but he didn't follow. I found myself in another hallway with another metal desk at the end of it. The guy behind it was named Adam, and he didn't smile when he stepped up at my side.

Together, we walked down a corridor as long and as bare as the one outside my room, crossed what would have looked like a lobby if the windows weren't covered and the door wasn't barred, and headed down another corridor identical to the one we'd just come out of. The only difference was that in this one, I could smell the heavenly scent of bacon.

Oh, it should have, but not even the thought of those covered windows and that barred door was enough to ruin my appetite. That's how hungry I was.

I stepped up the pace and followed my nose to a room on my left. The place was as big as a gymnasium, and like a gymnasium, there were no windows in it. There was one long wooden table set up in the middle of the room and ten chairs placed around it.

I did a quick count. There were only four people seated there, an empty chair between each. Without a word to any of them, Adam showed me to my place and disappeared into an open doorway across the room. I hoped it was to get me breakfast. Wherever he went, I had a funny feeling he wouldn't be gone long. I had to get down to business. And fast.

"Hi. I'm Pepper." I slid into the empty chair to my left, next to a stick-thin woman with stringy blond hair and dark, dark roots, and when nobody bothered to greet me—or even look at me for that matter—I knew this wasn't going to be easy. I beat my brain for some idea to get their attention and was surprised (not to mention grateful) when a memory bubbled up from beneath the ocean of drugs that had been pumped into my veins.

"Oscar Zmeskis," I said, and waited for one of the people at the table to show some kind of reaction. "Are any of you Oscar Zmeskis?"

When no one responded, I struggled to remember the rest of the names Sister Maggie had given me. "Becka Chance?"

Hopeful, I looked at the woman next to me, who was wearing a hospital gown that hung from her scrawny shoulders. She, however, was busy staring into a bowl of oatmeal that looked as if it had gone cold long ago. "Are you Becka Chance? Or maybe Athalea Misborough? I can't tell you how happy I am to finally see somebody. What's the deal here? How long have you been here? What day is it? Where's the phone?"

The woman continued to stare into her oatmeal.

I checked to make sure Adam was still busy before I changed seats again. This time, I found myself next to a middle-aged guy with open sores on his arms. He was drooling. I made it quick. "Alan Grankowski? Leon Harris? Lony Billberger?" I tried the names out on him, and when he didn't flinch, I moved to the other side of the table.

My third candidate was sound asleep, so I opted for breakfast guest number four, who was a thirtyish African American guy with bad teeth and a maroon cardigan over his hospital gown. He just so happened to be talking to his pancakes when I showed up. In my book, that was a good sign. At least he was talking.

"So, what's going on here?" I asked him. I looked over my shoulder. Still no sign of Adam, though I could hear the rumble of his voice and the clank of dishes as he loaded a tray that I prayed was mine. "Why are we here? And where is here, anyway? Who are all these people? What do they want from us?"

He looked up from his pancakes. "I'm one of the lucky ones. I see people who aren't there."

"Yeah, me too." I heard Adam thank someone for helping him. His voice sounded closer. I didn't have much time. "When did you get here? What's your name? And how do we get out? I mean, all the doors are locked, and the windows are barred and—"

Adam appeared in the doorway, but lucky for me, he was in the process of saying something to someone back in the kitchen, and he was looking over his shoulder. By the time he finished up and arrived with my breakfast, I was waiting in my original seat.

Adam, it seemed, was not as dumb as his WrestleMania physique made him look. He eyed my breakfast companions carefully, and it wasn't until he'd satisfied himself that they looked just as spaced out now as they had when he went into the kitchen that he set a plate of food down in front of me.

The bacon was too greasy, and I am always careful about how many fat grams I consume.

The eggs were too runny, and I got the willies just looking at them.

The toast was rye, and I much prefer wheat.

I dug in practically before the plate was on the table.

"Doctor Gerard wants to see you after breakfast," Adam said.

"Great." I wasn't sure if I was talking about the bacon I wolfed down or about finally having the chance to confront the doctor. "'Cause I want to talk to him, too." I swallowed down a plastic forkful of scrambled eggs and talked with my mouth full. "And another thing—"

Another fork filled with eggs was halfway to my mouth when something just outside the door of the dining hall caught my eye.

I was out of my chair practically before Adam could say, "Hey, you're not allowed to get up," and out the door long before Mr. Muscle-Bound had a chance to stop me.

The way I figured it, that gave me a couple seconds to talk to Ernie before Adam caught up.

I ignored the big bruiser escorting him and plucked Ernie's sleeve. When he stopped and turned to me, his eyes were glassy and his expression was blank. Just like the expressions on the faces of the people back in the dining hall.

My stomach went cold.

"Ernie, it's me, Pepper. You remember, from the alley next to the clinic." The big guy accompanying Ernie put a hand on his left arm. I held on tighter to his right. "I came to find you. Are you all right? How long have you been here? You didn't tell Doctor Gerard you can see ghosts, did you, Ernie? I'm sorry I ever mentioned that to you. I should have known you'd use it to get into the study. Please, tell me this isn't my fault, that you didn't—"

"Gettin' three squares a day. And a nice, warm bed." Ernie grinned, and for just a second, his eyes brightened with recognition. "Did you bring Alberta?"

I remembered the photograph I'd left in the box in the alley. "She's back at home, Ernie. She's waiting for you. She says you need to get back to her and—"

Turns out that for a big guy, Adam was pretty quick on his feet. He lumbered out into the hallway and latched onto my arm.

Like that was enough to make me let go.

"You're going to see her again," I told Ernie even as his attendant tugged him away. "I promise you that, Ernie. You're going to see Alberta again."

"There's no fraternizing." Adam's grip tightened enough to make me wince. He yanked me away from Ernie, and helpless, I watched the other guy lead Ernie away.

"Doctor Gerard is not going to be happy when he hears about this," Adam said.

"Great. Fine." It wasn't easy shaking off his grip, but somehow, I managed. Maybe that's because Adam wasn't used to the folks around there fighting back. At the same time I backed out of his reach, I glared at him. "Let's go see Doctor Gerard, why don't we? Because I'll tell you what, I'm plenty anxious to talk to him. I'll bet my attorney will be, too. You know, the guy who's going to file the couple dozen lawsuits that are going to put this place out of business."

Did Adam take me seriously? Darned if I know. But my comment did make him snap to. He motioned me to get moving, and maybe he did believe the line of attorney bullshit, because he was really careful to keep his distance. Side by side, we walked back the way we'd come, through the locked-down lobby and back into the wing of the building where I'd woken up that morning.

A few minutes later, I found myself outside a closed office door.

"Doctor Gerard?" Adam tapped on the door politely. "Patient JK6345 is here."

The door snapped open, and once again, I found myself face-to-face with Hilton Gerard. I had planned on playing it cool, tossing around that attorney threat again in that oh-so-unconcerned-because-I-know-I've-got-you-by-the-balls tone of voice I'd learned at my parents' knees. I might have succeeded, too, if my arm didn't ache from where Adam grabbed me. And if I didn't remember that spacey, stripped-of-all-humanity look on Ernie's face.

I popped off like a science fair rocket.

"You son of a bitch!" I pushed past the doctor and into his office so I had more room to stare him down. "What are you doing to the people here? Why are they so out of it? And while we're on the subject, what happens to them after you're done with them, huh? You can't just scoop people up and think that nobody's ever going to miss them, and—"

My own words sunk in and cut me off short.

"Of course you can scoop them up and nobody misses them." Astounded and appalled, I grappled with the idea. "They're homeless. Nobody's going to look for them. That's why you started that clinic of yours in the first place. You aren't a great humanitarian, you're a son of a—"

"Yes, yes. You said that before." Hilton Gerard's smile was as gracious as if we were trading quips over canapés. "And may I remind you, you also were kind enough to share with me that you're not from this area, that your father is currently and unfortunately incarcerated, and that your dear mother is somewhere in Florida. My, my, but to me, it sounds like—"

"Nobody's going to be looking for me anytime soon, either." My insides froze. The next second, the ice melted under a healthy dose of anger. "That's not true. Plenty of people know I'm here. There's Doris and Grant from the conference. And my boss, Ella. She's the one who sent me here in the first place. And Quinn, he knew I was coming to Chicago, too, and just for the record, he's one tough cop. He'll be plenty interested in hearing about those folks in the dining hall. You've got them drugged, don't you? Every single one of them."

"Of course they're drugged." Doctor Gerard sneered. "They are mentally ill, after all. They need their medications."

"And you need them to be compliant. Why?"

"Pepper, Pepper, Pepper . . ." The doctor signaled Adam to leave and close the door behind him, and after it clicked shut, he got down to business. "You know what I'm looking for, don't you?"

There didn't seem to be much point in denying it. "Ghosts. You're looking for someone who can contact the Other Side. Why?"

His shrug said it all. "Why not? Let's face it, if I can prove there is life after death, well, it would be the most incredible scientific breakthrough of this century. Or any century for that matter."

"You want to go down in history?"

He laughed. "You are a shallow thing, aren't you? I'm not looking to see my name in lights, not for finally being the one who can put the living in touch with the dead. But think about it, Pepper. If I did that, think about all the great things I could accomplish."

I tried. And couldn't think of one. "In my experience, the only thing dealing with the dead gets you is trouble."

"Maybe because you haven't been dealing with the right dead. Or not in the right way. What if . . ." He tipped his head back, thinking. "What if we could make contact with the spirit that was William Shakespeare? If he could give us the words of his next drama?"

"Not a good idea." I knew this for certain because I'd already dealt with a sorcerer who was channeling a rock star's songs. I remembered all too clearly that the last time I saw him, he had a knife sticking out of his chest. "Things like that never end pretty."

"All right, what about the ghost of Albert Einstein, then? Think of what he could tell us. Or the spirit of some unsung hero of a doctor who died just before he had a chance to complete a study that would have cured cancer? Don't we owe it to the world to be open to the possibilities?"

"And you think I can help you?"

"Dan does."

"Dan doesn't—" It was hard to get the words past the sudden sour taste in my mouth. Something told me it had nothing to do with the scrambled eggs. "Dan would never be all right with what you're doing to those people in the dining hall."

"You think so?" Doctor Gerard looked at me hard, but he didn't wait for me to answer. He got up and went across the room, and when he rummaged around in a file cabinet over there, he turned his back on me.

I saw my chance and made a move toward the phone on his desk.

"I really wouldn't do that if I were you." When he turned back around, the doctor was holding another big, honkin' syringe. "You have to have the PIN code to get an outside line," he said.

"I'll bet." I backed up toward the door and watched him close in on me with that syringe in his hands. "Look..." I ran my parched tongue over my dry lips. "If you're looking to contact the dead and do all those great things you talked about doing, I really might be able to help you."

"I know that."

"Then you really wouldn't want to—" My butt slammed against the door knob. "You wouldn't want anything to happen to me. I mean, if I'm your best bet, you want me to cooperate, right?"

"Oh, you'll cooperate." Doctor Gerard closed in on me.

"But I can tell you stuff." I watched both the doctor and the syringe get closer. "I can tell you about Gus, the first ghost I met. And Didi. I helped her get recognition for a book she wrote fifty years ago. And—" He was right in front of me now, close enough for me to see the flare of his nostrils. "I can't do that if I'm drugged."

"You're absolutely right." Doctor Gerard backed off, and I breathed a sigh of relief. Right before I yelped when he lunged at me and stuck that needle in my arm.

"But you see, Pepper..." When my knees gave out, he was there to catch me. "It's not the stories of how you work with the dead that I'm interested in. It's duplicating your Gift. And I can't do that..." He dropped me into the closest chair. "Not until I get inside your brain."

13

When I was a kid, my dad would come home from a long day of nipping, tucking, and surgically enhancing and watch *MacGyver*. Between his office hours and rounds at the hospital, I hardly ever saw him, so even though I thought any show that was long on science and short on fashion was basically boring, I was starved for attention as only an only-child can be. I spent many a Monday night sitting on the couch next to Dad, trying hard to be interested.

I guess I absorbed more than I thought. That's the only thing that would explain why, when I woke up again and found myself back in my room, I decided (in an obsessive-compulsive, I've-got-to-do-this-and-I've-got-to-do-it-now sort of way that I blamed on the aftereffects of the drugs) that I needed to concoct some brainy invention that would allow me to escape.

I rushed around the room, scooping up everything I could find.

Then, for an hour or more, I found myself staring at a toothbrush, a hospital gown that I had—so far—managed to avoid changing into, and the entire contents of my purse (minus the missing cell phone, of course). Lipstick, compact, blusher, perfume, mascara, eyeliner, hand sanitizer, hand lotion, lip gloss, tampons, breath mints, wallet. Everything a girl could ever want or need. Except an idea of how to use it all to get out of there.

MacGyver, I was sure, would cobble together something simple yet brilliant.

Pepper Martin?

Not so much.

Exhausted, I flopped back on the bed, my brain tired and my stomach queasy from the fatty bacon I'd never had a chance to finish. I don't know how long I lay there staring at the tiles of the drop ceiling and wondering what to do next. I do know that it was frustrating, but it beat worrying about what was going to happen to me if I stayed in Doctor Gerard's clutches. If history repeated itself—and as much as I tried, I couldn't think of a reason it wouldn't—I was about to become a statistic. Just another one of the missing.

I wondered if Doctor Gerard had pegged me correctly as someone no one would come looking for.

My dad? No way he could.

Mom? Between her tennis league, her yoga class, and her book club (they didn't read a thing, it was an excuse to meet at the martini bar down the street from her condo) and my schedule as detective to the dead, we talked maybe once every couple weeks. She wouldn't even know I was gone for days, and by that time, something told me it would be too late.

Quinn?

We hadn't exactly promised we'd see each other again when I returned from Chicago, but I kind of figured we would. If he did, too, he might show up on my doorstep, and if I wasn't there...

I twitched the thought aside.

If I wasn't there, Quinn would go on his merry way, no doubt about it. I wondered if he'd ever bother to stop and think of me again.

Of course, there was always Dan.

There was a time this thought would have actually made me feel better. After all, Dan had once saved my life. But now I suspected that he was so hell-bent on contacting Madeline, he'd do anything to make it possible. Even if that meant locking me up in some loony bin and turning his back when Doctor Gerard poked around inside my brain.

Had I tipped my hand with Dan when I told him I'd spoken to Madeline? Or was it the comment about the missing patients that had sealed my fate? Was that why I was being held prisoner?

My stomach rebelled again, and this time, it had nothing to do with greasy bacon or runny eggs. My heart bumped and lurched, but even the bumping and the lurching weren't enough to kick my brain into gear. What the hell was I going to do to get myself out of the predicament I'd gotten myself into?

The daylight outside my room faded from afternoon to evening, then disappeared altogether, and the ceiling tiles above my head washed out from white to gray. Still, I was no closer to figuring out how I could escape.

Except for those ceiling tiles, of course.

The idea hit, and I sat up like a shot. I didn't know how often they did a bed check or how early breakfast might be served the next morning, but I wasn't taking any chances; I didn't have a moment to lose. My boots were next to the bed, so I slipped them on, turned on the light, then carefully and quietly positioned the room's one and only chair so it was close enough to the dresser for me to step from one to the other. I was all set to start climbing when I decided I'd better take my purse, too. It was, after all, a Juicy Couture. I slipped the shoulder strap over my neck and left shoulder, and with my hands free, I got to work.

Lucky for me, the dresser was sturdy. Luckier still, the first ceiling tile I tried moved easily. I slid it aside and waited, my breath caught behind a tight ball of anticipation in my throat. One minute went by. Then another. There was no sound from out in the hallway, nobody running to see what I was up to, no alarms. In fact, the only sound I heard was my heart beating double time in my chest.

Before my heartbeat could deafen me, I stuck my head into the hole in the ceiling and took a look around. The nearly total darkness took a while to get used to, but once my eyes adjusted, I saw confirmation of what I'd thought when I took that walk to the dining hall: the building was old and once upon a time long ago before the drop ceiling had been added, the real ceiling was twelve feet or more from the floor. There wasn't plenty of room, but there was room enough to move around between the new ceiling and the old. At the same time I prayed I wouldn't run into any of the spiders that had coated the space with webs, I hoisted myself into the opening. There were support beams between the tiles, and I sat down on one, cautiously eased the tile I'd moved aside back into place, and squinted into the darkness.

I was in a maze of air-conditioning ducts, electrical wires, and years of accumulated dirt. I knew when I scrambled up into the ceiling that I was facing the doorway. That meant if I crawled straight ahead, I would be over the hallway outside my room. I also knew the desk—and the attendant who manned it—were down the hall to the left. On my hands and knees, I went to the right.

I am not a good judge of distances, and in the dark, it was hard to say how far I'd come to begin with. I only knew when it felt like far enough. When another passage intersected the one I was in, I went to the left, listening as I did for any sounds from below.

The place was as quiet as Garden View at midnight.

If this was a good thing or a bad one, I couldn't say. I only knew I couldn't spend the rest of my life in the ceiling. I stopped, and choosing a ceiling tile at random, I hooked my fingers under it—and broke a nail. Past caring, at least until I could get out of there and schedule a manicure, I latched on tighter, winced when another nail snapped, and moved the tile aside.

I found myself looking down into a room with an open doorway on the left. Beyond it, there was a light on in the hallway. Through the mishmash of light and shadows, I saw what reminded me of the biology lab back at my high school. Never the scene of any academic triumphs, at least not for me. On my right, the wall was lined with glass-fronted bookcases. There were windows on another wall. Yes, they were barred. In the center of the room were a dozen or more individual lab stations, complete with Bunsen burners and sinks. Carefully, I lowered myself onto the countertop of one of the lab stations, and from there, I hopped to the floor.

I didn't dare move from the spot, not until I was sure the coast was clear. I had just about convinced myself it was and that it was time for me to dart out of the relative safety of the lab and into the hall to try and find a door that led outside when I heard a voice.

It was a man, and he was headed my way.

I ducked under the lab station, curled into a ball, listened, and waited.

"Everything's secured." The man's voice was punctuated by the bleeping sound of a walkie-talkie. "Gonna take another swing through the east wing, but I'm guessing we're set for the night. Then I'll—shit."

The walkie-talkie beeped and squawked before another voice responded. "What's up, Glenn? Something wrong?"

"Just the lab." Glenn was right outside the door, close enough for me to hear the exasperation in his voice. And close enough for him to hear me if I lost my nerve and whimpered. I dug the fingernails—broken and unbroken—of one hand into the palm of the other as a way of reminding myself to stay focused and keep quiet. "Somebody left the door open again and damn, I didn't bring the keys. I'll have to come back to the security desk to get them, then head back up here. You're still down there, right, Dwayne? You want to wait for me to get back, then we can duck into the stairwell for a smoke?"

Dwayne's confirmation came with another squawk. "No problem, buddy."

I waited until the echo of Glenn's footsteps died away before I dared to budge. Looking back on it, maybe that's where I made my mistake. I should have moved faster, sooner. The way it was, I pulled myself out from under the lab station, inched over to the door, and took a look around. The hallway outside the lab looked much like the other ones I'd seen earlier that day, except that way down at the end of this one, there was a door marked with a red exit sign.

I had just started toward it when I heard Glenn's footsteps again.

Apparently, the security desk was not as far away as I'd hoped.

With no place to hide in the hallway and no other options, I scurried back into the lab, shot under the lab station I'd just crawled out from under, and listened, helpless and losing heart, as Glenn arrived. When he pulled the door shut and locked it, there was nothing I could do but wait for him to leave.

Grumbling a curse, I looked back up at the dirty, dusty, cobwebby hole in the ceiling and knew I had no choice but to get back up there and return to my room. Of course, that didn't mean I couldn't take a moment to look out the windows and think about life on the outside.

I had just gone over that way when the clouds outside parted and a nearly full moon shone above the waters of Lake Michigan. Its light glistened against a few snowflakes that floated past the window. It tipped the lake water with silver and glittered against the coating of ice along the shoreline.

It also glanced against the glass-fronted cases in the room, and when it did, something in them caught my eye.

Curious, I closed in for a better look.

"Patient XK545." I read the label on a glass jar just inside the door, then looked beyond the paper label to the contents.

"Holy shit!" I jumped back as fast as I could, but even if I wanted to (and believe me, I wanted to), I couldn't look away. I stared in stunned horror at row after row of glass jars that filled the shelves.

Each one of them was labeled with a patient number.

Each one contained a human brain.

"So, how are we feeling this morning?"

The last thing I was in the mood for was chipper, and Doctor Gerard, with his tweedy suit and cheery voice, was definitely going for chipper.

With a sneer of epic proportions, I let him know I didn't appreciate it. "*I* feel like shit. That's all that matters. And it's your fault. What the hell did you shoot me up with yesterday? And why? What the hell is going on around here, Doctor, and—"

"I am so sorry about that." We were in his office, and morning sunlight streamed through the windows. It was nearly as bright as his smile. "Forgive me, Pepper, but you have to understand, there are certain scientific procedures—"

"Screw your scientific procedures." I wasn't in any frame of mind to sit down and get comfortable, but after the walk from my room to the cafeteria for breakfast (where I didn't see Ernie or the oatmeal lady, come to think of it, and where everyone else was as stoned as they had been the day before), and from the cafeteria to Doctor Gerard's office, I was wiped out. I plunked into his guest chair. Set right next to it was a table with two china cups and a plate of flaky croissants. They sure as hell looked better than the scrambled eggs and toast I'd had for breakfast, but I wasn't taking any chances. There were more ways to drug a girl than simply by pumping the poison right into her veins, and I was too smart to fall for any tricks.

"And screw you, too," I told the doctor.

"I can't blame you for feeling this way." There was one of those thermal coffee carafes on the credenza behind his desk. He got it, filled one cup, and looked my way.

"No?" I guess my expression—the one that had *I don't trust you, buster*, written all over it—told him everything he needed to know. "I can prove it isn't spiked, if that's what you're worried about." Doctor Gerard took a sip of coffee. "The croissants are drug free, too. You don't need to worry about them. Go ahead." He set the carafe near my elbow, and when he did, the aroma of coffee filled my nose. One sniff and I knew this wasn't the watered-down version they served in the cafeteria. This was the real deal and it smelled heavenly. I waited for him to take another drink, and when he didn't choke or pass out, I figured it was safe to take a chance; I poured myself a cup.

I gulped it down, hot and black, and without the sweetener I always added. Doctor Gerard beamed me a smile. "There. Now we're on better footing." There was a chair next to mine, and he sat down in it. His long-sleeved blue shirt was so starched, it crackled as he settled himself. "You have trust issues. I can understand that. I haven't been as forthcoming as I might have been."

"Oh, you've been plenty forthcoming." I wasn't exactly sure what the word meant, but I liked the way it sounded when I added an acid twist. "And now you're going to go forth right now and pick up your phone and make a call and then a cab is going to be coming to get me. I'm getting out of here." To prove it, I stood.

"Not yet." The doctor put a gentle but insistent hand on my arm. "We're almost done with our testing, and I have to tell you..." He stood, too, and he was taller than me. When he looked down, his eyes glittered with excitement. "The tests I've done, Pepper...The results I've seen...You're the only one I've ever met who really might..." He was so overcome, he couldn't finish.

I wasn't all that emotional. Not when it came to ghosts, anyway. I backed out of his reach. "You mean when it comes to talking to the dead, right? What, you didn't believe me when I told you I could do it?"

"I've heard it before. Dozens of times." The doctor turned and walked behind his desk. There was a mountain of file folders on it, and he picked up a batch of them. "So much promise! And so many people who I thought just might..." He dropped the folders back on the desk where they landed with a *smack*. "They disappointed me. All of them. Then I saw your brain scans. You're the answer to my prayers, Pepper. You're the key to the whole mystery. Working together—"

"Hold on there, Hilton." I held up a hand to stop him. Since I'd been unable to resist and I'd just grabbed a croissant, it dropped flaky crumbs around me. "Who said this was a partnership?"

He leaned forward, his palms flat against the desktop. "But it can be! It will be! Don't you see? Working together, we can change the world!" His voice shook when he said, "Go ahead. Do it now. Call on one of the dead."

"Call on? You mean like demand they show up? I can't just—"

"Of course you can. And don't worry about all the messy little details. We'll get our attorneys involved later and—"

"Lawyers?" OK, it might have been the drugs messing with my mind, but honestly, I didn't think so. I finished the croissant, brushed the crumbs from my hands, and got down to business. "Why do we need lawyers to talk to ghosts?"

"We don't. Not now. Not when you're simply demonstrating." The doctor rubbed his hands together. "But once we're in full start-up mode, then, of course, I wouldn't expect you to not get some portion of the profits. After all, you—"

"I'm the one you think can get Shakespeare to spit out the words of his next play. And Einstein the formula for . . . for whatever a guy like that would come up with a formula for." I chewed over this new thought. "You want to contact the dead to make money from them?"

His laugh was a little nervous. "You make it sound so vulgar. And besides . . ." He smiled in a way that reminded me of the greasy bacon I'd eaten for breakfast the day before. "We're getting way ahead of ourselves. Until I know you can really do it . . ." His look was expectant. "Go ahead, Pepper. Don't worry about doing anything difficult. Not this early in our study. We'll forego Shakespeare and Einstein and the rest of them for now. You can simply talk to one of the ghosts you've already been in contact with. The ones you mentioned that day in my office. Gus Scarpetti or Didi Bowman or—"

"Madeline Tremayne?"

I wasn't imagining it. The light was too good in the office for it to play tricks on my eyes. Doctor Gerard's face really did get pale.

He ran his tongue over his lips. "Madeline? My former assistant?"

"One and the same." Something told me that for the first time since I woke up and found myself wherever the hell I was, I had the upper hand. I used it to my full advantage. "Want to know what she has to say?"

Doctor Gerard's smile fluttered. "Of course I do. Madeline...my goodness..." Like he was trying to take it all in, he blinked fast. "How I've missed her! What has...what has she told you?"

"Well, for one thing, she's the one who told me the patients here come in and don't go out again."

"Yes, of course." He sat back down in the chair he'd gotten out of only a little while before. "She doesn't think...she doesn't think there's anything sinister happening here, does she?"

"Sinister?" I laughed. After days of worrying, it felt good. "You sound like a sci-fi movie. If what you mean is that Madeline thinks you're a shady little son of a bitch who's scamming people to get them in here then doing who-knows-what with them...well, yeah, I guess you could say she thinks you're doing something sinister."

"She would think that, of course." Doctor Gerard ran a nervous hand over his shirt sleeve. "She doesn't know—"

"What?"

"That I help them as a way of showing my thanks, of course." Some of the tension went out of his shoulders, and he smiled more freely. "I mean, when they leave here. Madeline doesn't know...She didn't...I hadn't started that part of the program yet. She'd have no knowledge of it. When I've finished studying those other patients..." He drew in a long breath. "Well, you see, Pepper, I don't mean to brag, but I find them homes. And jobs. Of course no one sees them on the streets again. I help them start new lives."

He sounded so sincere, I actually might have bought into the line of bullshit.

If not for those jars of brains I'd seen the night before.

"Funny, Madeline never mentioned it," I said. It seemed a better strategy than saying anything about the brains. "She hangs around at the clinic, you know."

Doctor Gerard's gaze darted around the room. "Is she here now?"

I looked around, too. "Not that I know of."

"Has she told you..." He licked his lips again. "What else has she told you?"

Of course he was nervous. He was worried word might get out about that bungalow in the Bahamas. And the cooked books.

And I wasn't stupid. The coffee was terrific. The croissants were tasty. But my sudden status as Princess of Patients would disappear in a flash if Doctor Gerard knew that I knew more than I should have. Or more importantly, if he knew that I knew something damaging. And if he thought I'd spill the beans to the authorities.

I shrugged like it was no big deal. "She hasn't told me a whole bunch. She's pretty boring. Oh!" I added this as an afterthought just so he didn't get any ideas about how I had to be shut up permanently. "She thinks you walk on water. You know, the whole helping the homeless and the mentally ill and blah, blah, blah. I'd hate to disappoint her and let her know how unhappy I am with the way I've been treated here."

"Yes, yes, of course." When he got up and went around to the other side of the desk, Doctor Gerard looked relieved.

When he came back with some sort of machine that reminded me of one of those old portable CD players, I was less so.

He held out what looked like a set of headphones. "Go ahead, put them on. Then when you make contact with Madeline again, I'll be able to monitor what's happening inside your head."

"But I can't just make contact. Don't you get it?" I didn't like being that close to one of his weird brain-reading gizmos, so I turned and walked to the other side of the office. "They come to me. The dead, I mean. And when I want them to show up, well, sometimes they do. But most times—"

"We'll find a way to conquer that little problem."

When Doctor Gerard returned to his desk, I breathed a sigh of relief. I'd dodged the test-Pepper's-brain scenario. At least for the moment.

Or at least I thought I had.

Until I realized he'd pressed a buzzer on his desk and that when he did, Thaddeus the hulking orderly showed up.

"Get her into the chair," Doctor Gerard ordered, and Thaddeus closed in on me.

There was no use fighting. He was bigger and I wasn't on top of my game. When he grabbed me and hauled me to a chair, I sat as directed, and when Doctor Gerard put the gizmo on my head, I knew that if I didn't sit still, Thaddeus would make me.

"Call them," Doctor Gerard ordered me.

I looked from him to Thaddeus who was standing nearby, his arms folded across his big-as-Hoover-Dam chest. "I can't. I—" A tingle like electricity prickled over my scalp, and I let out a tiny screech of surprise.

"Call them," the doctor said again.

"You're not getting this, are you? It doesn't work—" Doctor Gerard hit a button on the CD player look-alike he held on to. The tingle intensified.

"Call them now," he said again. Poor ol' Doc Gerard. He was dying to talk to the dead, but he didn't know how stubborn I could be, and by that time, I was pissed. Co-operating was the last thing on my mind. Even when he turned up the juice on the machine and I screamed.

14

Just my luck. That night, after I went through all the trouble of moving the ceiling tile in my room and sneaking up inside the filthy crawl space, I found that somebody had remembered to lock the door to the lab.

I stood in front of it, my heart slamming my ribs and my spirits as deflated as I had no doubt my hair looked after who-knew-how-many days without the right shampoo and the proper conditioning. That's when I heard it.

Footsteps out in the hallway. And they were getting closer.

Whoever was out there stopped right outside the door to the lab.

I would have held my breath if I wasn't so busy letting it out in a gasp of horror.

Because the next sound I heard was someone unlocking the door.

I gulped. I'd never replaced the ceiling tile. I was dead meat.

Unless I could hightail it out of there before the person could raise the alarm.

When the lock clicked and the door eased open, I grabbed a stool from one of the lab stations, reared back, and swung.

I hit him in the midsection, and the man in the doorway gasped and staggered back, but damn, he didn't fall down, and that meant I couldn't get past him and out the door.

In fact, instead of collapsing in a heap like any self-respecting adversary should have, the guy pivoted and grabbed me. The bad news was that the stool clattered to the floor and I was left without a weapon. The good news was that even though he had a hold of my left arm, my right hand was free. I took a chance and threw a punch. He ducked and swerved, and my fist glanced off his cheek.

Before I could even think about trying another jab, he had my other arm in an iron grip. Still hanging on with one hand, he grabbed me around the waist with the other, turned, and flipped. The next thing I knew I was on my back on the floor and he was on top of me. I looked up into the face of—

"Dan?" Not sure I was seeing clearly, I blinked. When I looked again, the man sitting square on top of me was still Dan.

And I still wasn't sure if this was good news or bad.

I didn't want to take a chance, so I squirmed and kicked, but as Dan had proved back at Garden View when he fought off the attack of a vicious hit man, he was no pushover. The more I twisted, the tighter he held me, and when I took a breath to let out a scream, he put a hand over my mouth.

He hissed my name, and trying to make sure he was getting through to me, he looked into my eyes. "I'm not going to move until I'm sure I can take my hand away and you won't scream. OK?" He waited for me to nod my agreement, and when I finally did, he sat back. "What the hell are you doing here? You nearly scared me to death."

"I nearly scared you?" I pulled myself out from under him and sat up, my back propped against the nearest lab station. "What's going on? What are you doing here?"

"I came to find you." Dan got to his feet and offered me a hand up, and when I took it, he didn't waste any time. He dragged me toward the door. "I'll explain later," he said. "For now, we've got to get out of here and we've got to get out fast. I think maybe we made a little too much noise."

I looked down at the stool, still spinning against the green linoleum. "You mean—"

"Somebody must have heard us. They're going to be coming."

That was all I needed to hear. With Dan leading the way, we tore down the hallway toward the exit door I'd seen the night before. Good thing I hadn't wasted my time with it then; it was locked. When Dan hesitated in front of the door, I tugged on his hand to get him moving again. "We can't get out this way."

"Sure we can." He pulled a set of lock picks out of the pocket of his winter coat. I remembered I'd seen them back in Cleveland when I was investigating the death of

Vinnie Pallucci. Now, like then, Dan knew exactly what he was doing. He messed with the lock for just a couple seconds before I heard the satisfying sound of it clicking open. I grabbed the doorknob and pushed open the door, but before I could step through it, Dan stopped me.

"Not so fast." He leaned forward and listened, but I guess he didn't hear anything, because he took a careful step out into the stairwell. I followed along, and when he looked over the railing at the winding stairs that led down into the darkness, I looked, too. There was nothing to see.

"I dunno." Dan's voice was a whisper. His hair was mussed from our scuffle. He brushed it back. "It's too quiet down there. Makes me nervous. Let's head up."

"To where?" I stopped him when he made a move to climb the steps. "We'll end up on the roof or somewhere. Then what are we going to do?"

In the dim light, I saw him grin. "We'll shimmy down a rain gutter."

This was not the reassurance I needed, but who was I to argue? I didn't know how Dan knew where I was or why he came to find me, but I did know that now that he was there, I wasn't about to let him out of my sight. When he took the steps two at a time, heading up, I followed right behind him.

We'd already gone up a couple floors when he stopped suddenly and held out a hand to hold me back.

"What—"

He turned long enough to put a finger to his lips to signal me to be quiet, and I got a whiff of what spooked him—cigarette smoke. "Somebody's up there." Dan's mouth worked over the silent words and he pointed up. I got the message. Carefully, I turned to head back down the stairs. I would have made it, too, if I didn't bang my knee into the metal bannister.

"Shit!" I wasn't sure if I was cursing because my knee hurt or because I forgot myself and grunted the word. I only knew that the next second, a light snapped on on the landing above us.

"Who's down there?" Glenn the security guard looked over the railing. He might not have recognized me on sight, but he knew trouble when he saw it. And two people who didn't belong in the stairwell meant nothing but trouble.

I'd barely had time to register any of this when Dan zipped by me and grabbed my hand. We raced down the steps to the next landing, and he went for the door.

"It's going to be locked," I warned him, but he wasn't listening.

He punched the door open. "Only from the inside," he said.

We found ourselves in a hallway that was a duplicate of the one outside my room—down to the burly attendant who was mopping the floor behind the desk. He saw us, dropped the mop, and closed in. Just as Glenn banged through the door.

Dan pushed me out of the way and yelled, "Find another way out of here, fast!" right before he turned to face the security guard and the beefy attendant alone.

Adrenaline pumped through my body and fed the fear that bubbled into every corner of my being. I raced down the hallway, then slowed my steps. No matter how many doors I found, I knew they'd all be locked. But the door Glenn had barreled through had banged against the wall and stayed open. With the attendant and the security guard busy beating on Dan, I just might be able to slip behind them, get out the door, and head back upstairs and to the roof where he thought we'd find a way to escape.

With that thought in mind and the sweet idea of freedom calling me, I doubled back.

Until another thought took its place.

Dan.

Facing two burly guys.

Alone.

I am not by nature a brave person. At least no braver than I've ever needed to be. But I'm not a quitter, either. Especially when it comes to my friends.

Hell, I didn't know how to fight, but I guess I didn't know how not to, either. I screamed, leaped, and joined the battle.

I slammed into the attendant just as he threw a punch at Dan that landed with a *boof*. The attendant staggered one way; Dan stumbled the other. But as I'd seen back in the lab, it would take more than that to knock Dan down. When the attendant turned on me with fire in his eyes, it was just enough of a distraction for Dan to launch a counterattack. He landed a nasty right hook to the attendant's face. Blood exploded out of the man's nose. It polka-dotted his white scrubs. The attendant froze—right before he looked down at all the blood and passed out cold.

That left Glenn and believe me, he was plenty pissed. Cursing a blue streak, he came at me. I kicked him in the shins and darted behind him. But when Dan moved in, Glenn took something out of his pocket. Even I knew a Taser when I saw it. I also knew that Dan was in big trouble.

I grabbed the mop the attendant had dropped, and as hard as I could, I smacked Glenn over the head with the wooden handle.

I wasn't sure if the *crack* I heard was the mop handle snapping or Glenn's skull. I did know that when his eyes rolled back in his head and he fell to his knees, we were home free. At least for the moment.

Dan didn't waste a second. He latched onto my hand and we were off running again. This time when we hit the stairway, we went down, and by the time we got all the way to the bottom and we slammed through a door and found ourselves in a boiler room, all I wanted to do was curl up on the floor and hide.

Dan tugged me along. "We'll be out of here in a couple minutes. Then you can rest. But not now, Pepper. Not yet. Can you keep going? For just a couple more minutes?"

I was pretty sure I couldn't.

I shrugged, anyway, and said, "Of course." It was the first I realized that my sleeve was ripped and hanging from my sweater. In just about any other situation, I actually might have cared. But somewhere above us, we heard a commotion. People running. Walkie-talkies blaring.

I gulped. "How are we going to get out of here?" I asked Dan.

He gave me a wink. "Not to worry. I know this place. It's the old Gerard Hospital for the Insane and Mentally Feeble."

I remembered something Madeline had once told me. "In Winnetka? Is that where we are? I thought . . . the hospital . . . it closed years ago."

"Apparently not." He pulled me behind the boiler, and

from there, through a maze of pipes that traveled along the wall. "There's an old tunnel near here somewhere. It hasn't been used in years, but if the stories I've heard about it are true, it leads out to the lakeshore. Back when the hospital was open, they didn't want to get a bad reputation, so that's how they transported the dead bodies out of here."

"Bodies?" The very thought froze me in my tracks, but hey, who was I to argue? Especially when an alarm sounded through the building.

I got moving—fast.

An escape tunnel was better than imprisonment any day. No matter how many dead bodies were in it.

Once we were so far back in the sprawling basement that he figured no one would see us, Dan pulled out a flashlight. It was one of the high-tech ones with a halogen bulb, and its light was pure and bright. With it, we were able to find a metal door that looked as if it hadn't been touched in fifty years.

The door weighed about a thousand pounds, and it took both of us to open it. I broke another fingernail, but in the long run, it was worth the sacrifice, because we slipped out of the hospital and into a cavern that had been chipped from the rock beneath the building. The ceiling of the tunnel was rounded, and not more than a foot above my head. The walls were covered with ice. The floor was rocky and pitted, and at the same time Dan warned me to be careful and watch my step, he put his shoulder to the door and inched it closed.

The moment it snapped shut behind us, I knew we weren't alone.

*   *   *

"Shit!"

Dan patted my arm. There was no heat in the tunnel, and his hand was ice cold. That didn't stop him from slipping out of his coat and helping me put it on. I would have felt guilty if I wasn't freezing, and if he didn't have another, lighter-weight jacket on beneath it. "Don't worry. I know tunnels are scary for some people, but we're going to be OK, Pepper. There's nothing here to be afraid of."

"You think so, huh?" In the light of Dan's flashlight, I looked down the shaft of the tunnel. The flashlight was bright, and in its glow, I could see maybe a hundred yards ahead. Every single one of those yards was filled with ghosts.

Young and old, men and women, some in hospital gowns, others in street clothes, they stood two and three deep in places.

Until they saw me.

That's when they surged forward.

It was a solid wall of spirit, and I knew what would happen if either Dan or I came in contact with it. The cold of a Winnetka winter night was nothing compared to the icy chill that happens when flesh and blood meets even one spirit. If our flesh and blood touched that many ghosts . . .

Well, I wasn't exactly sure what would happen, but I did know that I, for one, was not willing to be the guinea pig who found out.

I stepped back, my body pressed to the frosty metal door.

"What is it?" Dan looked down what he thought was an empty tunnel, then back at me. "You're pale and you're breathing hard. It's not—"

"Ghosts? You bet it is." I had never confronted so many spirits at once, and though I was long past being surprised by their presence, it didn't mean I wasn't scared—especially when I realized the ghost nearest to me was the woman I'd seen in the cafeteria only a few days earlier. The one who'd been staring into her oatmeal.

"There are a lot of them." The least I could do was share this information with Dan. Then maybe he'd understand why I grabbed onto his arm and held on so tight, I was pretty sure he'd have a bruise by morning. "They must be the spirits of the people who died in the hospital. The ones whose bodies were brought out this way."

"And you really can see them?" Dan was as excited as a kid on the first day of summer vacation. Grinning, he glanced around, as if he thought that if he just looked hard enough, he could see the ghosts, too. "Does that mean . . . ?" He gave up on the ghost hunt and looked into my eyes, his voice clogged with emotion. "You weren't lying when you told me . . . Maddy? You really have seen her? You've . . . you've talked to her?"

"Well, duh! I told you that, didn't I? And Madeline's the least of our problems right now." The ghost of a man with sad eyes and gaunt features stepped toward me. I hung onto Dan and whispered, "I'm not sure they're going to let us out of here."

"Well, we can't go back."

I knew Dan was right. Even with the heavy metal door closed, we could hear the distant sounds of the commotion in the hospital and the constant blare of the alarm that signaled that one of the inmates—me—was missing.

"What are we going to do?" I asked Dan.

He slid me a look. "You're the expert."

Just for the record, I don't like being responsible. Not for anything. But I did know he was right. Thanks to the Gift that kept on giving, I was the only one who could get us out of the trouble my Gift had gotten us into.

Oatmeal Lady reached out a hand for me, and the other ghosts took their cue from her. They closed in on us.

"Oh no!" I held up one hand to stop them. "You know who I am, right?"

A man in an Indiana Jones–type hat spoke up. "You can help us move to the Other Side."

"I can. I will." Even I knew this was a line of bullshit, but hey, talk about an impossible situation. No way I could ever investigate the deaths of all those ghosts. But no way I could stay in that tunnel, either. "But here's the thing . . . I can't start helping you until I get out of here. And I can't get out of here if you don't let us pass." I bent my head, listening. A whole lot of people were running down the steps and into the basement.

"If I can't get away from here, then I won't be taking any more cases. Ever. And if I can't do that—"

"You can't help us."

This comment came from Oatmeal Lady. I was grateful. I nodded.

"So what do you want us to do?" the man in the hat asked.

It really was pretty simple. I asked most of the ghosts to stand flat up against the wall so we could get by without touching them. The rest I had stand near the door. I didn't think they could hold it closed, being incorporeal and all, but maybe—just maybe—the presence of that many spirits would somehow make the searchers feel uneasy and keep them from even trying to come through the door and into the tunnel.

I can't say if my plan worked or if plain old dumb luck played some role.

I do know that the crowd of ghosts parted just like I asked them to, and Dan and I raced through that tunnel. Less than ten minutes later, we were standing on the icy shores of Lake Michigan.

15

Dan didn't think it was safe for us to go back to Chicago that night, and I wasn't about to argue. Almost an hour after we stepped out of that icy tunnel, we found ourselves in a no-tell motel somewhere north of Winnetka. Our room was right off the just-about-deserted parking lot and was furnished with a lumpy bed, a nightstand that hadn't been dusted in a couple weeks, a dresser topped by a cracked mirror, and one chair. All of it looked as if it had been new long before I was born. The walls were pumpkin orange, a color that had never been one of my favorites. The carpet was lime green shag, and let's face it, that is so yesterday. The bedspread? Gold and black paisley. I will not even comment on the splotchy stains that dotted it.

It was the most beautiful place I'd ever seen.

The results were predictable; I was so hopped up on

adrenaline, I couldn't keep still. I stripped off Dan's parka, tossed it aside, and paced from one end of the room to the other. When he opened the bag of burgers we'd picked up at a McDonald's near the freeway, I never bothered to consider calories or fat content. I tore into a Big Mac, snaffled it down in a dozen ravenous bites, and started in on the supersized fries.

"Here's what I don't get." I hadn't bothered with ketchup, and when Dan opened a little pouch of it, I darted forward and dipped my fries. "What's he trying to prove? Doctor Gerard, I mean. I mean, you know who I mean, right? I don't get what he's up to. I mean, you do know what I mean, right? You know that I was right when I said he—"

"You told me the people who go into the study aren't seen or heard from again." Even though he hadn't taken a bite, Dan set aside his fries. I grabbed a few of his and wolfed them down. "I didn't believe you, Pepper."

"But now you do, right? That's a good thing. You—"

I am not by nature an emotional person. At least not when it comes to warm and fuzzy. Chalk it up to the drugs; I teared up. When I swallowed down another mouthful of fries, my throat ached.

"You believed me when I told you something fishy was going on at the clinic, didn't you? You said you didn't, but you really did. That's why you came to rescue me."

Instead of gloating like any self-respecting knight in shining armor should have, Dan looked away. "If I would have listened to you sooner, maybe…"

Just like he didn't want to say it, I didn't want to hear it. Suddenly, I wasn't all that hungry anymore. I set down my container of fries and wiped salt from my hands. The adrenaline—all that had kept me going—vanished, and I suddenly felt as if I'd crawled through a ceiling, fought my way out of a creepy mental hospital, and dealt with an army of ghosts. I dropped down on the bed. "How did you figure it out?" I asked him.

Over by the window, Dan slipped out of his light-weight jacket and tossed it on a chair upholstered in a shade of orange that didn't match the walls. "I thought about what you said, you know, about the missing people. But I've got to tell you, Pepper, as much as I like you... well, I just couldn't believe it. Hilton Gerard..." He shook his head and his hair flopped in his eyes. He didn't bother to push it away. "I've known Hilton for years. I've worked with him. He would never—"

"But he has."

"So you said. And while you've always been a lit-tle... well, how should I say this? A little different..." Apparently satisfied that I wasn't going to jump up and punch him in the nose, he went on. "But I knew you wouldn't tell me those things about a man I respect if you didn't think it was important. I spent a couple days deciding what to do. That's why it took me so long to find you. If only..." He dashed the thought away with a twitch of his shoulders.

"There was a fundraiser for the clinic the other night, so I knew Hilton would be wining and dining the city's elite. While he was gone, I went to the clinic and looked through the files."

This sounded encouraging. I sat up. "And you found out I was right, right?"

"I found out that the information in his research files isn't complete."

I guess this was supposed to be an *aha* moment. To me, it was more like *huh?*

Dan must have recognized this, because he explained. "No research scientist worth his weight in salt would be such a sloppy record keeper. That was my first clue that something was wrong. The second one came when I realized Hilton has done no follow-up with his subjects. It's part of the research protocol. He should have done it. Maddy would have if she were still in charge. She did everything by the book."

Pardon me for bristling, but since I was the one who'd just been held prisoner and drugged by a mad scientist...

And I was the one who'd helped in my own escape by clunking Burly Attendant Guy over the head...

And I was sitting there in that motel room with Dan...

Well, I didn't think it was exactly fair for him to play the dead wife card.

I knew it wouldn't do any good to point this out, so I didn't bother. Instead, I reminded him, "Now you've seen the truth with your own eyes. The files aren't complete like they should be, and I think that's because there's no one to follow up. He's got jars of brains, Dan!" I yelped, and I could have gone right on yelping if I didn't control myself. I took a deep breath.

"Once his experiments are done, Doctor Gerard doesn't care about those poor people anymore. And he kept me prisoner. You saw that, too. He wanted to experiment on my brain. And you..." Something told me Dan wasn't going to listen unless I made this as clear as clear can be. I got up and closed in on him and looked him in the eye. I didn't want to play the dead wife card, either, but I couldn't think of any other way to make Dan see the truth. "Doctor Gerard took advantage of you, Dan. He knows you want to communicate with Madeline and he knows you're the only one brilliant enough to figure out how to do it. He figured if he funded your research—"

"I'd lead a whole bunch of people right to him and then he could experiment on them for his own purposes." Dan's shoulders drooped beneath the weight of his responsibility.

"Neither of us has the luxury of feeling sorry for ourselves. We've got to save everyone else. We're going to call the cops, right?"

"Sure." Dan said it, but he didn't look convinced. "We will. I promise. It's just that—"

"What?" I couldn't believe I was hearing this from him. "You saw what's going on there, Dan." Just for emphasis, I pointed, though whether it was in the direction of the Gerard Hospital for the Insane and Mentally Feeble was anybody's guess. "You know it's not right. Locked rooms and bars on the windows and weird experiments." The very thought made me queasy. I stuffed a few more fries in my mouth to keep my stomach from rebelling. "We've got to help those people. If you won't go to the cops, I will. I—"

He grabbed my shoulders to stop me. His voice was calm, but his grip was steady. "I will. I promise. After I talk to Hilton."

"But—"

"Nothing's going to happen to anyone. Not tonight. For one thing, the staff has an escapee to worry about. They're going to be too busy looking for you to do anything else."

"But I have a list of their names and everything. The missing people, I mean. We could just—"

"I know how he thinks, Pepper. He sees you as his best chance ever. He's not going to worry about the others. Not for a while, anyway. And I'm going to talk to him first thing in the morning. I'll give him a chance to explain himself. I owe him that."

"But why wait?" No way I could stand still. Not when I was so hyped, and so frustrated by Dan's convoluted logic. I spun away. "We've got all the proof we need to go to the authorities. Oatmeal Lady was down there in the tunnel, Dan. I saw her. I had breakfast with her a couple days ago. Now..." I didn't want to take the chance of clogging up again, so I wiped the image from my mind. "She's a ghost. She's dead. Believe me, she wasn't dead the last time I saw her. That means something happened to her at that hospital, and that means somebody's got to stop your buddy Hilton. Before it happens again to someone else."

"You saw a ghost in an old tunnel. You think the cops are going to believe that?"

"Do you?"

Dan let out a sigh. "I want to. Really, Pepper, I do."

"Then if the cops raid the place—"

"They're going to find some very sick people who they'll be thrilled to know are off the streets and in locked rooms where they can't hurt themselves or anybody else."

"And when I tell them what happened to me?"

"Hilton is going to paint you as just as crazy as the rest of them. I'll bet he's dummied up the records to prove it. And he's got your brain scans. They *are* strange. There's no denying that."

Before I had a chance to defend my brain scans, Dan went right on. "Believe me, Pepper, my way is the best way. We'll wait until morning. I'll talk to Hilton and then—"

"And then?"

His shrug wasn't exactly the reassurance I needed. "If he can't provide a good explanation, then I'll have no choice. I'll go to the cops."

It's not the way I would have handled the situation, but it made sense. Sort of.

With all the pacing and spinning going on, I found myself near Dan's fries again. I reached for a couple and chewed thoughtfully while I sorted things out. I guess it was all the chewing that made me start asking questions.

"How did you find me, anyway?"

"I knew you were scheduled to give your talk on the Resurrectionists at the conference and—"

I gulped. "Oh my gosh, I forgot all about it! Did I miss it? Is the conference over? Ella's going to freak."

A smile touched Dan's lips. "She might understand when you tell her you were kidnapped."

"She might." I couldn't help but smile back. Right before I shivered. "It's kind of what Doctor Gerard must be doing," I said, thinking out loud. "When his patients die, he studies their brains. Just like the Resurrectionists did. They dug up bodies to dissect them." Suddenly, the ketchup didn't look all that appealing anymore. I didn't bother dipping the next handful of fries I ate. "Maybe he's not even waiting for them to die," I said, talking with my mouth full. "Maybe he's—"

Dan held up a hand to stop my wild imaginings. "Let's not get ahead of ourselves, OK? After I talk to Hilton tomorrow, I'll know more."

I realized Dan had dodged my original question. I chewed and stared at him. "And you were saying . . . about how you found me . . . ?"

He blushed like any humble hero would have. "After I went to the clinic and saw the files, I knew something wasn't right. I wanted to talk to you about it, but you weren't at your hotel. And you didn't answer your phone. So I went back to the clinic and talked to a couple of the homeless guys outside. One of them said he saw a woman who matched your description leave the clinic a couple days earlier. I've gotta tell you, I breathed a sigh of relief when I heard that. If you were at the clinic and then left, I figured you were all right. But then he mentioned that you left, all right, but you left in a wheelchair. He said it looked like you were sleeping, and that he saw Hilton Gerard put you in a van and drive away."

"Which explains how I got to Winnetka, but not how you knew to go there. Unless . . ."

My face must have betrayed what I was thinking, because Dan stopped in the middle of taking a slurp of a chocolate shake. "I didn't know what was going on in that hospital. That's the God's honest truth, Pepper. I didn't even know the hospital was open. I was there once. With Maddy. I'd read so much about the place in my studies, I talked her into taking me there just so I could look around. It was years ago, and I swear, when we were there, I didn't see any signs of life." As if it would prove it, he held up one hand, Boy Scout–style.

"Anyway . . ." Dan rolled the milkshake cup between his palms. "After I talked to that homeless guy, I spent a few hours trying to figure out what might have happened. I thought maybe when you were at the clinic, there was an accident of some sort, that what that guy had seen was

Hilton taking you to a hospital. I called every one in the area. I even checked with the police. I went to your hotel again. Then I thought about Winnetka."

"Pardon me for the sarcasm, but from what I saw, Winnetka isn't a place anybody thinks about."

"That's true. Except…" He bit into a cheeseburger. I was glad he'd gotten two for himself because I'd eaten just about all his fries and I didn't want to see him go hungry. "The hospital in Winnetka is a huge part of the Gerard history. It was the only place I could think of. I took a chance."

"I'm glad you did." I reached for the second chocolate shake. "But hey, maybe I could have gotten myself out of there. That was pretty cool, wasn't it? The way I bashed that guy over the head with the mop?"

Dan grinned, but it was short-lived. "It was pretty cool. You're one tough cookie."

"You don't sound impressed."

He took a bite of burger and chewed it over thoughtfully, holding up one finger to tell me he'd answer as soon as he was done. "Oh, I'm impressed, all right." He washed down his food with some of his own chocolate milkshake. "It's just that…"

Dan set down his burger so that he could cross the room and take my hand. When he walked over to the bed, I naturally went right along. The mattress was mushy and it sagged when we sat down.

As if he was getting ready to make a confession, he drew in a breath. "I've sent people to him, Pepper." Dan's voice was so low, I could barely hear it.

I leaned closer. "You've sent people to…Doctor Gerard?"

He nodded. "As I've been working on my part of the

study, you know, in places like Cleveland. When I found people I thought showed promise, people who I thought might have the ability to get in touch with the Other Side, I recommended they go to Chicago and see Hilton. I was blinded by my desire to contact Maddy again. I thought if I could find him the raw materials, Hilton could really make it work, and when he did..." We were sitting close, and his sigh rippled against my skin. It smelled like ketchup and onions. "I was just thinking..."

I could see why he'd put down his burger. My stomach felt a little queasy, too. "You're not blaming yourself for what happened to those people, are you?"

He shook his head, but I wasn't convinced. I mean, how could I be? He looked miserable, poor guy. That's why I slipped an arm around his shoulders.

"It's not your fault," I said. "You didn't know."

"I should have asked more questions."

"Knowing you, I bet you asked plenty."

I guess I was right on the money, because Dan looked relieved. At least a little. He sighed again, and when he adjusted his weight to make himself more comfortable, his thigh pressed against mine.

Dan isn't at all like Quinn. They don't look alike, they don't act alike (well, except for the being-around-to-save-my-life-once-in-a-while thing). With Quinn, there's always a hint of sensuality simmering just below his extra-large ego. As I'd found out firsthand and much to my delight, when that sensuality bubbled to the surface, it was a thing of wonder.

But Dan...Dan is one of those deep guys who feel things through and through but don't always like to let on. I mean, look at the way he still carried a torch for Madeline. It was creepy, sure, but it was sweet, too. It showed how much he could love, and how devoted he could be.

As for me, well, I had just been as close as I ever want to be to having my brain pickled and put in a jar. Like anyone could blame me for craving a little comfort?

"There are a lot of questions that need to be answered," Dan said. His voice was huskier than I'd ever heard it.

I took that as a good sign and leaned in close so I could whisper my response against his lips. "And we'll find the answers. Just not tonight."

"You mean . . . ?" For a moment, I thought Dan was going to say he didn't know what I meant. Or worse, that he was still so into Madeline that he wasn't interested. But the truth dawned, and I saw his pupils widen. A smile touched his lips. Before I knew it, his arms were around me.

Dan looked into my eyes. His mouth was only a hairbreadth away from mine. "I thought once you knew about Maddy, you wouldn't want to—"

"She's got nothing to do with this." This was the truth. At least for right then and there. "Besides, I've been held prisoner and drugged. I've had weird electrode thingees attached to my head. I was scared, Dan. I just need you to hold me."

He, being the knight in shining armor that he is, didn't refuse.

From there . . .

Well, I won't go into details. I mean, what's the point? Let's just say that before either of us had a chance to second-guess what we were doing or why, we had that black and gold bedspread—and our clothes— stripped off.

"You're sure?"

Leave it to Dan to ask permission even while he was trailing a series of kisses down my throat.

"No." I lay back against the flat-as-a-pancake pillow and smiled up at him. "But being sure has nothing to do with this. Are you sure?"

"Sure I want you?" He kissed me hard, and when he was done, he grinned. There was heat in that smile of his. It tickled over my skin and set me on fire. "Right now, you're the surest thing in my life. I'm sure I can't wait. Not for another minute."

Again, I don't need details, do I? At least I wouldn't if everything happened the way it was supposed to happen. But let's face it, this is my life, and lately, the way things are supposed to happen and the way they do happen...

Well, I guess that's why I wasn't exactly surprised when I realized I wasn't feeling all the things I should have been feeling at that particular moment.

Instead of snap, crackle, pop and sizzle, I felt a weird pull. Like suddenly my spirit was made out of metal and there was a giant magnet in the room tugging it.

That was kind of weird. Because my body was doing exactly what it was supposed to be doing. In fact, the last thing I remember is looking up into Dan's dreamy blue eyes.

Right before my spirit was sucked straight out of me.

I found myself sitting on the dresser. Only it wasn't me. I mean, it couldn't have been.

Because I was still in bed with Dan doing you-know-what.

Or at least somebody was.

My mouth open in surprise and horror, I watched as the Pepper who wasn't Pepper went through the motions.

This did not seem possible, and just to check, I looked at myself in the mirror.

I was me, Pepper Martin, and my hair was red and curly and my face was a little pale, what with the lack of light and the drugs and all. But still, I looked like me, all right. Only I didn't.

Maybe that's because I was wearing a long, shapeless black skirt, glasses, and a lab coat.

I jumped off that dresser in an instant and hurried over to the bed, but by that time, it was too late. Dan and the Pepper he was in bed with were done doing what they'd been doing and they were both looking pretty darned happy. The Pepper in the bed winked at me over Dan's shoulder. She didn't move her lips, but her voice reverberated through my head. It sounded smug and a little too academic for my taste.

"Thank you, Pepper. I couldn't have planned this any better."

16

Certain things are way more interesting to do than they are to watch. Especially when the person I was watching do them was wearing my body.

Madeline had been dead for three years. When it came to the physical world, she had a lot of catching up to do.

And Dan? Well, the good news is that he might love Madeline to the grave and beyond, but he liked me. I mean, he really, really liked me. He showed it in lots of different and interesting ways.

The bad news was that now that Dan had gotten over his shyness, he had a lot of catching up to do, too.

And me? I spent the rest of the night in the bathroom, my fingers in my ears, so freaking panicked, I couldn't think straight.

The next morning when Madeline and Dan came in to shower (together), I ducked back into the room. Even with a change of scenery and the sounds of running water drowning out (mostly) the moans and the groans coming from in there, I didn't feel any better.

I paced and worried. I paced and cried. I paced and screamed every swear word I could think of (and a few I made up on the spot), and I didn't have to care that I might be causing a commotion.

No one could hear me.

Tears welled in my eyes again, and I didn't bother to wipe them away. Heck, why should I? No one could see me, either.

"So, how does it feel?"

OK, I wasn't exactly accurate about the no-one-could-see-me. Madeline could. Done doing what she'd been doing, she was wrapped in a paper-thin towel that scarcely covered her breasts (*my* breasts!). She sauntered into the room with a smile on her face that was as bright as the song Dan was humming in the shower. I think it was a Broadway show tune.

"Now you know how I've felt these past years," she said. "You're invisible."

"No shit, Sherlock." I raised my chin and looked into eyes that used to be mine and a face that just yesterday had looked back at me from the mirror. It was weird. "You've had your fun." I didn't need to elaborate. She knew exactly what I was talking about, and to prove it, she grinned and purred and stretched like a contented cat. "Now give me back my body."

"*My* body." The voice was mine, but the attitude—and the sarcasm—was all Madeline. "Once a narcissist, always a narcissist. I've got news for you, Pepper. My body." She poked her finger at her chest (*my*—well, there's no use dwelling). "My hair." She tugged on it.

"My clothes." She looked down to where they were tossed on the floor just as Dan switched to something that sounded like opera. He didn't have a bad voice.

Madeline paused for a moment to listen. "My Danny," she said.

"And you think I'm the narcissist?" Since I didn't have to worry about my image, I snorted to emphasize my point. So tacky, but it helped me sound tough, and tough was exactly what I needed. Without the tough, I'd be a basket case. "Get over it, girlfriend. You're dead. And when you died, the world didn't stop spinning. Life goes on. Without you."

"Without you." Madeline giggled. Even coming out of my mouth, it was not a pretty sound. "Don't you get it? I arranged this whole thing just so I could get your body."

"How—?"

Apparently, my question wasn't even worth listening to. Not in Madeline's opinion, anyway. "Hilton was so obsessed with this whole ghost, paranormal thing. He made me do hours and hours of research. It's amazing what you can learn in some of those dusty, old books of his. Séances, shape-shifting, time travel, spirit possession of a live body when the stars and the moon are aligned just right...I never believed any of it, but hey, I'm a researcher, remember. I figured it was worth a try. I was waiting for the right test subject to come along. According to that book of Hilton's, my live subject—you— had to make love to the one person—Danny—who was still in love with the person who passed on—me. I set this whole thing up like an experiment. You fell for it. And it worked."

I couldn't believe what I was hearing. I swallowed hard. "Then the people at the hospital, the ones in Doctor Gerard's study. They aren't—"

"Missing? Sure they are." Madeline dismissed the information with a wave of one hand. "The point is, who cares?"

"You do. At least you said you did."

"I told you Danny was involved, too. I thought that was a nice touch. He's got that whole cute-as-a-button thing going for him. And the broken heart shtick, too, of course. Most women can't resist. I figured you were no different. He has to get on with his life. He needs to find a woman who will love him as much as I did." When she spoke these last two sentences, she pressed her hands to her heart. She sounded like her old self. Except for the cackle of a laugh at the end. "I've proved it again. I'm smarter than you. I came up with a great way to sucker you in."

No way I could get beyond the desperation that ate away at my composure, but still, I couldn't help but feel a wave of relief. "So Dan isn't really in trouble?"

Madeline shrugged. "Does it matter?"

"Shouldn't it?"

Another shrug. The towel that was all she was wearing came loose, and Madeline tossed it aside and went to stand in front of the mirror. She turned this way and that, assessing her new body. "Not bad," she decided. "With this body and my brains, I'll go a long way. I can't believe you didn't think of it, or maybe you did, but without the smarts to carry it off, you just weren't very good at it. What do you think? Can I sleep my way to the top?"

"Sleep? Top? Top of what?"

"A hospital research program. A university psychology department. What's the difference? I'm not all that particular." Madeline grabbed the thong that had landed on the dresser when Dan and I ripped off our clothes. She stepped into it and made a face. "I've got to go out and get myself some real clothes."

"Real? Like…" Why this hadn't occurred to me before, I don't know, but I glanced down at my own fuddy-duddy outfit. My long black skirt had an elastic waistband, and I plucked it away from my stomach and took a peek.

White cotton briefs!

If I wasn't already invisible, I would have died from embarrassment. "You've got to be kidding. You don't really expect me to wear this?"

"Personally, I don't care what you wear. I don't care about you at all." Madeline reached for my jeans and slipped them on. She put on my bra and my sweater. The ripped sleeve didn't seem to bother her. The fit, though, did. She squirmed. "Your boobs are too big. They make me feel top-heavy. Maybe I'll get a reduction."

"You wouldn't dare, you no-good, sneaky—"

"Ah, is that a little bit of jealousy I hear?" Dressed now, Madeline peered into the mirror and ran her fingers through her curls. She tugged at a ringlet and made a face. "This has got to go. Too high maintenance. I'm thinking a nice, short cut. Wash and wear. It will give me more time for—"

"What?" I crossed my arms over my chest, holding in my temper and my panic. "You want to give yourself more time in the shower with Dan?"

"You think that's what this is about? You're dumber

than I thought." She looked toward the bathroom. "He's a sweet guy. Really. And so enthusiastic when it comes to . . . well, I guess you noticed, right? It's just that . . ."

My temper dissolved beneath a wave of nausea. I couldn't believe what I was hearing. Force of habit; even though I knew Dan couldn't hear me, I lowered my voice. I couldn't bear the thought of hurting his feelings. "Are you telling me—"

"What, that I don't give a damn about Danny?" Finished preening, Madeline spun and leaned against the dresser. Since I was standing directly opposite her, I could see us both at the same time. Looking at the physical me standing in front of the dresser and the essence of me in the mirror was too weird for words.

Maybe Madeline realized it. Maybe that's why she smiled.

"How can you think that I don't care about sweet Danny?" Her smile inched up. "He's obviously good for a few things. But then, I guess you noticed that, too."

The sourness in my stomach shot up into my throat. "That's not the way a wife should talk about the man who's carried a torch for her for three long years. He loves you."

"He loves a memory."

"Which has to be based in fact." A new thought struck, and if I wasn't afraid that my hand would *whoosh* right through my head, I would have slapped my forehead. "Not much fact, right? You put on a show for Dan. You pretended to be someone you weren't. Just so he would marry you. Now all he remembers is the warm and fuzzy stuff, and he's spent three years of his life missing a woman who never really existed. He doesn't know that you're really a bitch."

"You think so?" My purse was on the dresser. Completely unconcerned about my criticism, Madeline opened the purse, plucked out a tube of "Paris Nights," swiveled it open, and made a face. "Isn't this color a little obvious?"

"Isn't that the whole point of wearing lipstick? And beauty tips aren't what we were talking about. We were talking about Dan."

"And I said he was a sweet guy." Madeline tossed my practically new tube of lipstick in a nearby trash can. She followed it up with my blusher, my mascara, my eyeliner, and the Missoni Parfum Rollerball I'd paid too much for and never regretted. "If you had more self-confidence, you wouldn't need all these things to shore up your ego."

"I thought I was a narcissist. That means I don't need anything to shore up my ego. I've got ego to spare."

"And you hide behind cosmetics." Madeline shook her head sadly. "That ends today. From now on, the world sees the real me."

"The real me, you mean."

She slid me a look. "Not anymore. You're not dead, Pepper. But you're not alive, either. That means you don't belong in this world or the other one. And that means you can't stay. You're going to fade and then *poof!*" She snapped her fingers. "Disappear completely. Then I'll never have to worry about you again."

The nausea intensified. I hugged my arms around myself. I'd go crazy if I thought about what she said, so I concentrated on the problem at hand. "Did you ever love Dan?"

"Love is a fickle emotion. It can't be quantified."

"Most people don't want to quantify it."

"Most people are morons."

"Is Dan?"

She glanced toward the bathroom just as Dan shut off
the water, and when she answered me, she made sure he
couldn't hear. "He was a brilliant student. I knew he'd be
successful someday. He's Nobel Prize material."

"So you hitched your wagon to his star."

"It would have worked. If I hadn't died."

"The mugging. Is that story bullshit, too? Maybe you
just made it up so I'd feel sorry for you."

She had already opened her mouth to respond when
Dan stepped out of the bathroom. He had a towel
wrapped around his waist, and I had a chance to admire a
body I hadn't had nearly enough time to check out the
night before. Nice shoulders, abs that were too well de-
veloped to belong to a brain researcher, a chest that
wasn't nearly as broad as Quinn's, but just as yummy. I
winced when I saw the red welt I'd caused when I bashed
him with that stool back at the mental hospital, but apparently Dan didn't hold it against me. Or at least he
didn't hold it against the me he thought was me. There
was a glimmer in his eyes and an expectant expression
on his face. Both dissolved when he saw that the woman
he knew as Pepper was already dressed. "You're all set to
go. I thought we could—"

"We have a long day ahead of us."

He gave in with the kind of accommodating smile I'd
always wanted from him and never got. "You're right, of
course. And we'll have plenty of time later for…" Hot
under the sheets and as shy as a violet when it was all
over. I wasn't surprised when Dan blushed. He reached
for his clothes, and damn, he turned his back on me when
he dropped the towel and put on his boxers. He slipped

his jeans on, too, and turned around again just as he was zipping them. "Before we leave, I want to make sure I have my story straight. Let's go over the details. What do you know about the clinic, Pepper, and how did you find it out?"

All right, I admit it...I gloated more than just a little when I saw the blank expression on Madeline's face and realized she couldn't answer any of his question. She might have my body, but the bitch didn't get my memories.

That's why she tried to buy some time when she said, "Well, as you know, I'm not very bright..."

"Oh, puh-leez!" Needless to say, this comment came from me.

Just as needless to point out, Madeline ignored it. She went right on.

"But I was able to put two and two together. About the ghosts, I mean. That's why I went to the clinic in the first place, to talk to Hilton about ghosts."

Dan's eyes gleamed. "You really do communicate with the dead. You've seen Maddy. You've talked to her!"

Sensitive guy that he is, Dan realized talking about his dead wife might not be the politically correct thing to do when the sheets were still hot. He scrambled for an apology that Madeline didn't give him time to deliver.

"It's OK." Her voice more cloying than mine had ever been, she closed in on him. "I understand, Danny, I really do. From everything I've heard about her, I know Madeline was a truly remarkable woman." How she got this out without gagging, I don't know, and just so she didn't think she was getting away with anything, I opened my mouth, poked a finger toward my throat, and made a choking sound. She shot me a look before she turned her attention back to Dan.

"From everything I've heard about her…" She took Dan's hands in hers. "I know she was kind and giving and caring. I understand how impossible it must be for you to forget her. Just as I understand that what we had here…well, sex is just sex, isn't it? And a man has needs. I'm a realist, I never thought it was any more than that. Don't worry, Danny, I'm not expecting more from you in the way of commitment or caring."

"You're not?" Dan looked at Madeline closely. "I never thought you were—"

"That understanding? Oh please, darling!" She briefly skimmed a finger along his cheek before she headed over to the mirror to check her hair.

And watching her, Dan whispered below his breath. "That shallow."

"See?" I followed Madeline and pointed back toward where Dan stood watching her, his eyes narrowed. "Did you hear that? He expected more from me than wham, bam, thank you, ma'am. He knows I'm not that much of a loser."

Madeline stopped in her tracks. When she turned back to Dan, she had a smile firmly in place. "I hope you don't think I'm that much of a loser." I wondered how she'd learned so quickly to turn on the waterworks at just the right time. A single tear slipped down her cheek, and she sniffed. "I just want you to know that I understand how I could never take Madeline's place in your heart. I've come to grips with that. I'm at peace with it. She was your soul mate. I can never be half the woman she was."

Dan drew in a breath. "You're right, of course. I mean, about the soul mate thing, not about how I feel about you." He waited for her to smile before he glanced at the bed and continued. "I never would have... I mean, we never would have... I mean, what happened last night, it never would have happened if I didn't have feelings for you."

"I knew it!" I punched a fist in the air.

Madeline pretended not to hear me. "That's so sweet." She kissed Dan's cheek, and in the kind of blatant attempt at flattery I had never needed and never would have stooped to, she touched a hand to his sleeve and batted her eyelashes before she grabbed the coat I'd worn into the room the night before. "Now let's get back to Chicago."

For a second, Dan stared at her. When she just twinkled back (it was not a pretty picture), he waved a hand in front of her face. "It's the drugs, right? That's got to be it. Have you forgotten what you said last night? You wanted to call the cops. You wanted to march back to that hospital yourself. Last night you said—"

"Of course!" Not a chance Madeline had any idea what he was talking about; she hadn't been in the room when Dan and I discussed going to the authorities the night before. Still, she recovered in a heartbeat and covered even faster. "I would have said that! I'm such a feisty thing. That's why they call me Pepper, you know." She was going for a brilliant smile. Instead, it looked as if she'd bitten into a lemon. Hell, I could have done better, and I was incorporeal. "It's this crazy, peppery personality of mine."

I rolled my eyes.

Madeline looked the other way.

Dan just looked confused.

He put on his shirt and pulled a bulky Aran knit

sweater over his head. "I told you I wanted to talk to Hilton this morning," he explained, giving her the benefit of the doubt (which he shouldn't have done since she was a lying sack of crap, but of course, he didn't know that). He grabbed his own lightweight jacket and slipped it on. "And you said you had a list of the names of the missing patients. It would really help me to have that kind of ammunition when I talk to him. You've got it with you?"

Pardon me for pointing out that I had another chance to gloat. Madeline was shocked to hear about the list. Oh yeah, I could tell she was plenty surprised, all right. But once a liar, always a liar, and she went right on pulling the wool over Dan's eyes. She patted down her pockets. "Silly me, I left the list back at the hotel. But let's not worry about that. What we really need to do, Danny honey, is get out of here. Fast."

As if it could help him better see the logic of her argument, he slipped on his glasses. "So last night you wanted to go after Hilton with both barrels, and today you want to forget the whole thing? Those drugs have really messed up your mind. I'm going to get over to the hospital. And you—"

"No way in hell you're leaving here without me." I'd stepped forward and voiced my opinion before I had a chance to think, and the next second, I cursed myself. I should have let Madeline hang out to dry. This way, she knew exactly what she should say. Never one to let an opportunity pass, she threw back her shoulders and lifted her chin.

"I'm going with you to talk to Hilton," she said.

"That's my girl. I knew you would." Dan gave her a kiss. When he was done, he looked at her hard. "Are you all right?" he asked.

Madeline being Madeline, she couldn't imagine that she wasn't always all right. She wrinkled her nose and tipped her head. "All right? Why wouldn't I be?"

He stepped back. "I dunno. It's just that..." Uncomfortable, he laughed. "It just feels different, kissing you now than it did kissing you last night. It's as if you've changed."

Madeline smiled. She wrapped an arm through his. "Of course I'm not the same," she said. "Everything's different today. Everything's changed, Danny."

It was enough to satisfy him, and really, how could I blame him for giving in so easily? Dan might be into the whole woo-woo scene, but something told me even he couldn't imagine the body-changing scenario that had played out right in front of his eyes.

This time when he laughed, it was without reservations. "You're right." He wrapped an arm around Madeline's shoulders. "Everything has changed. It's like the world has opened up for me again. And you know what's weird, Pepper, it's like Madeline had something to do with it all." Dan went around the room, turning out lights and tossing our McDonald's bags. "Wherever Madeline is," he said, "I finally know she's at peace. See, you may not realize it, but you used his first name. Hilton Gerard's. You didn't call him Doctor Gerard, you called him Hilton, just like Madeline always did. And you called me Danny. Even my mom never did that. Madeline was the one and only person who ever called me Danny."

Oblivious to the truth staring him in the face, Dan unlocked the door and stepped into the frigid morning sunshine. "Before we get over to the hospital, we should probably stop somewhere so you can replace that ripped sweater of yours."

Madeline followed Dan outside. "That will be fine."

He headed over to the car. "I'm afraid the only close store is a Wal-Mart," he said, an apology in his voice.

Madeline nodded. "Like I said, that's fine."

"Fine?" Laughing, Dan stopped just as he was about to open the car door. "Boy, you weren't kidding when you said you changed last night. No way the Pepper Martin I know would agree to go clothes shopping at Wal-Mart."

He was still laughing when he held the door open for Madeline and she got into the car.

Me? I wasn't laughing at all. Firmly ignoring the pissed look on Madeline's face, I climbed into the back-seat.

Wal-Mart or no Wal-Mart, I'd be damned if they were going anywhere without me.

17

As it turned out, Hilton Gerard had split for Chicago long before we got back to the Gerard Hospital for the Insane and Mentally Feeble.

Too bad.

I was spitting mad and in the mood to give the good doctor a piece of my mind. Don't ask me how I was planning to do this (being invisible and all), but I sure would have liked to have had the opportunity.

The way it was, Dan thanked the receptionist who turned us away in that locked-down lobby, and when we were back in the parking lot, he held the front car door open so Madeline could get in. I knew nobody was going to bother to open the back door, so I slipped in ahead of her, and maybe it was a good thing I was invisible, at least for that moment. Me in my dorky black skirt climbing over the seat so I could ride in the back . . . well, it was just as well Dan couldn't see.

He came around to the other side of the car, got behind the wheel, and turned the key in the ignition before he reached across the seat and patted Madeline's hand. "There are plenty of people who wouldn't have had the nerve to walk back into that place. Not after what you went through. And you—"

"I just kept my chin up and put on a brave face."

From the seat behind her, I snarled. "That's because you don't know what really happened in there."

"That's because I'm peppery." Madeline giggled.

Dan smiled, too. "I'll say. And now—"

"Now we can get back to the city." She stretched, closed her eyes, and made herself comfortable. Not exactly an easy thing to do in Dan's Honda Civic Hybrid, but then, Madeline didn't have my exacting standards.

"You're sure?"

If she'd been paying attention, she would have noticed Dan's quizzical expression. She popped open one eye. "Sure? Why wouldn't I be? You tried to talk to Hilton. It didn't work. There's nothing to be gained from belaboring the point."

"And the cops?"

"Oh." Madeline sat up. While she thought of a way to talk herself out of her little faux pas, she played with the climate control buttons on the dashboard. When she had the heat turned down to a temperature I never would have tolerated and the blower going strong enough to muss her hair, she gave Dan a sidelong look. "I think we need more evidence. And I think we're only going to find that back in the city."

"Like that list of names you said you had. The missing patients."

"That's right, Danny." In a move designed to distract him, she skimmed a hand along his thigh.

"Oh, come on, Madeline! He's never going to fall for that," I wailed, at the same time Dan purred like a cat with its whiskers in a bowl of cream.

The smile Madeline shot me said it all.

I was up Shit Creek without a paddle.

And getting in deeper every moment.

I needed a plan and I needed one bad, but instead of coming up with one, I sat in the backseat like a lump and worried and panicked my way back to Chicago.

Of course, there's only so much worrying and panicking a person can do. Even a person without a body. Did that stop me? Hell, no. Because I didn't know what else to do, I worried and panicked my way into the hotel on Madeline and Dan's heels, and I'd just about convinced myself that all that worrying and all that panicking was getting me nowhere when Doris from Detroit stepped off the elevator.

There was so much honest relief on Doris's face and in the mammoth hug she gave Madeline, even I got teary-eyed. She let go of the woman she thought was me and stepped back to give her a once-over. "Oh my gosh, Penelope. We were so concerned! Where have you been? What happened? Are you all right?"

"I'm fine. Of course I'm fine." Madeline had slipped out of Dan's parka the moment they were through the hotel's revolving door, and she tugged nervously at the new white polyester blouse she'd paired with a calf-length polyester blend skirt printed with black fern leaves on a taupe background.

As if.

I pulled my gaze from the offending clothing so I could watch the little drama unfolding before me.

"Well, you look..." Doris checked out Madeline again. As long as Madeline was at Wal-Mart using my MasterCard with wild abandon (where—it should come as no surprise—none of my credit cards had ever been used before), she'd tossed in a pair of thick-soled black shoes with low heels, dark stockings, and one of those black cotton cardigans the middle-aged and the tres unchic insist on wearing—the kind with stubby wooden buttons and sleeves that have to be rolled up so they don't stretch beyond the length of the wearer's hands.

"You look different," Doris said.

I can't explain how much this cheered me. I whooped and yelled, "You got that right," and I was about to slap Doris a high five when Madeline turned and aimed a sneer in my direction—just to remind me I was wasting my time.

She looked plenty frickin' smug when she grabbed Dan's hand and turned back to Doris. "You're absolutely right," she cooed, and damn, but if there was ever a clue that this Pepper wasn't the Pepper that Doris and Dan knew, this should have been it. Even on my worst days, I've never sounded that corny. "As of today, everything is different. My life is different. I am different. No more self-centered egotist. No more airhead. No more—"

Doris's laugh cut her short. "Like you're any of those things!" She glanced from Madeline to Dan before she leaned in close and lowered her voice so Dan couldn't hear. "You are all right, though, aren't you? This guy isn't bothering you? He isn't—"

"Don't be silly!" When Madeline giggled, it set my teeth on edge. "This is my Danny."

Relief swept over Doris's expression. "Well, good! It's just that when you didn't show up to give your talk—"

Madeline dismissed this comment with a very un-Pepper-like snort. Her words dripped with contempt. "I never miss a professional commitment. I would never—" She caught herself at the same time Dan gave her a funny look.

"I haven't been well," Madeline said, suddenly all sweetness and light. "You understand, I'm sure. When a person is as emotionally unstable as I am—"

Doris laughed again. She patted Madeline on the shoulder. "You're so funny. As long as things are OK, kid, that's all that matters."

Madeline stepped nearer to Dan. She slipped an arm around his waist just as the closest elevator doors opened. When she stepped into the elevator, Dan went with her willingly. "Everything is fine." She looked past Doris to where I stood, and just as the elevator doors closed, I saw her sleek smile and heard her say, "Everything's going to be fine from now on."

Call me crazy, or maybe I was just hoping against hope. I had the funny feeling that Doris didn't actually believe this. She stood there staring at the closed elevator doors for a long time, the expression on her face halfway between befuddled and amazed. Again, my hopes rose. If Doris suspected something was wrong and if she was willing to find out what it was...

With a twitch of her shoulders and a shake of her head, Doris headed over to the concierge, and I heard her tell the woman she needed a taxi. She was headed to the airport and on her way back home to Detroit.

My hopes plummeted like a rock. Doris might have had a gut feeling that something was wrong with the Pepper who wasn't Pepper, but none of it would matter once she was on that plane.

There I was in Chicago. All by myself and invisible to boot.

I didn't have to worry that my lipstick would look like hell, so I chewed on my lower lip and stood there for a while, holding my panic at bay while I thought about my options. I can't say I'm one of the world's great brains, but I did know one thing for sure: if anybody was going to get me out of this mess, it would have to be me.

I also knew where I had to start—the Gerard Clinic.

No sooner did the words form in my invisible brain than a weird thing happened. I felt a tug, as if a hand grabbed me and pulled hard. The world around me rushed by, like the scenery during a roller coaster ride.

The next thing I knew, I was standing in the street right in front of the clinic.

"Cool!" I told myself.

It was. At least until I saw a yellow cab not three feet away and heading right for me.

It was especially not so cool as I watched the front bumper of that cab get closer—and *whoosh* right through me.

I needed no more proof that invisibility sucked, and no more motivation to get moving. Traffic was heavy, and before another vehicle could zip straight through the ectoplasm that was me, I raced to the sidewalk. Just as I got there, I ran smack into what felt like a wall of ice.

There was nothing there I could see, but I could feel it, all right. Cold that penetrated deep inside me. Ice that would have chilled me to the bone, if I had any.

And fear.

Oh yeah. I recognized that the moment it climbed up my spine and sent my brain into terror-mode.

By this time, I knew what was happening, so I wasn't surprised when the cold coalesced and the nothing in front of me swirled and collapsed in on itself.

All that was left in its place was a black hulky shadow.

I'd never been this close to the thing, and this close was not the place I wanted to be.

I stepped back.

The shadow stepped forward. It lifted one of its massive arms and reached for me with a paw tipped with razor-sharp claws, and I closed my eyes and held my breath, not sure what was about to happen.

One paw (hand? talon? hook?) still raised, it stopped.

As if it were thinking, the shadow cocked its head. It leaned closer. It didn't exactly have a face, so I can't exactly say it had a nose. Even so, I swore I heard it sniff.

It snuffled to the right of me. It whiffed to the left of me. It got right up into my face and sniffed, and the next thing I knew, it shot upright—and disappeared in a *poof*.

"Well, pardon me for not having time to spritz on a little perfume this morning," I snarled, braver now that it was gone. "I've been a little busy being invisible."

And I was more than sick and tired of it. With that thought in mind, I decided to delay a trip into the clinic and headed instead into the alley.

I didn't knock on Ernie's box. I mean, why bother? As far as I knew, Ernie was back in Winnetka at the Gerard Hospital for the Insane and Mentally Feeble, and besides, not having a real hand, I couldn't really knock on anything, anyway. Instead, I closed my eyes, held my breath, and walked right through the tarp that covered the opening of the box. Once I was inside, though, I was nearly knocked for a loop. There was Ernie sitting on a milk crate! I was so relieved that he was safe and back home, I just about cried. I was talking even before I thought about how there was no way he could hear me.

"Thank goodness you're back! You weren't hurt at that crazy hospital. You're not—"

"Dead?"

Ernie looked right at me, and I would have jumped out of my skin if I had any. Being the smart cookie I am, it didn't take more than a moment for me to realize what was going on.

Ernie confirmed my worst fears when he said, "I'm dead, all right. How else would I be able to see you and talk to you? Looks like you're pretty dead yourself. That's a real shame, you being so young and all. I was hoping you'd find a way to get out of that place."

"I did get out." I was so upset to hear that Ernie had met the fate of the other people in the study and so happy to finally have someone who could hear and see me, I couldn't think straight. I hurried over and sat down next to him. There was one good thing about not having a body: the cold didn't seep into me the way it had last time I visited. "I escaped from the hospital through the ceiling and Dan came and got me out and we left Winnetka and I was safe, but then..." This part was hard to explain so I didn't even try. "I'm not dead," I told Ernie. "Someone just stole my body."

He pursed his lips and looked over my shapeless black skirt, my white blouse, and my lab coat. "Someone who doesn't have your sense of style, that's for sure. You look like that Doctor What's-Her-Name, the one who used to work at the clinic."

"Madeline Tremayne. She's the one who's using my body. She learned how to do the switch from the research she was doing for Doctor Gerard."

Thinking, Ernie shook his head. "Never did trust that woman. Didn't like the way she looked at folks. You know, like they were invisible."

"She's the one who's been invisible. She was a ghost. After her murder, I mean. And her husband wanted her back more than anything in the world. And now he has her, only he doesn't know it's her, and he thinks it's me and—"

"Hold on there." Ernie could tell that what little of my composure was left was about to self-destruct. To calm me down, he looked me in the eye. "We'll talk about all that in good time. Let's start with what's most important. You're telling me you're not dead, right?"

I nodded.

"Then it seems to me that this is all wrong. If you're not dead, you shouldn't be in spirit. That's unnatural, and I may be crazy, and I'm for sure dead, but I can tell you one thing, I know we've got to set things straight and get you back in your body where you belong."

I couldn't have agreed more.

"Where should we begin?" he asked.

I wasn't sure, and I told him so. "I thought maybe if we could get into the clinic—"

"Easy as pie." Ernie rose from the milk crate. "But you already know that, right? You walked right in here like it was no big deal."

"I took a chance. I wasn't sure." I thought back to all the ghosts I'd dealt with in the past and how they'd come and gone at will. "Are you telling me I can go anywhere?" I asked him, and call it force of habit, but the thought of being loose in Saks in the middle of the night...or all alone with the Roberto Cavalli bags at Nordstrom...well, it made me tingle from head to toe.

As if Ernie knew exactly what I was thinking, he chuckled. "Like a hot knife through butter," he said. "One of the few advantages I've found to being a ghost. It's easy to get around."

He made it sound like being dead was no big deal, but remember, I had experience when it came to this sort of thing; I knew better. Before we got distracted by the task of putting the spiritual me back in physical form, I needed him to know that I understood.

"How...?" Sure, I was used to talking to the dead, but none of them had ever been such recent deaths. And I hadn't known any of those ghosts in their lifetimes. Face-to-face with all that remained of someone who'd been alive only a short time before, I found myself with a lump in my throat. "How...did it happen?" I asked Ernie.

He shrugged off my concern. "Same way it happens to everyone Doctor Gerard takes out to that hospital of his, I suspect. They start out hooking you up to these crazy machines—"

"They did that to me."

"And they keep turning up the juice."

I swallowed down the sour taste that filled my mouth. I remembered that, too.

"But when they find out you aren't the real deal, that you don't really see ghosts like you say you do—"

"He killed you? He kills all of them? Just like that?"

Another shrug. "Not just like that. I mean, they're humane enough about it. I guess they don't want any of us going back on the street, talking about what happens out there. You know, so we don't scare away anyone else and they always have folks they can experiment on. They take our brains, too, you know, after we pass. That way they can look at the way they work, and the way those machines of theirs affect different parts of the brain. As for the dying itself . . ." He was quiet for a few moments, and I knew he wanted to make sure he could say this without breaking down.

"They gave me a shot of something, I think," Ernie said. "All I remember is lying on a bed and drifting away. That, and thinking about Alberta as I went." He looked down to where the photograph of his wife rested against the milk crate. "Last thing I remember is thinking that I should have gone over to her library after all. You know, just to say hello to Alberta. Just so I could hear her voice one more time."

"You could go now."

"Don't seem to be much point now," he said, and he didn't sound bitter about it, just resigned. "Only I was thinking that at least if Alberta knew I was dead, she could check and maybe she could get some of my veteran's benefits. That would be something I could give her. You know, as sort of a gift. Never did much else for the woman." Ernie shook himself out of his thoughts.

"Enough of that," he said, "or I'll start sounding pathetic, and I don't want to go through eternity like that. Let's see what we can do about your problem. If that

Doctor Tremayne said she found out how to switch bodies through Doctor Gerard's research, maybe there's
something in the clinic that will tell you how to switch
back. Only before we go..." Ernie stooped down and
picked up the photograph of Alberta. "Not going to leave
here again without this," he said.

I stared at him in wonder. "How did you do that?"

"Do?" He was confused, but only for a moment. "Oh,
you mean pick up the picture? I get it! You think your
hands are going to go right through things, am I right?"

Now that Ernie mentioned it, I realized I'd never even
tried to touch anything. After all, I'd met my share of
ghosts, and they weren't able to touch anything. There
was no use frustrating myself even more by trying.

Was there?

As if Ernie was reading my mind, he grinned. "Guess
you don't know," he said. "You, not being officially dead.
But I found out right away. I can touch things. I'll be able
to keep touching them, too. Right up until the next full
moon."

This was not something I'd ever heard from a ghost,
but then, the ghosts I knew were long dead and gone.

Except for Madeline, of course.

"But she sent me a postcard," I said, even before I
realized Ernie might not know what the hell I was talking about. "She's been dead for three years, so that means
the first full moon after she died was a long time ago. But
she sent me the postcard of the Palmer memorial."

Ernie scratched a finger alongside his nose. "Can't
say I know what you're getting at," he said, and really,
I think he was trying his best to understand. "But if
that there postcard came from a dead person, and if

that dead person was dead for a while, my guess is your dead person had help. You know, from another dead person."

"Like one of the people whose brains ended up in those jars." It made sense. "So you're telling me I can—"

"Touch things. Hold things. Pick things up. Sure." Just to prove it, he tossed me the photo of Alberta. I caught it with no problem.

"Yes!" I punched a fist into the air and Ernie laughed.

"May last even longer for you," he said. "You not really being dead. I mean, maybe for you, you just got to prove you believe."

My momentary triumph vanished just as quickly. "Believe I can get my body back?" Yeah, I sounded gloomy. Like anyone could blame me?

"You've got to believe, Pepper." His words were soft, but the look in his eyes was encouraging.

I couldn't stand to let him down. "I do believe," I told him.

Ernie slanted me a look. "Except for the part about how you don't. I can't say how this whole thing works, but maybe you just gotta tell yourself that it's possible. Like…"

"Like me fitting into those jeans I bought on sale last fall that were a little tight the first time I tried them on, only eventually I got into them?"

"And I bet you looked like a million bucks!" He grinned. "What do you say, young lady? Let's see what we can do about getting you back in the body where you belong."

It was weird walking past the clinic receptionist and realizing she couldn't see us. It was even weirder when we went straight through the locked door and into Hilton Gerard's office. Fortunately, he wasn't there, and I had this vision of him scrambling to cover his tracks now that the Pepper Martin he'd kept prisoner was on the loose and he didn't know where. Or what she might say to who.

And if he ever found the Pepper who wasn't Pepper? Since Madeline didn't have my memories, I suspected she didn't have my Gift, either. It would serve Hilton right to find her after she couldn't do him any good. Since Madeline wasn't nearly as clever as I was, and since she didn't have half the nerve, she'd never get away from Doctor Gerard's clutches.

Was it small of me to like the sound of that? Sure. But the thought of Madeline's brain in one of those jars back at the lab...I had to admit, it made me smile.

Ernie noticed. "No time for thinking whatever you're thinking." He looked around at the wall lined with file cabinets and the credenza behind Hilton's desk where more files and books were stacked. "If we're going to find anything, we'd better start looking."

We did. We looked through every file in Hilton's office, and after a couple hours of finding nothing helpful at all, I was more than ready to throw in the towel.

Discouraged, I plunked down smack-dab on a three-foot-high pile of file folders that I'd yanked out of the file cabinets and stacked on the floor. "At this rate, by the time I'm able to get my body back, it's going to be too old for me to want it." No sooner were the words out of my mouth than I felt guilty. "I'm sorry. That was tacky of me. Here I am talking about getting my body back when you...you know...you can't..."

"You mean would it bother me all that much if you

got your body back and I couldn't?" Ernie looked up from the folder he was looking through. "I'm dead, and you're not. That's the big difference, isn't it? And just so you don't go feeling all bad about it, I can't say I'm all that sorry about being conked out. I got a nice warm bed to sleep in those last few nights. I didn't have to spend my final days in a dusty, dirty alley."

"Dusty." Why the word resonated, I couldn't say. I only know that hearing it got my brain working. "She said *dusty*," I screeched, and suddenly feeling energized again, I jumped off the pile of file folders and did a turn around the office. "Madeline said she found the information about a ghost switching places with a living person in one of Hilton's dusty, old books. But we're not looking through dusty, old books. That's why we haven't found what we need."

Ernie glanced around the room. We'd already been through every file cabinet and every desk drawer. He shrugged. "Maybe he keeps those books at home."

"Or maybe they're too precious for that." I'd already been through the credenza once, and I'd seen there was a safe behind one of its doors, but damn, there I was being shallow again. Back before he ended up in the clink, I knew the only thing my dad kept in his office safe was my mother's jewelry, and I assumed everybody thought the same way. Jewelry was valuable. Books? Not so much.

Jazzed, I knelt on the floor in front of the safe and looked over my shoulder at Ernie. "What do you think?" I asked.

He knew exactly what I was talking about. "I'm pretty new at being dead," he said. "Never tried anything like it. But if you believe . . ."

I did. I think. And if I didn't, I told myself I did, anyway. That was the only thing that gave me the courage to shove my hand right through the inch-thick steel plate door. When I brought it out again, I was holding a sheaf of brittle papers and a book. A dusty, old book.

"Got it!" I jumped up and plopped the book on the desk, then dropped into Doctor Gerard's chair to start reading. It was no picnic. The book was old, the printing was faded, the font was gothic and tough to read. Still, I was lured by the tantalizing possibility of finding the information Madeline used to steal my body.

Even an hour later, I hadn't given up, and it was a good thing.

"Here!" I pointed to the page and called Ernie over. "It says exactly what Madeline said the night she pulled the switch. It says the stars and the moon have to be aligned and—"

I read the rest of the sentence and my voice faded.

"What? What is it?" Ernie's eyesight wasn't all that good. He squinted and bent for a closer look. "It says you can do it again, right? You can switch back?"

I slammed the book shut. "Sure, it says I can do it again. But not until the stars and the moon are aligned the same way. It also says that's not going to happen again for another seven hundred years."

18

I might not have been able to help myself, but there was no way I was going to let Hilton Gerard keep pickling people's brains.

As certain as I was of that, I was even more certain that there was only one person who could help me. Talk about believing in the impossible!

The last I'd seen him, Dan was at my conference hotel with Madeline, and I guess that's where I expected him to stay. But this was Chicago, remember, and in Chicago, hotel rooms are at a premium. I was scheduled to leave town the same day Doris hit the road, and I'd seen the sign in the hotel lobby that said the American Association of Water Purification and Pollution Professionals was due at the hotel next for their big annual conference.

That meant some poor AAWPPP schlep was in my room.

I should have thought of this before I told Ernie I'd

see him later and hocus-pocused my way back to the hotel, but hey, I was new at this whole incorporeal thing, and I was still more than a little shaken by the news that if I waited for the stars and the moon to be aligned just the way they were when Madeline snatched my body in the first place, I wouldn't want the seven-hundred-year-old carcass anymore, anyway.

Not sure what else to do, I stood in the hotel lobby and said, "I need to see Dan Callahan," and sure enough, just like before, I felt a tug and a pull. The world around me zipped by in a blur. The next thing I knew, I was standing in a short-term rental condo near Lincoln Park. Don't ask me how I knew this, I just did. It was actually kind of cool.

So was the condo itself.

The living room was tastefully furnished with a burgundy-colored leather sectional, arm chairs in stripes of brown, purple, and the same winey color as the sectional, and a gorgeous Oriental rug that sat on a polished hardwood floor. One wall featured a brick fireplace; another was filled floor to ceiling with bookcases. A single expansive window revealed a million-dollar view of park and buildings gilded by the setting sun.

I could get used to a place like that.

It looked like Madeline, though, was a little tougher to please.

Even as I stood there, she shuffled (just for the record, I have never shuffled; eight years of ballet, tap, and jazz lessons made sure of that) into the room wearing a gray and red flannel robe I wouldn't have been caught dead in. Without even a look toward the fireplace near where I stood, she tossed the latest issue of *Elle* down on the sleek, I-wish-it-were-mine coffee table.

"Boring," she grumbled. "Boring, boring, boring. How can anybody—"

"What's that you said?" The bathroom was down the hall, off the kitchen, and Dan stuck his head out of it. His right cheek was coated with shaving cream. There was another poof of it in his left palm. "You talking to somebody?"

Madeline flopped down on the sectional. "Can't we do something interesting this evening?"

He wiggled his eyebrows. "We already did a couple interesting things," he said. When he didn't get a response from her, he walked out of the bathroom and crossed the kitchen into the living room. He was wearing nothing but a pair of those clingy boxer briefs that look great on the models in the ads and even better in person when the guy wearing them happens to be Dan.

Once he was in the living room he could see into the dining room, and he glanced that way and at the stack of file folders on the table in there. "I told you, I've made some notes and lists. After I'm out of the shower, we'll go to dinner and talk about the situation at the clinic. Nobody could say that's not interesting! And don't worry, I know how anxious you are for us to get all our information in line so we can confront Hilton, but he's not there tonight, anyway. I know for a fact he's over at Northwestern. He's giving a lecture on homelessness and the mental health crisis. We'll take care of the due diligence tonight and talk to him at the clinic tomorrow. And before you can tell me you can't wait that long..." He gave her a smile she didn't return. "I'll make it quick." He ducked into the bathroom, then just as quickly was back out again in the hallway.

"While I'm getting dressed," he said, "you might

want to go over all of it again. You know, what happened where and when. That way we'll be on the same page when we do finally talk to Hilton. And believe me, Pepper, I swear, if he doesn't answer my questions the way I think he should—"

"I know, I know." She waved a dismissive hand in the air, and I saw, much to my horror, that her nails were cut short and not polished. Did the woman have no standards? "We'll go to the cops."

Dan cocked his head and narrowed his eyes. He came back into the living room. "Are you feeling all right?"

She clicked her tongue. "Why shouldn't I be? I've got just what I wanted, don't I? I've got you, and you're going to help me investigate at the clinic. That certainly should satisfy my sense of self-importance. And my delusions of grandness. Like all narcissists, I believe I'm special. Every little success feeds my sense of entitlement."

He stared at her as if he'd never seen her before. "Sure, but what it doesn't do is explain what the hell you're talking about. Or why you're using terms right out of a psychology textbook. I've never heard you talk like that before Hilton got ahold of you."

I cannot put into words how happy I was to hear this. I'd come to Dan for help because of all the people I knew, he was the only one who was open-minded enough to not only believe in ghosts, but in ghosts switching bodies with live people, too. I hoped. Now that he saw that there was something really sketchy about the Pepper who wasn't Pepper, maybe he'd see the light.

Then again, that scenario counted on Madeline continuing to act like a moron. I should have known there was no way that was going to happen.

She saw the slippery slope she was headed down. That's why she shook herself out of her funk and smiled. "Am I talking crazy? I know it isn't like me, but really, Danny, I think there has to be more to life. You know, more than solving dumb crimes for dead people nobody cares about anymore anyway."

"Is that what you do?" Dan's eyes lit, and it was no mystery why. Sure, I'd told him I'd seen and talked to Madeline, but I never mentioned any of the other ghosts. Or the other cases I'd investigated. This was news to him, and Dan being Dan, nothing could have thrilled him more. Well, maybe realizing he was actually in the same room with the woman who'd tricked him into marrying her, lied so that she could benefit from whatever success he had, and made him pine over her for three long years when he should have given her the one-finger salute, turned his back on her grave, and gone on with his life.

But I digress.

Dan being Dan, he was blown away. He said, "That's amazing. And no way you can possibly think it's dumb," and I was glad he was having the conversation with Madeline and not with me, because most of the time, I thought it was dumb, too. "That's the coolest thing I've ever heard! I can't imagine you'd ever want to do anything else. And now that I know what you're actually doing is solving crimes for them . . . reaching out a hand from this world to those on the Other Side . . . Wow! I'm more impressed than ever. And you should be, too. You're special."

"I am." Madeline simpered. "Special and bored." She got up and went over to where Dan stood so she could run a finger from his collarbone down to the elastic waistband of his boxers. "Let's forget this whole thing,

Danny, honey. Let's head somewhere else. Do something else. Who cares what Hilton is up to at that clinic of his."

He looked her in the eye. "You do. You just told me—"

"I did. But I'm so tired of the whole thing. And I nearly got killed, remember. I think it's smarter—and safer—to just stay out of it."

"You are definitely not acting like yourself." Dan put a hand to her forehead. Satisfied that she wasn't burning with fever, he kissed the tip of her nose. "You need to focus. Once you do, everything will come back in line and you'll feel better. Have you called Ella to ask for a couple extra days off? And have you had a chance to look through your suitcase for that list of missing clinic patients you told me about?"

Her smile was a little tight, but my guess was that Dan didn't notice. That's because she was busy tickling a finger over his abdomen. "I've got the extra days off all taken care of. As for that list . . . I'll look. I promise."

"That's my girl!" Dan grinned. He glanced at the coffee table and the magazine she'd tossed there. "After all you've been through, you should just sit back and put your feet up and read that magazine I picked up for you downstairs at the newsstand. I've got to admit, it was a stab in the dark. I don't know much about women's fashion. But I figured you'd like it."

This time, she didn't even try to hide her opinion. She grimaced. "I told you, I'm not the fashion-conscious airhead I used to be. Why do you think I went out and bought this nice comfy robe this afternoon? It sure beats that slinky, nasty one I brought here to Chicago with me."

Since *slinky* and *nasty* equaled the sweet emerald

green satin wrap I'd bought to treat myself, I didn't appreciate the criticism. I'd kept my mouth shut to this point, but enough was enough. I stepped to the center of the room to let her have it.

"You'd look like hell in my wrap, anyway," I snarled at Madeline. "Even with my body, you couldn't pull it off. Your true essence would somehow show through, and let me tell you, girlfriend, we aren't talking attractive."

This was, I admit, pretty bratty, but since it was true, I felt justified. Besides, who could blame me? For all she'd done to me, it was the least Madeline deserved.

Except she didn't respond. I mean, not even with a snarling look.

This caught me off guard, and while I was still processing, Dan gave Madeline one more kiss and turned to go back to the bathroom. "Don't think I don't know what you're doing," he said. "You're pretending to be all serious and unconcerned about things like fashion and makeup, but Pepper, nobody changes that much. Not that fast! Which is why I'm not buying it when you say you don't want to have it out with Hilton. You think it might be dangerous, right? You're trying to protect me. I know exactly how you think. But remember, I can take care of myself and besides..." He looked over his shoulder long enough to give her a wink. "You don't have to pretend with me, Pepper. Not ever. I liked you fine just the way you were, so don't think you've got to put on a show."

"He liked me fine. Just the way I was." I tried to point this out by stepping even closer to Madeline and stabbing a finger toward Dan.

She didn't seem to care. She growled, "Show, my ass," but not until Dan was out of earshot. When he had the bathroom door closed behind him, she sat back down on the couch looking awful (I mean, even more awful than anybody would have in a robe that should have been hanging in a stable). "God, I can't wait to get out of here," she grumbled, and she got up, went into the dining room, and snapped open Dan's laptop.

I leaned over her shoulder. "What, you're going to Google *apology* and *woman whose body you stole*?"

Except to shiver, Madeline didn't acknowledge me.

And that's when it hit.

She'd told me I'd fade away. She'd said that eventually, nobody would be able to see me.

I just never expected it to happen that fast.

I've got to admit, this gave me a jolt. Being invisible was hard enough to get used to. Knowing that little by little, I was disappearing completely...

I swallowed hard. Not an easy thing to do considering there was a lump in my throat.

There was also new determination in my every step.

While Madeline logged on to some psychological association website I couldn't pronounce much less spell, I hightailed it into the bedroom. I ignored the mussed blankets and the tussled sheets and found my suitcase still sitting mostly packed near the closet. I rummaged around in it until I found the portfolio I had with me the day I talked to Sister Maggie. Don't ask me how these things work, but when I ripped the sheet out of my legal pad, folded it, and tucked it into the pocket of my dumpy black skirt, I guess it turned as invisible as I was.

That would explain why Dan didn't see either me or the list when I walked into the bathroom just as he finished shaving.

He turned on the shower and stripped off his boxers

and hey, invisibility is good for something. Completely guilt free, I stood and watched and enjoyed. Once he was in the shower and had the curtain pulled, though, I knew I couldn't waste any time. I had to get to work. If I was fading, I needed to make contact. Fast.

I looked around the bathroom and hit on an idea.

I grabbed the can of shaving cream, shook it, and went over to the mirror.

"What are you up to?" When he heard the *slurp* of the shaving cream whooshing out of the can, Dan's voice came at me from out of the shower. "Pepper, are you playing with my—"

He stuck his head around the shower curtain. His hair was shampooed and bubbles dribbled down his forehead.

He flicked a finger over his eyes to keep the soap out and looked around the bathroom. "Now I'm the one imagining things," Dan muttered. Until he saw the mirror.

When he stepped out of the shower for a better look, my hopes rose. And for once, I'm not talking about my hopes of getting a better look at Dan's body.

He stepped in front of the mirror, water puddling around his feet, and read my message out loud. "Not me."

With my hands clutched together and my heart in my throat, I waited for the epiphany moment when he made the connection and saw that he'd been wrong about the woman he thought was me.

Only he didn't. He mumbled, "Pepper, you're such a kidder," and wiped the mirror clean.

As soon as he was back in the shower, I reached for the shaving cream can again.

Even above the noise of the water running, I heard

Dan sigh. "You're doing it again," he said, and he wasn't mad, exactly. He sounded more exasperated, the way a parent would with a kid who was doing something cute, but annoying. "Another message, huh?" He turned off the water. "What is it this time?"

Dan stepped out of the shower, and when he saw that Madeline wasn't in the room like he expected her to be, his brows dropped low and he glanced around. He grabbed a towel, wrapped it around his waist, and because he wasn't wearing his glasses, he got closer to the mirror so he could read what I'd written there.

"Not me," he read under his breath. "Madeline."

For a moment, I thought I'd shocked him so badly that I'd killed him. That's how still he stood. He stared at the mirror and the words written there, and when he finally started to talk, I wasn't at all surprised by what he said.

"The magazine..." Dan's head whipped around and he looked at the door. I imagined he was picturing Madeline sitting in the living room. "The robe. She said she didn't want to investigate, and the Pepper I knew, hell, she'd go in with guns blasting if it meant finding the truth of a situation."

"Yes!" I punched a fist in the air and danced around as much as anyone can in a bathroom. Thrilled that Dan was finally getting the picture, I waited for him to take that final leap of faith that would tell me that at last, I had an ally.

"If Pepper isn't Pepper..." He spoke slowly, like even he couldn't believe what was coming out of his mouth, and I leaned forward and held my breath. "If she's not Pepper. If she's Maddy..."

He swallowed so hard, his Adam's apple jumped.

Grabbing another towel, he scrubbed it over his hair, tossed it aside, and walked out of the bathroom.

Anxious to have a front row seat for the big scene of our little drama, I followed. That meant I was right behind him when he quietly walked up behind Madeline. She was so busy clicking her way around a website devoted to job openings for psychologists, she was oblivious.

And Dan?

Dan watched her for a minute, then carefully backed out of the room and went into the bedroom. Stunned, he sat down on the bed.

"Somehow things got changed around and..."

I nodded some more and smiled, too, as if it could encourage him to finish.

"Pepper is really Maddy." He stood and looked out toward the dining room, and for the first time since I'd written that message on the mirror and he'd read it, the expression on his face changed.

No more shock.

No more confusion.

Oh no, that would have been too easy, and way simpler to accept than the smile as big as all of Chicago that split his face when Dan said, "I finally have my wife back!"

19

"Hey, you're not getting discouraged, are you?" I had a feeling Ernie would have put a comforting hand on my shoulder if he felt we knew each other well enough, and who knows, maybe I would have appreciated it. The way it was, I wasn't exactly in the mood for consolation.

"Discouraged? Why should I be?" Oh yeah, that was my voice, all right. The one that sounded cynical. Not to mention bitter. "The man who said he was going to bed with me because he liked me has just realized he's got his wife back and he's so happy about it, I doubt if he'll ever even think of me again. And hey, what about...?" I'd been so busy feeling sorry for myself, that when this new thought hit, it took my breath away.

"What about my mom and dad? Maybe they won't know she's not me, and maybe they won't care. And

Quinn?" I didn't like the picture that formed inside my head. The image of Madeline taking my place in bed next to Quinn. "Maybe he won't notice, either. Maybe he won't give a damn. Maybe nobody does."

Was it right to take my bad mood out on Ernie? Probably not. Which is why I felt lousy about it instantly.

"Sorry." I'd been pacing at the mouth of the alley outside the clinic and I stopped near him. "It's just that—"

"No apologies necessary." He waved away my words. "I understand. You thought you had one chance to set things right and now—"

"What am I going to do?" My shoulders slumped. My eyes filled with tears. "You should have seen the look on his face, Ernie. Happy doesn't begin to describe what Dan's feeling. This is what he's been wanting for three long years. It's what he's been praying for and working for. And it was impossible. I mean, it should have been, right? Madeline was dead and that should have been that, right? And there's no way Dan should have been able to have another chance at being with her. But it happened, anyway. And now . . . hell, I'll bet he doesn't even care how it happened. He doesn't care about me. Why should he? Why should anyone?"

"I do." Ernie wasn't looking for thanks, so I didn't give him any, even though these simple words of friendship meant more than I could say. "There's got to be something more you can do."

"I dunno." I shrugged. "I've tried to think, but it's getting me nowhere."

"Then let me try." Ernie did just that, his brows low, his mouth thinned. "What are they doing tonight? You know, Dan and that Madeline woman?"

Was my snort as monumental as I feared? I didn't much care, and from the way he snickered, I could tell Ernie didn't, either. "Now that Dan knows his precious Madeline is back, they'll probably never get out of bed."

"Is that where they were? I mean, when you left that condo and came back here?"

Thinking back to the scene in the Lincoln Park condo, I shivered. "I didn't wait to find out," I admitted. "I'd already seen enough. I mean, there I was, invisible, and there wasn't a thing I could do but stand there and watch the way Dan thought through everything that was happening, Madeline's weird reactions to everything, my message on the mirror. I knew the very moment he realized what was really going on. I saw the way his eyes lit. After that..." I didn't know I was crying until I had to sniff away my tears. "He's never going to help me. Not now that his dream has come true and he's got his precious Madeline back. Why would he?"

"Maybe because he's a good man?"

Another sniff. At least my tears weren't turning to ice in the frosty wind. "I thought he was."

"Then give him another chance."

"But—"

When Ernie looked me in the eye, he stopped my protest. "You've got to believe. Remember? You've got to— What is it?" When he saw that something had caught my eye, he turned to look over his shoulder toward the street.

And he saw just what I saw: Madeline got out of a cab, told it to wait, and walked toward the clinic.

"What's she doing here?" he asked. "It's the middle of the night."

I didn't know for sure, but I found out when a familiar-looking guy stepped out of the shadows and into the light thrown by the security lamp above the front door. Baseball cap, spiky hair, dirty Army jacket. I'd recognize Mr. Homeless FBI Agent anywhere.

I also couldn't fail to notice a big, fat noncoincidence when I saw one up close and personal.

"I'll be right back," I told Ernie, and OK, so I've bellyached about it plenty, but being invisible is good for something. I hurried over and joined in the meeting taking place just outside the illumination thrown by the security light.

"I was surprised when you called, Miss Martin." I was shoulder to shoulder with the FBI agent when he stepped forward and shook Madeline's hand. "Last time we talked, I didn't get the impression you wanted to help."

"Last time we talked..." I could practically see the wheels spinning inside Madeline's head.

"You remember," I told her, and it was too bad she couldn't hear me, because my words dripped with sarcasm. "The day that shadow chased me. And then I bumped into this guy. That day I went over to—"

"Graceland Cemetery! Yes, of course." I remembered too late that Madeline had been there. Damn it, she was able to recover and go on. "I hope you'll forgive me, Agent..."

"Baskins. Scott Baskins." He supplied the name along with a curt nod. "I'm just surprised, that's all. What made you change your mind?"

"Oh, this and that." Madeline giggled the way I never would have. "It's so easy for a girl like me to get all mixed up. I mean, thinking straight, well, it's not something I always do well. But when I finally had the chance to think about everything that was happening..." She lifted her chin. "I hope you understand, I just want to do the right thing."

"Right thing?" I stepped closer and spoke the question like a challenge. More than anything (well, just about anything, not including getting my body back), I wanted to pin her down on this. "Right thing about what?"

"So you're willing to talk? About Doctor Gerard?"

She nodded. "I've got some information about the finances here at the clinic. I can supply all the facts and figures to support what I say. I think you'll be surprised to see where some of the fundraising money is going."

"Oh, I don't know about that." Agent Baskins rocked back on the heels of his beat-up sneakers. "We have our suspicions about Doctor Gerard. Have had for years. But if you've got the proof you say you have..."

"I do." Madeline stepped forward. "I've got more than that. I've got everything to prove that Dan Callahan is involved in the fraud, too."

"What?"

Maybe I wasn't as faded as I thought I was. Madeline might not have been able to hear me when I screeched the single, disbelieving word, but she twitched. Like she could feel the anger that oozed from my every pore.

"You bitch!" I screamed. "You told me back in Winnetka that you'd made up all that stuff about Dan being in on Doctor Gerard's shady scheme. Now you're going to lie to this guy and tell him it's all true?"

"I'll tell you everything," Madeline said as if answering my outraged questions. "And I'll provide all the proof you need."

"Then we need to talk again." Madeline stepped toward her cab, and Agent Baskins stepped back into the shadows. "Tomorrow?" he asked. "I'm around here all day, but it might be best if you come after dark. If you bring me that proof you talked about, our people can start going over the numbers."

When the cab pulled away with Madeline in it, my mouth was still hanging open. That's how Ernie found me.

"So she's gonna turn him in, huh?" Ernie had been hovering in the background. He stepped forward and shook his head. "What are you going to do about it?"

"What can I do?" I pushed my hands into the pockets of my lab coat and started my pacing again. "Even if I could communicate with Dan the way I did back at the condo, I'm pretty much between a rock and a hard place. I mean, if I keep my mouth shut, he's going to end up in prison."

"And if you don't?"

I sighed. "If I can find a way to tell him...if he believes me...then he'll find out that Madeline is a no-good, rotten liar and that she never really loved him. And that would break his heart."

He thought for a moment. "Seems to me there's only one thing you can do."

I'd already decided that. Which would explain why I was grumbling again. "What do you think?" I asked Ernie. "Think I can *whoosh* my way into a library?"

He nodded. "What are we going to investigate?" he asked.

"The names on that list I got from Sister Maggie, for one. And we're going to need to steal a cell phone, too. One that can send text messages."

"I'm in." He stepped forward, and I knew he was coming with me, only before we went anywhere, I needed one more moment of reassurance.

"You don't think..." I looked down at the shapeless skirt and the lab coat that wouldn't have looked good on anybody, not even me back when I still had my own body. "I mean, you don't think the part of her personality that's good at research is kicking in, do you? That I'm actually starting to turn into her?"

Ernie laughed. But he never really answered.

It was not the reassurance I needed.

I may have been dressed like Madeline, but my brain wasn't anywhere near as dorky. Once we were inside the nearest library, it took a while to figure out what we were looking for and then even longer to find the information. Ernie and I researched long into the next morning. By the time we were done, though, I at least had some ammunition. We'd found newspaper articles that mentioned a couple of the people on my list. Both were brief police blotter–type blurbs. Both said that acquaintances had reported the people missing, and both used the word *homeless* prominently. I had no illusions. I knew it was code for *who cares anyway*.

Still, I wasn't discouraged. The articles confirmed what I knew, and with any luck, they'd provide the proof I needed.

Oh, not about how Madeline had stolen my body. Or even about how she was going to double-cross Dan.

Those were problems so huge, I couldn't wrap my brain around them.

At that point, all I was worried about was Doctor Gerard, that crazy hospital of his, and all the brains in those jars.

If I could do something about that, if I could keep him from scooping up anybody else from the streets and using them to try and contact the Other Side...

Well, I wouldn't exactly be happy, but at least I could say I'd accomplished something before I faded into oblivion.

By the time we were done and after all the energy I used looking through the library's computer files, I was pretty whooped. But I couldn't stop. Not yet. Like I'd actually done some purse snatching in the past, I cruised the library with an expert eye and found just the victim I was looking for as she was reading in the magazine section. She was young enough to understand technology and savvy enough (after all, she was wearing Armani, so she must have been) to keep up with the latest trends. I waited for her to get up and get a copy of the newest issue of *Vogue* and thanked my lucky stars that she didn't take her purse with her. It was a boneheaded move on her part; anyone smart enough to wear Armani should have known that. But I wasn't complaining. I slipped my hand into her Coach bag and came out with her iPhone.

"Done," I said. Phone in hand, I zoomed past Ernie quickly, as if I might actually get caught. "Let's get out of here."

He was right behind me when I stepped back into the street. "And go where?" he asked.

I hung on to that iPhone for dear life because I didn't want to lose it when we whooshed to wherever we were about to go. "There's only one person who will believe any of what's going on. Even if he doesn't want to help me, he'll want to help you. He'll want to help everyone who's been kidnapped and killed. You're right, Ernie, he's one of the good guys and I've got to trust him. That's why we're going back to see Dan."

Just like I expected, the world tipped and we whizzed across town. Yeah, I was a little afraid I'd land next to the bed in that Lincoln Park condo. That's why I squeezed my eyes shut and kept them that way, even after the world stopped whirring by. At least, that is, until I smelled the heavenly scent of morning coffee and the aroma of fresh-baked muffins.

When I opened my eyes, I grinned. I'd recognize the standard-issue decor anywhere. "Starbucks," I told Ernie, and glanced around. Madeline was sitting at a table for two over near the windows, and Dan was headed her way with a tray.

Before he came into her line of vision, he paused for a moment, just standing there, looking at her as if she were a banquet—and he were the starving man who found himself with an unexpected invitation.

My stomach flipped, but I reminded myself I couldn't lose heart. Not if I expected to help all the people who'd been killed by Hilton Gerard.

"She's going to do you wrong," I warned Dan, but of course, he couldn't hear me. He shook himself out of his daydream and sat down.

He set the tray on the table, put down a plate of blueberry muffins, and slid a Grande Latte across to Madeline. "I'm surprised you didn't get skim."

She had been reading the front page of the *Tribune* and looked up as if she forgot she wasn't alone. "Skim?

Milk?" She wrinkled her nose and gave her coffee a quizzical look. "Do I usually?"

His smile was a little strained. At least for a moment. The next second, it blossomed like the morning sun. "You're full of surprises these past couple days," he said. "That's why I want to talk to you."

She skimmed the front page while she took another sip of coffee. "About what?"

"About something important." He reached across the table and touched her hand, and Madeline got the message.

I could just about see the effort it took her to pretend she was actually interested. "Of course. You've always got something important to talk about, don't you? I forget sometimes. You know, on account of how I'm not very—"

"Bright. Yeah. I figured you were going to say that." He didn't sound happy about it. "That's what I have to talk to you about, Pepper. You're not acting like yourself."

"So..." Interested, I scurried closer. "You haven't told her yet, have you?" I asked Dan, fully expecting not to get an answer. "You've spent the last day thinking about your theory. About how Pepper isn't Pepper. About how Madeline is back. I can practically see the wheels spinning in that too-smart brain of yours. You want to make sure you don't make any mistakes, say anything stupid. She doesn't know that you know!"

This scenario had never occurred to me, of course, because if I were in Dan's place, it's not how I would have handled the situation. The moment I found out the person I was with might not really be the person I thought I was

with but might really be a dead person who I really wanted
to see only I never thought I would again because—

Well, anyway . . .

I would have pounced with a thousand questions and
demands to hear the whole truth and nothing but, and I
wouldn't have rested until I did.

But that's not how Dan worked.

Dan was smart and very cautious. Of course he'd take
his time. No doubt he'd been hard at work on the problem ever since the day before when I broke the news with
my shaving-cream message. Now he was past the thinking phase and into the probing stage, and I didn't want to
miss a word. There was an empty chair nearby, and I sat
down, leaned forward, and listened.

The whole time I'd been thinking about this, Madeline was fussing and fidgeting, obviously trying to get
her story straight in her head. She squeezed Dan's hand
and said, "I told you, Danny, I'm a new woman."

"And I appreciate how that could happen. I mean,
with what you went through at that hospital and all." He
picked up his coffee cup, but he didn't take a drink. "That
was really something, the way you grabbed that empty
bucket and threw it into the middle of the floor so that the
attendant tripped and we could get past him and escape."

I didn't appreciate the revisionist history. Offended, I
sat up. "It wasn't a bucket," I said, "and I didn't trip him.
I grabbed the mop, remember? I hoisted it in both hands,
swung, and—"

And the sense of what Dan was saying hit. I perked up
and listened, anxious to see if Madeline would fall into
his trap.

"I can be spunky, all right!" She giggled.

"And when we found that open back door and ran out into the parking lot..." Dan watched her carefully.

"It was cold," Madeline said. It was the perfect generic response.

I knew an opportunity when I saw it, and before the moment passed and she did anything to squelch his suspicions, I pulled out the pilfered iPhone.

Oscar Zmeskis

I sent the text message and didn't worry about cost. After all, Armani woman was paying. At least until she discovered her phone was gone and disconnected the service.

When Dan's phone signaled a message, he dug it out of his pocket and read the words on the screen. "Oscar Zmeskis?" He looked at Madeline. "That name mean anything to you?"

Oh yeah, it meant something to her, all right. That would explain why her cheeks went a little chalky.

Now that I had the advantage, I struck again.

Becka Chance

Again, Dan read the message out loud. This time, Madeline pushed back from the table.

"Somebody's playing a trick on you," she said. She looked all around, and I had no doubt she was looking for me. "Why would somebody just send you random names?"

"Unless they're not random." Dan watched the screen on his phone, and who was I to disappoint him?

Alan Grankowski, Leon Harris, Lony Billberger, Athalea Misborough

He read the names over once, then read them again. "You don't suppose..."

"What?" By now, Madeline was on her feet. I've got

to say, I was surprised my messages got such a rise out of her. "Obviously, somebody's got the wrong number. They're sending you information that should be going to someone else."

"I thought you said they were playing a trick on me?" Dan watched her carefully.

And I struck one last time. I sent him the dates and page numbers of the newspaper articles Ernie and I had found. The ones that talked about Alan and Lony being missing.

As if it would all make him see better, Dan took off his glasses and rubbed the lenses against his Aran sweater. When he put them back on, his blue eyes glittered. "What are the chances these are the names on that list you can't find?" he asked her. "What if someone else knows who's on the list? I mean, I know you said you didn't remember, but—"

"No. Those names aren't familiar at all." Madeline stepped back from the table. "It's a wrong number, that's all it is. And I..." She looked over her shoulder. "I have to go to the ladies' room. I'll be right back."

He couldn't argue. Not with an excuse like that. Instead, Dan pulled a notebook out of the laptop case on the chair next to him and wrote down the names I'd sent along with the newspaper names, the dates, and the page numbers. He sat looking at the information, tapping his pen against the tabletop.

And I watched Madeline disappear into the restroom, and I was more surprised than I can say.

Why?

Because though I was anxious to get the names of the missing to Dan so that he could start investigating on his own, I hadn't expected that kind of reaction from Madeline.

It made me wonder if she was lying again; if she recognized the names.

And if so, if she knew exactly what was happening to those people out in Winnetka.

20

By the time Madeline came back from the ladies' room, Dan was ready to hit the road.

"It's time to talk to Hilton," he told Madeline, "but not until I stop at a library and check out these names. I'm guessing you don't want to come along. I'll call you when I'm done." He gave her a peck on the cheek that was loving enough, but when he looked into her eyes, it was to send an unspoken message. "We're going to get this thing settled once and for all."

I knew what this meant. Dan was headed out to do research, and research—it goes without saying—is boring. Something told me it would be far more interesting to tag along with Madeline.

I was glad I did. When she hailed a cab, I crawled into the backseat next to her, and when she gave the cab driver the address of the Gerard Clinic...well, I can't really say I was surprised. I was curious, though. She wasn't carrying a briefcase or a file, so I didn't think she had the proof with her that she was supposed to have when she met Agent Baskins, so that's not why she was headed to the clinic. So what trick did Madeline have up her polyester sleeve?

Anxious to find out, I stuck close, even when she marched right past the receptionist and walked into Hilton Gerard's office without knocking.

When he saw the woman he thought was Pepper Martin walk in, his surprise couldn't have been more complete. (Well, maybe it would have been if he knew she wasn't me and I was right next to her.)

For a couple moments, he simply sat there behind his desk, his mouth opening and closing like a fish that had been hooked and dragged onto dry land.

But hey, the guy is an expert, right? I mean, about brains and research and psychology. And also about cheating the government, hiding money, and, oh yeah, murder, too.

He wasn't about to be caught off guard for long.

When the receptionist came running in on Madeline's heels, falling over herself to apologize, Doctor Gerard told her not to worry, got up, and closed the door in the poor woman's face. He stood with his back to it, his eyes hooded as he sized up his guest.

"Miss Martin. I must say, I'm surprised to see you. I can't believe you'd have the nerve to walk back in here. Not after—"

"Cut the crap, Hilton." Madeline breezed behind his desk and took the seat he'd just vacated. Not wanting to miss any of the fun, I sat on the edge of the desk and watched the show. "We've got more important things to talk about than how you tried to snatch that stupid girl's brain and how she got away from you."

He smiled in a way that said he didn't actually trust that he was safe in a closed room with the woman. "You're talking about yourself as if you're someone else. You're so stressed that you can't handle reality. You're having what we call a dissociative fugue."

Madeline was one step ahead of him. She clicked her tongue and waved off the bullshit explanation. "I know exactly who I am," she said. "That's what I'm here to talk to you about."

"The hospital experience?" Hilton's smile faded. His laugh sounded as uncomfortable as he suddenly looked. "You remember what happened to you there?"

"Not what happened to Pepper. Who the hell cares what happened to Pepper! I do remember, though, what happened to the others. You know, Oscar Zmeskis, Becka Chance, Alan Grankowski, and the rest of them."

Hilton was back to the fish impersonation. While he stood there staring with his mouth open, Madeline laughed.

"Surprised?" she asked. "You shouldn't be."

"You're bluffing."

"Are you willing to take that chance?"

He thought about this while he walked over to the desk and dropped into one of his own guest chairs. "What do you want?" he asked.

"The same thing I wanted before. A million ought to do it. At least to start. That will keep me quiet about what I already know. You know, about all those brains you've been studying out in Winnetka. And about how you murdered Madeline Tremayne when she found out what you were up to."

"Huh?" Still sitting on the desk, I spun around so I could give Madeline a closer look. Then I glanced the other way to catch Doctor Gerard's reaction. She was looking happy. And him? He was as guilty as hell. I could tell, and I wondered why I'd never seen the truth before.

"Madeline was killed by a mentally ill patient," Doctor Gerard said, and if I hadn't seen that fleeting look that told me he'd been caught with his pants down (only proverbially, of course, thank goodness), I actually might have believed him.

Madeline didn't. Then again, no one knew this part of the story better than she did. "Madeline was in on it from the start. She knew exactly what you were doing to those homeless lowlifes. She wanted you to pay her in return for her silence. A million dollars, right? The same thing I'm asking for." She let this sink in before she went on. "You didn't want to share. You paid John Wilson to kill her, and then you supplied him with enough drugs to make sure he OD'd. It was the perfect way to keep him quiet."

Hilton's voice was breathy. "You can't know that."

"But I do." Her smile was sleek. "And if you think about it, you'll know how I know. Remember, Hilton, I did a lot of research for you."

The truth of the matter dawned, but just as quickly, he dismissed the possibility with a shake of his head. "No. It isn't possible. You . . . er . . . Madeline . . . Madeline was the only one who knew what was really happening in Winnetka. No one else knew. You couldn't know."

"You think?" Stretching like a cat, she rose from the

chair. "Remember, Hilton, there's more in those books of yours than just information on ghosts. Shape-shifting, body switching. Did you ever think it was really possible?"

Honestly, I almost felt sorry for the guy. That's how upset he looked. Before he had a chance to say anything, though, the door banged open again, and Dan raced into the office. He rushed around the desk, grabbed Madeline's hand, dragged her toward the door, and tried to push her out into the hallway toward the receptionist who was, again, stuttering out her apologies to the doctor.

"Out," Dan said, and when Madeline wouldn't budge, he tugged her again. "Out, now. It's too dangerous here for you. Hilton and I have things we need to talk about."

"Not you, too." Doctor Gerard groaned. "Your friend here has been telling me some fantastic stories, Dan. I hope she doesn't have you believing them."

"I've got some stories of my own." Dan had a piece of paper clutched in one hand, and I was sitting close enough to see that it was a computer printout of the same two articles I'd found about the missing homeless men. "What do you do with them, Hilton?" he asked, poking the paper in Hilton's direction as if he could see it. "Where are the people who've gone into your study? Please tell me that it's not true that you—"

"Can't you keep your mouth shut?" It was Madeline's turn to slam the door in the face of the receptionist. When she was done, she turned to Dan with fire in her eyes. "I was taking care of everything. Why did you have to show up and ruin it all?"

"What?" He looked at her as if he'd never seen her before. "What are you talking about? Ruining everything? Terrible things are happening out in Winnetka. I've got documentation." He waved the newspaper articles at her, too. "It's not proof, but it's a start." He turned to Hilton. "You owe me some answers."

"You think so?" This time when Hilton laughed, it sent chills up my spine. To put some distance between myself and him, I walked to the other side of the room and stood near the bookcases there. Too bad Madeline had the same idea. She came to join me, and I sidled into the corner, the better to avoid the bad vibrations that rose off her like the electrical charge from a thundercloud.

"I've got news for you, Dan." Hilton strolled back around his desk and stopped behind it. "I don't owe you anything, and I don't owe anything to your friend here, either. So when she tells me I've got to pay her a cool million—"

"What!" Dan spun to stare at Madeline, and I was busy staring at him staring at her.

Which is why none of us noticed when Hilton Gerard opened his desk drawer. By the time we realized what was happening, he already had the gun in his hand.

Hilton pointed with the gun, encouraging Dan and Madeline to stand closer together. "Don't you get it?" the doctor asked. "Don't you see what happened before your very eyes? She isn't Pepper Martin. She's Madeline. She has to be. It's the only way she could know everything she does."

"Then it is true!" Dan's eyes misted. He grabbed her arm and looked into Madeline's eyes, and for a moment, I thought he'd actually be corny enough to kiss her, even while Doctor Gerard was pointing that gun at them. Big points for Dan, he didn't go for the obvious. Then again, Dan never did.

"What did you do with her?" he asked, and since I knew he was talking about me, I perked right up. "Where's Pepper? Is she safe?"

"Oh please!" Madeline yanked her arm away. "You always were a sucker."

"A sucker to believe that you really loved me? A sucker to miss you for three long years?" Dan could barely choke out the words. "Are you telling me—"

"She knows everything," Doctor Gerard said. He stepped closer. "You see, Dan, Madeline was part of my scheme. It was working pretty well, too, until she got greedy."

"No." Dan dismissed the very idea with a shake of his head that sent his shaggy hair flying. "It can't be true. Maddy wouldn't—"

"But I would. I did!" Her laugh was almost a shriek. "And I had you fooled since day one," she told him. "I had you all fooled."

"It's an unfortunate situation." Doctor Gerard trained the gun on Dan, and I tensed, wondering if I could spring at him and knock the weapon away. Before I could, though, he swiveled toward Madeline and fired.

After that, everything moved so fast, it's hard to say what happened when. Even over the noise of the deafening gunshot, I heard Madeline scream and watched her crumple to the floor. I wasn't taking any chances. When the doctor turned toward Dan, I launched myself through the air and knocked into his gun hand. At the same moment, the office door burst open and Agent Baskins rushed in. He tackled the doctor and had him handcuffed before Dan could recover and help, and when some of the clinic employees ran in to see what was happening, he ordered them to call 911 and hurried over to where

Madeline lay, a trickle of blood pooling on the floor around her.

"Hang on," Agent Baskins told her, and it was weird, but I kind of wondered if he was talking to me. Because even as I watched, the scene in front of my eyes blurred and faded. Then again, that was apt to happen since I was watching myself bleed to death right before my very eyes.

When Agent Baskins spoke again, his voice sounded like it came from a million miles away. "Hang in, Pepper," he said. "You're my star witness against these guys, remember."

Dan knelt on the floor and took Madeline's hand in his. He pressed it to his heart.

"You heard this guy," he told her. "You've got to hang in. You can't leave yet. You've got to tell me what you did with Pepper."

Something told me that Agent Baskins would have liked to ask what the hell Dan was talking about, but he never had the chance. Outside, we heard the pulsing sound of police car sirens. Inside, well, something really weird happened. While they knelt there and hung on to Madeline, the floor beneath my feet shifted and disappeared, and I couldn't tell if I was right side up or upside down. I looked down at my ugly outfit just as it—and I—faded. Pretty soon I was nothing but a mist hanging high above the scene.

That's why I had a bird's-eye view when Madeline's spirit swooped out of my body, kicking her clunky black shoes and screaming all the way.

"Oh no," she shouted, her angel face twisted with anger. "I'm not giving up this body. I'm staying here. I'm staying alive. I'm not going anywhere."

Apparently, somebody had other ideas.

I heard a noise that sounded like thunder, and I'll tell you what, though I suspect Agent Baskins would never admit it, I think he heard it, too. His head came up and he listened closely. Dan, of course, was another story, and an intuitive thinker if I ever met one. Both men felt a shift in the air, just like I did, and just like I did, they looked at the far wall of the office just as that spooky black shadow exploded right through it.

Did Dan and Agent Baskins know the thing was there?

I can't say, but maybe they didn't have to. I was scared enough for all of us.

Shaking in my chunky shoes, I watched as the creature reached a hand out to Madeline. She automatically jumped back.

"No. Don't take me," her spirit screamed. "I'm alive. I have this body. Take the girl it belongs to. She must be here." She looked around, and for the first time, she spotted me. She stabbed a finger toward me. "Take her spirit in exchange for mine."

The shadow turned its fiery eyes toward me. "Don't want you," it said, and while it was still looking in my direction and Madeline was caught off guard, it snaked one arm around her and pulled her closer.

Her scream was like nothing I'd ever heard before and hope to never hear again. The closer she got to the massive creature, the more muffled her cries became, and when it put both its arms around her and she was folded into the black cloud, the screaming stopped altogether.

I barely had time to breathe a sigh of relief. The next thing I knew, that invisible hand was on me again, yank-

ing me through time and space. The world around me
faded and blurred, and I moved a thousand miles an hour
toward I-don't-know-where.

I did know that when the spinning stopped, my left
side felt as if it were on fire and there was something hot
and wet and sticky all around me.

When my eyes fluttered open, I found myself in a position similar to where I'd been when Madeline snatched
my body—looking up into Dan's blue eyes.

B y the time I stepped foot in Garden View again, the
last of the daffodils were up and the tulips outside
the administration building were starting to bloom.

Ordinarily, I would not even have noticed.

But a funny thing happened once I had my body
snatched and I got it back only because somebody shot
me: I started paying more attention to the little things.

Like the looks of genuine delight on the faces of my
fellow employees as they lined the hallways to welcome
me back to work. Of course, Ella was at the end of the
line, but that was because she was planning one of those
hugs of hers—the kind that never seem to end. For once,
I didn't mind.

"You look terrific," she said. Since she had tears
streaming down her face, I'm not sure how she could see
me clearly. "Six weeks in Florida with your mom did
wonders for you."

"Yeah, that and those couple weeks in the hospital."
That part was not a pleasant memory, and I didn't want
to think about it, so I shook it away. "I'm still moving
kind of slow," I told her, just so she didn't equate first-

day-back-at-work with anything like actually working. "I think I'm going to need to take it kind of easy for a while."

"Of course you are." She patted my arm. "That's why I've got something new and wonderful all lined up for you. But before I tell you about that, I have to tell you that a woman named Alberta called you early this morning. She said to tell you that the memorial service for someone named Ernie is going to be in June, on Father's Day weekend. She said she hoped you'd be there, because after all you did for her, she thinks of you like family. Do you know what she's talking about?"

"You bet." I could still remember the vision I'd had as the paramedics were taking me out of Doctor Gerard's office on a stretcher; a vision of Ernie and Stella and all the others who'd been experimented on at the hospital as they went into the light. Even Oatmeal Lady looked happy, and just thinking about it, I couldn't help but smile. "Maybe you'd like to go with me. We could explore Graceland."

The look of sheer joy on Ella's face was all the answer I needed. I made a move toward my office door. "I'll call Alberta right now," I told her.

"Oh, not right now." Ella slid a look toward my closed office door and leaned in to whisper, "He's waiting for you."

I wasn't exactly sure who she meant, but since it was the perfect opportunity for me to get away from the crowd, I opened the door and went inside. There was a bouquet of hot pink roses on my desk, and the *he* in question was sitting in my guest chair. It was Dan, and I hadn't seen Dan since the day I got shot.

"Hey." He rose the second I walked in. His hair was a

little longer than it had been when I last saw him, and he was wearing rumpled khakis and a blue polo shirt. He looked cute. And more uncomfortable than I'd ever seen anybody look in my whole entire life.

"I'm sorry I didn't have a chance to call since you left the hospital," he said by way of explanation, even though I hadn't asked for it and wasn't expecting one. It was part of my new don't-sweat-the-small-stuff attitude. He sat down, then stood up again. "Once I knew you were going to recover..."

"You figured I could do it all on my own."

Dan's cheeks went ashen. "I was pretty busy for a while with the guys from the FBI," he said. "Now that Hilton's confessed, they're finally satisfied that I didn't know anything about what was happening out in Winnetka. I've got to tell you, you had them going for a while. They were pretty confused, what with the woman they thought was you telling Agent Baskins she had the proof to put me away for a thousand years, then with you in the hospital, claiming you didn't know anything about it."

"I don't." I shrugged, because after all, what else could I say? There didn't seem to be anything to gain from pointing out that Dan's late wife was the one who was out to get him. The dark circles under his eyes told me he'd already spent plenty of time thinking about that.

He didn't want to talk about it, either. That's why he went right on. "Once I knew you were safe and sound with your mom... well, I figured you'd have a quicker recovery without me around."

His nervousness was contagious. I shuffled around behind my desk. "It would have been nice to talk to you."

"Pepper…" As quick as lightning, Dan was around the desk and had my hands in his. "I almost got you killed. I can't tell you how that made me feel. Guilty. Terrible. Awful. Damn, I didn't even realize you weren't you, that Maddy was you. I don't know how she did it, but…" He drew in a breath and let it out slowly. "I can't believe how stupid I was."

"It's not exactly an everyday situation," I said, because it was true, and because I didn't have the heart to watch him suffer. "There's no way you could have known what Madeline was up to."

"No, but I should have. That first time I kissed her, I knew something was different. If only I'd been paying more attention. She wasn't you. She never could be." He dropped my hands and backed away. "After Hilton shot you…shot her…" He shook his head, clearing it. "Maybe it was the stress of the situation, maybe I was just imagining the whole thing, but I swear, Pepper, I swear I saw her spirit rise out of your body and for the first time, I saw Maddy for what she really was. It wasn't pretty."

"I'm sorry," I said, and I meant it. "I didn't want you to know."

"Thanks." His smile was fleeting. "But it's better for me to face reality, and the reality—"

"The reality is that even when you knew that was Madeline there inside my body, you wanted to help me. You didn't let me down. I thought—"

"That I'd want her more than I wanted you. I know. That's why…" Dan looked toward the chair where he'd been sitting, and I saw that there was a full-to-bursting backpack on the floor next to it. "I made a huge mistake thinking I could have Maddy back in my life again and nothing would be changed. I can't take that chance again. I've got to learn that the past is the past, and I need to put the past behind me. I can't do that here. I'm going to London. This afternoon. There's some really cutting-edge paranormal research going on in the UK."

"So you don't want to study my brain anymore?"

It was his turn to shrug. "Right now, that would feel a little intrusive."

"Even though you know I can see and talk to ghosts?"

Another shrug. "There are more important things than finding out the truth. I'm thinking giving you a little peace and quiet is one of them."

"And you're thinking that if you go away and don't see me for a while, you won't feel so guilty."

Did I sound like as much of a baby as I was feeling?

Maybe, because Dan came over and put his hands on my shoulders. "I'm not doing it to hurt you, Pepper." He dropped a kiss on my forehead. "Maybe once we've had a chance to process everything that happened—"

"Yeah. Maybe." I stepped back and out of his reach, and like I've said, he's an intuitive kind of guy. He knew what it meant: it was time for him to leave. He got his backpack, and his hand was already on the door when I spoke.

"Only it doesn't seem fair, does it?" I asked him. "I mean, Madeline got to go to bed with you and all I could do was—"

"Watch?" Dan had apparently not thought of this before. That would explain why color shot up his neck and into his cheeks.

I grinned. "Maybe a little."

He stepped closer, but only long enough to kiss me quickly. "We're going to see each other again."

"Yeah. OK." I opened the door for him.

And found Ella standing right outside.

Dan stepped around her. "I'll call," he said. "I promise."

I watched him walk away, and when he turned the corner, I went back into my office. Ella was already in one of my guest chairs.

"You OK?" she asked.

"Yeah." I said it even before I realized I was telling the truth. "There's a lot for Dan and me to think about. We'll both be better off with a little time away from each other."

"Exactly!" Ella hopped to her feet. "That's why I know you'll be thrilled to hear what's happening. I'm going to be giving you something very exciting to keep you occupied for the next couple months. There's a committee working to restore Monroe Street Cemetery. It's a wonderful urban burying ground, but it's been neglected for years and years. These are wonderful, enthusiastic volunteers."

From experience, I knew this wasn't the end of the story, and I leaned forward, urging her on. "And..."

"And it's going to be a once-in-a-lifetime opportunity," she said. "And it's not that I'd like to see you leave. Heaven forbid! But it will look great on your résumé, and you'll have a chance to write and publish articles about everything that happens, too." She sashayed her way to the door.

Only I wasn't about to be satisfied with so little of the

story. "Ella." I stopped her before she could leave. "What am I doing with this wonderful group of volunteers?"

"You're chairing the committee, of course," she said, and before I could pin her down—or protest—she pulled open my door and walked out of my office.

I was all set to follow her when I ran smack into an Italian silk tie that cost more than any cop should have been able to afford.

"Careful!" Quinn Harrison put his hands on my shoulders much as Dan had done just a couple minutes before. But instead of using it as an adios move the way Dan had done, Quinn back-stepped me into my office and kicked the door closed behind him. "You don't want to irritate that gunshot wound of yours the first day back on the job, do you?"

"I'm fine." I was. The doctors in Florida had assured me. I grinned. "You know that. You've called me a couple dozen times. And the flowers…" I bent to smell the roses. "They're gorgeous. Thank you."

"They are." Quinn cocked his head. "I didn't send them."

"You didn't? I thought…" I tripped over my blunder.

Quinn stepped forward. "Maybe we should read the card?" He plucked the little envelope from the center of the arrangement, but before he had a chance to open it, I snatched it out of his hands and ripped it open. The card inside was blank except for the sender's name: Scott Baskins.

"They're from…" I shouldn't have been embarrassed and I knew it, but that didn't keep me from being uncomfortable. I stuffed the card in my pocket. "A friend."

"Your friend has good taste."

"You do, too. You sent plenty of flowers while I was recovering."

"I've got to tell you, I wasn't exactly sure how you'd feel about the flowers. Or the phone calls. I mean, the last time we saw each other..."

He didn't need to remind me. The sex was terrific, but the morning after was a little tense.

"So..." He let the single word hang in the air between us, and though it wasn't a question, I knew he was expecting an answer.

"I've learned a lot over the last couple months," I told him. "A lot about myself, and a lot about relationships. Where we were headed...well..." I swallowed my misgivings. "We need to get to know each other better. You know that, don't you?"

"Absolutely." He'd never agreed to anything that quickly, so I knew either we were on the right track or we were making a huge mistake. "I've had time to think about it, too. I like being with you, Pepper. We need to date and establish some kind of real relationship before...you know."

"Right." I tried to sound enthusiastic, because after all, it was exactly what I'd said, and it made a whole lot of sense. Right? "We'll be grown-ups about the whole thing."

He started for the door. "Agreed. So I'll call you sometime. And we'll have dinner. Or meet for a drink."

"Perfect!" I watched him walk out the door and close it behind him, and for a couple moments, I thought about everything that had happened, everything we'd said, and everything I'd learned about life and love.

That's when I made up my mind.

I raced for the door and pulled it open only to find that

the hallway outside my office was filled with ghosts. There were tall ghosts and short ghosts, skinny ones and fat ones. Most of them were dressed as if they'd just stepped out of one of those dreary *Masterpiece Theater* productions.

Aside from saying, "Excuse me," to get around them, I didn't even stop to give them the time of day. I knew who they were; the bunch from that cemetery I'd be helping to renovate. That meant I'd have all summer to worry about them.

Right now, I had something more urgent to take care of. I moved faster than I'd moved in months, and I was out the door and in the parking lot just as Quinn was unlocking the door of his unmarked police car.

"Hey, Quinn!" When I called to him, he looked up. "That stuff you said, you know, about being grown-ups and establishing a relationship. Does that mean we can't have sex?"

His green eyes glittered in the spring sunlight. "I don't know. What do you think?"

"Me?" I grinned. "I think we don't have to be that grown-up."

Penguin Group (USA) Online

What will you be reading tomorrow?

Tom Clancy, Patricia Cornwell, W.E.B. Griffin,
Nora Roberts, William Gibson, Robin Cook,
Brian Jacques, Catherine Coulter, Stephen King,
Dean Koontz, Ken Follett, Clive Cussler,
Eric Jerome Dickey, John Sandford,
Terry McMillan, Sue Monk Kidd, Amy Tan,
John Berendt…

You'll find them all at
penguin.com

*Read excerpts and newsletters,
find tour schedules and reading group guides,
and enter contests.*

Subscribe to Penguin Group (USA) newsletters
and get an exclusive inside look
at exciting new titles and the authors you love
long before everyone else does.

PENGUIN GROUP (USA)
us.penguingroup.com